GU00027901

James Nelson Robinson was born in Reading, Berkshire, England in 1949. At the age of eight, his family migrated to New South Wales, Australia. Finishing his schooling in 1965, 16-year-old James enlisted in the Royal Australian Navy as an apprentice Aircraft Maintenance Engineer.

Resigning his commission from the Navy in 1985, ex-Warrant Officer Robinson then joined the Australian Department of Civil Aviation where he worked until his retirement from the workforce in 2004.

While he was encouraged by his wife to write seriously for many years, it wasn't until the forced lockdowns that came with the spread of COVID-19, that, at the mature age of 73, he finally sat down and, as they say, 'put pen to paper.'

(Please note that James Nelson Robinson is the nom de plume of the author.)

To Pam – for being the mortar that has held my life together for 51 years.

James Nelson Robinson

THE QUARRY

AUSTIN MACAULEY PUBLISHERS™

LONDON * CAMBRIDGE * NEW YORK * SHARJAH

Copyright © James Nelson Robinson 2022

The right of James Nelson Robinson to be identified as the author of this work has been asserted by the author in accordance with sections 77 and 78 of the Copyright, Designs and Patents Act 1988.

All rights reserved. No part of this publication may be reproduced, stored in a retrieval system, or transmitted in any form or by any means, electronic, mechanical, photocopying, recording, or otherwise, without the prior permission of the publishers.

Any person who commits any unauthorised act in relation to this publication may be liable to criminal prosecution and civil claims for damages.

This is a work of fiction. Names, characters, businesses, places, events, locales, and incidents are either the products of the author's imagination or used in a fictitious manner. Any resemblance to actual persons, living or dead, or actual events is purely coincidental.

A CIP catalogue record for this title is available from the British Library.

ISBN 9781398487406 (Paperback)
ISBN 9781398487413 (ePub e-book)

www.austinmacauley.com

First Published 2022
Austin Macauley Publishers Ltd®
1 Canada Square
Canary Wharf
London
E14 5AA

I'm writing this novel at my home near Forster, on the New South Wales Mid-North Coast.

It is with a sense of profound wonderment that I sincerely acknowledge the indigenous Worimi and Biripi people as the traditional custodians of the land where I live and work, and pay my utmost respect to the Elders both past and present.

Names of persons in this novel have been borrowed from people I have known over the years so if you happen to have the same name as a character in my book, you must have left a lasting impression.

The early chapters of the story take place in a purpose-built Australian Government Migrant hostel comprising uninsulated corrugated Nissen huts dotted over a barren hill a few hundred meters from a large salt-water lake.

If you are reading this book and you recognise the camp, I hope the unpleasant memories of the living conditions have faded over the past 60-odd years and my description of the camp and the surrounding area only revives the good ones.

Table of Contents

Introduction

I was a 'Ten Pound Pom'; actually, it was my parents that earned the right to that colloquial title as my passage to Australia was free. That fact obviously went over the heads of many of my teenage mates who seemed determined to attach a label to everyone that wasn't, in their eyes, 'Australian'.

Many of the British families we immigrated with became disillusioned within weeks of disembarking and couldn't wait to return 'home'. As a child, I was insulated against the invariable and mostly exaggerated, comparisons newly-arrived migrant adults made between the two countries. (Here's a good example; '*My dinner stayed hotter in England*'. Really?)

As an eight-year-old, England was a place where I had lived and played—Australia was exactly the same—only warmer! Those early days in the Hostel were full of adventure and excitement; who'd have thought you could actually play *under* a house? Everything was new and different, with every day revealing another wonderful and sometimes weird, facet of my adopted country.

This is my first attempt at writing a novel. While not an autobiography, the story encapsulates many vignettes of my life; yes, I was a migrant and lived in a hostel; I served in the Royal Australian Navy for 20 years and my first car was a 1965 Mk1 British Racing Green Ford Cortina—sadly, not a GT but a '440' (it did have one advantage over the GT—it had a front bench seat! Wink, wink, nudge, nudge, say no more, say no more, know what I mean, eh, eh!—*thank you, Eric Idle and Monty Python*).

I hope you enjoy reading, as much as I enjoyed writing, this book.

Prologue

August 1942

On 25 March 1942, nearly 1,000 Jewish women and girls were 'deported' from Slovakia. They were packed into enclosed airless rail cars and sent to Auschwitz Concentration Camp in German-occupied Poland. That same year, as part of Adolf Hitler's 'final solution to the Jewish question', Auschwitz began exterminating Jewish prisoners in large gas chambers disguised as shower blocks.

Jewish prisoners were also being used as guinea pigs by German doctors in experimental medical procedures.

It didn't take long for the Polish resistance movement to send details of what was happening inside Auschwitz back to the British Intelligence service.

****

"Good luck, Jimmy."

Wing Commander Jessop, Commanding Officer, Special Operations Group extended his hand to the man standing in front of him. Warrant Officer Jimmy Schreiber shook his CO's hand.

"Just another day at the office, Sir."

"At the risk of repeating myself; make sure you stick to the plan because I don't need to explain the consequences if you get caught!"

"That's right, you don't and I won't—get caught that is!"

Their farewell was cut short when the Wright Cyclone R-1820 radial engines that powered the all matte-black Douglas DC-3, they were standing beside, roared into life in a cloud of blue smoke.

With the noise of the engines preventing any further conversation, Jimmy saluted his CO and climbed into the spartan interior of the 'Gooney Bird'. The aircraft had been stripped of all non-essential fittings—this included any passenger comforts; Jimmy strapped himself into one of only six canvas sling seats attached along the fuselage.

The aircraft climbed unhurriedly out of RAF Winfield near Berwick on Tweed, to a cruising altitude of 20,000ft. She didn't have a great rate of climb to begin with, but with the additional long-range fuel tanks fitted, it was almost painful. Their route would take them out over the North Sea on roughly an easterly heading towards Sweden. Once in neutral air space, the aircraft would turn south towards the designated drop zone in the heart of Poland. Being outside the normal bomber aircraft approach lanes, with any luck, they wouldn't encounter any German fighter patrols.

Once they had levelled off, Jimmy adjusted his leather helmet, fitted the oxygen mask, pulled the fur collar of his sheep skin-lined leather jacket up around his ears and settled back against the cold aluminium skin. He closed his eyes and automatically went through the operation from whoa to go for probably the hundredth time. However, the steady drone of the propellers soon had him nodding off to sleep.

The plan had sounded absolutely bonkers but Jimmy's trust in the many people behind the scenes had grown with each successful mission into enemy territory so, despite some nervous anticipation, he was able to sleep for most of the three-hour flight.

This was Jimmy's sixth mission behind enemy lines in the last twenty-four months. He only had to look in the mirror to understand why he was selected. With his pale skin, blond hair and piercing steely blue eyes, he was by all accounts, the 'typical' Aryan German that Hitler dreamed would rule his world.

****

Jacob Werner Schreiber had been born in Dresden, Germany to parents who were highly regarded University Lecturers.

Following in their footsteps, Jacob had been on the cusp of gaining his Bachelor of Engineering degree when his family had fled to England; his parents totally opposed the 'realignment' of the education system by Adolf Hitler.

While it hadn't taken his parents any time at all to find positions at Cambridge University, 19-year-old Jacob was distraught with leaving his home, his friends and worst of all, having to suffer the insults and slurs that came with being a German in England in 1933. However, the family's arrival hadn't gone unnoticed by British Intelligence.

Once his parents had started lecturing full time and had a regular source of income, his father had purchased a beautiful 2-story house on the outskirts of Chesterton on the banks of the River Cam.

Jacob just couldn't adapt to the radical changes in his life and dropped out of University within the first six months of enrolling. Much to his mother's disgust, he took up smoking and was spending more and more time in the pubs in and around Cambridge.

It was following a rather unsavoury incident just on closing time in the *Green Dragon* pub between him and a rather large—and extremely drunk—navvie, that he found himself in a cell in the Chesterton Police Station. His father, having been informed of his incarceration, thought it a good idea to let him stay there where he could give some serious thought about changing his attitude.

Thirty-six hours later he was taken from his cell in handcuffs and escorted by two policemen to a sleek black 1932 8-litre Bentley Saloon waiting at the kerb outside. A young lady in an Army uniform held the back door open as he was bundled somewhat harshly inside. Sitting on the other side of the seat was a Royal Air Force Squadron Leader.

"Mr Schreiber, my name's Jessop, Terry Jessop. Here, let's get those handcuffs off."

And so began the second coming of Jacob Werner Schreiber, soon to become Corporal James Schreiber and, on completion of the hardest—both mentally and physically—4 years of his life, Warrant Officer Schreiber.

British Intelligence surveillance of the Schreiber family had paid dividends. While the parents were hard-working and definitely anti-Nazi, Jacob was a square peg trying to fit into a round hole. It had been Squadron Leader Jessop's team's task to whittle away the brashness and plain pig-headedness and turn the obviously talented youngster into something that not only his adopted country, but Jacob himself would be proud of.

Five years and many—mostly successful—operations later, Jimmy was beginning to wonder whether turning down the now Wing Commander Jessop's recommendation for promotion to Lieutenant, together with the promise of a cushy desk job, was such a smart move after all.

The pilot's voice came through the headset stirring him from his reverie, "2 minutes, Sir." No response was expected, the pilot simply flew to the drop zone, waited for 15 seconds after illuminating the green drop light and then turned for home.

Exactly 2 minutes later, Jimmy dropped the headset and oxygen mask onto his seat, donned his goggles and jumped from the 'Goony bird' into the inky-black moonless night.

First part of the plan—tick. The second part; locate three lights located on hilltops several kilometres apart roughly signifying the drop zone.

Operations had waited 2 weeks before giving the go-ahead. Waited until the weather conditions were optimal. Jimmy smiled at that—'optimal' meant the best they could hope for and was a long stretch from 'ideal'. But as he descended from 20,000ft through a thin layer of cirrostratus cloud, he easily spotted the three lights slightly off to his left.

Second part of the plan—tick.

The dominant resistance movement in Poland was the *Armia Krajowa* (the Home Army). It was the AK who had advised Ops that the area of occupied Poland he was dropping into was only patrolled irregularly by the German Army so it would be highly unlikely the enemy would witness his arrival.

Once on the ground, however, Warrant Officer Schreiber became a fluent German-speaking Oberfeldwebel Jacob Schreiber and the latter would welcome meeting a German patrol unit—even if it was only to exercise his native language.

Soon-to-be Jacob deployed the main black silk canopy and steered towards what he hoped was the centre of the three lights. He knew he was close to the ground when he could no longer see the lights and he spotted the red brake light of a vehicle flash. Flaring the parachute, he bent his knees and braced for the inevitable hard landing.

He was gathering up the deflated 'chute when a very English accent came from a few yards away.

"Do get a wriggle on James old boy; my bloody tea's getting cold."

Major Percy "Curtains" Draper had been 'inserted' into the AK several months earlier for the sole purpose of arranging the extraction of Jimmy and, hopefully, his so far unidentified package in 24 hours hence.

"Curtains, trust you to get the cushy jobs. I suppose a beautiful young Polish girl is cooking you *Kotlet Schabowy* and warming your slippers as we speak?"

"Firstly James, I don't eat pork and secondly, when I get home, I don't have time for wearing slippers!"

The pair greeted each other with a laugh and a friendly embrace and then got down to the matter at hand.

"Welcome, Oberfeldwebel Schreiber. I hope you had a pleasant flight?" Curtains asked in fluent Polish.

"Ja, Major Drapelski," Jimmy replied in fluent German, "although the meal was absolutely tasteless!"

****

"We're about 2 kilometres from the rail crossing, Sir" Victor, the driver of the laden cattle truck announced a short time later.

"Part three begins" Jimmy mused as he eased open the passenger door and stepped out onto the doorstep. "See you at the rendezvous tomorrow night, Major." And with a snappy salute, he was gone.

The trains carrying the 'deported' Jews to Auschwitz didn't run to a set schedule, but most of them arrived during the early hours of the morning when higher priority goods trains transporting troops and armaments were less frequent. Jimmy hoped that tonight's train would arrive between 0200 and 0400.

Apparently—although he had never personally proven the theory—this was when a person's senses were at the lowest level of awareness and were most vulnerable. If he was to board a moving train unseen and dispatch any guards that got in his way, he needed all the help he could get. Hopefully, Step 4 of the plan would slow the train enough for him to board without sustaining any injuries.

The cattle truck that had been Jimmy's transport lumbered slowly and noisily towards the rail crossing. As it drew nearer, a German soldier stepped from the gatehouse and signalled the truck to stop. With much shouting and gesticulating, the driver pulled up next to the soldier who said "Papers please" in German.

The shouting and gesticulating continued until an obviously bored young German Officer joined the soldier. "Papers please," this time in Polish, "and I really don't care if these forsaken-looking beasts are for the Fuhrer himself."

"My apologies, Lieutenant. It's just that this truck; she is so old she's hard to get moving once she stops," he explained as the appropriate documents were handed over and duly scrutinised. "I'll be returning from the market this time tomorrow, perhaps you could wave me through?"

"In your dreams, Dziadek," as he handed the papers back to the driver.

"Grandfather!" the driver muttered as he jammed the truck into gear with all the grinding he could elicit without permanent damage. "Bloody cheek!"

"Easy Victor, you need to watch your blood pressure!"

"You can go fuck yourself too, Curtains!"

The truck jerked onto the crossing and then with a bang and a cloud of blue smoke, came to a stop half on and half off the tracks. The small charge and some strategically placed oil sprayed onto the hot exhaust worked perfectly.

The driver and his passenger were lifting the bonnet to the still-smoking engine when the German Lieutenant and his offsider came running over.

"We have a train due through here anytime soon so I would strongly advise that you get this heap of shit moving or risk the ire of some already pissed-off SS soldiers!" shouted the now highly agitated Lieutenant.

"Sorry, sir, but it's the clutch bearing deflecting arm, I think it shattered. It's the stopping and starting you see. It puts excessive pressure on the release module which in turn overheats and then POW! No more drive. If you and this fine example of a German soldier here can give us push, we'll park on the other side where we can work on it."

No sooner had they started to push the truck when the strong light mounted on the front of the train picked them out from 100 metres away. They heard the hissing of the steam as the train started to slow and then the urgent blast of the locomotive's whistle. This had the desired effect and the truck lurched from the extra effort the two German soldiers suddenly discovered. A few seconds later, the train rumbled through the crossing; a familiar figure standing on the running board at the rear of the train.

"Clutch bearing deflecting arm, Victor? What if one of them was a motor mechanic?"

"No chance of that, any German soldier with an ounce of skill is on his way to the Eastern Front."

****

Dawn was breaking when the train stopped outside the gates of the last place most of the passengers on the train would ever see. Jimmy wasn't prepared to watch the disembarkation so he hopped off as the train was still pulling up and marched confidently through the main gate and into the Commandant's Office.

"Welcome to Auschwitz, Sergeant," said the SS Major as he studied Jimmy's papers. "As you can tell," he wafted an arm around his office, adorned with all its Nazi SS citations, flags and other paraphernalia, "we don't get many regular army personnel being posted here. With your distinguished career, you must have really pissed off some high-ranking General to get posted to this shit hole?"

"Actually, the General in question gave me the option of either here or joining General Paulus with the 6th Army near Stalingrad."

"In my opinion Sergeant, you made the wrong choice."

"I agree, Major, but that just pissed the General off even more."

The Major chuckled. "I think you and I are going to get along really well," and extended his hand in greeting. "I'll have the orderly show you to your quarters where you can freshen up after your journey. Report back to me at 0730 hours and I'll have your duty roster ready."

Part 4—tick.

Jimmy already knew where the NCO's quarters were located. In fact, thanks to the briefings he had received over the last six weeks, he almost certainly knew where every building within the camp was located, its purpose, the distance between each one and how many German guards were stationed at each building at any time during the day and night. But there was only one building that he was interested in and after tonight they could remove it from the records because it would cease to exist.

Considering the desolate and forlorn state of most of the camp, the NCO's Quarters were palatial. Jimmy didn't have a room to himself but he did have a decent size curtained-off cubicle with a wash basin, water and a towel, a small kit locker and a bed and a mattress—on which he allowed himself an hour's sleep.

At exactly 0730, Jimmy, refreshed from a nap and a cursory wash down, came to attention in front of the Major's desk "Oberfeldwebel Schreiber reporting for duty Herr Major" and snapped off a smart salute and received a half-hearted one in return.

"At ease, Sergeant, military procedure is reserved for the parade ground."

"Understood, Major."

"To tell you the truth Schreiber, I'm finding it difficult to assign you something that befits both your extensive military experience and your rank, so

I've decided to allow you the choice of several positions." He handed Jimmy a handwritten list, "Those three duties will still not have you bouncing out of bed with enthusiasm in the mornings but they will help pass the time."

"Thank you, Major. May I take the morning to walk around the camp and see what these duties entail?"

"By all means, however, I hold a Heads of Section meeting at 0800 hours— if you like I can introduce you to the Officer in Charge of the sections covered by that list to save you some time?"

"Thank you, Major. I'll see you at 0800."

Jimmy quickly scanned the list the Major had given him and swore under his breath "Damn!" Unfortunately, the list didn't include the "Research & Development Unit," which was where his target would be located during Part 5 of the operation. No matter, while it would have made the mission a whole lot simpler, the original plan was still viable.

****

"Sergeant Schreiber, this is Lieutenant Carl Matthias, OIC Security Division." The Lieutenant was the last in line to be introduced to their new recruit.

"Welcome, Schreiber." That was it. No handshake, no attempt at small talk, just a cold, interrogative stare from the lieutenant's steely-blue eyes. Jimmy was very good at assessing people at first sight and he didn't like Matthias one little bit.

"Lieutenant," Jimmy replied with what he hoped was an equally hostile glare.

A momentary pause later he relaxed the glare knowing that he had to defer to this slick and spit-polished arsehole; the last thing he needed was Matthias ringing Berlin for a copy of his service file.

"'Matthias', that name is familiar?" he mused. "Wait, your father wasn't Colonel Richard Matthias?" Jimmy caught the relaxation of the Lieutenant's eye muscles, '*Gotcha*'.

"No, no, the Colonel was my uncle," Matthias replied excitedly. "My father was a Commander in the Kriegsmarine; unfortunately, his submarine was lost in the North Atlantic 2 years ago."

"My condolences, Lieutenant." He had to recover the conversation quickly. "But you must be immensely proud to know he played such a vital role against the enemies of the Fatherland. Not only that but you also have an uncle in whose Regiment I had the pleasure of serving in North Africa. In memory of both great men, I salute you Lieutenant Matthias." All conversation in the room ceased when Jimmy snapped his heels sharply together and gave a loud 'Heil Hitler!'

He was pleased to note that Matthias actually blushed before lowering his eyes. "Thank you, Sergeant," he said genuinely, "if we can catch up later, I would like to hear about your time in Africa with my Uncle?"

Jimmy gave a small bow. "Most certainly Lieutenant, it will be my honour." But Jimmy had other plans for the little shit that didn't include any conversation.

With Matthias's section crossed off his list, he had the choice of the Motor Transport Unit or the Armoury. Both sections had their advantages; the obvious being the Armoury where he would be responsible for the maintenance and repair of all small arms, but in the end, he chose the MTU where he had access to any number of vehicles that might come in useful.

Reporting to a dour, overweight, overall-clad Lieutenant Marks a short time later, he was assigned the position of Supervisor, Engine Maintenance. He was pleasantly surprised to find that his charges were two very jovial Poles who, according to Marks, were 'volunteers' from Krakow. Jan and Radek were working under the bonnet of a Kubelwagen when Jimmy introduced himself in fluent Polish. He had in one short greeting, gained two allies who might be useful later on that day.

Jimmy squatted down next to them. "Does the fat turkey speak Polish," he whispered, pointing to the carburettor in the pretext of discussing what the Poles were working on. They caught on immediately, "Marks doesn't know shit!" one spat loudly while continuing to work on the engine. "He issues orders in English that we both understand and, I found out the hard way, he does understand the popular Polish insults, but apart from that, no, he doesn't speak Polish."

"OK, thanks. I'll talk to you both later."

"Is this my office, Lieutenant?"

"It certainly is not Sergeant, but you can use it while I'm in the workshop."

Jimmy opened the door to the windowless office and promptly closed it again; the combined stench of stale body odour and foul-smelling cigarettes was too much!

"No, that's OK, I'll set up shop on one of those workbenches at the back."

Unfortunately for Jimmy, there were no routine meal breaks during the day. The MTU opened at 0700 and closed 12 hours later—provided the assigned tasks had been completed.

Marks had lunch in his office while the Poles were fed when and if, they made it back to their hut by 2000. Jimmy was left to sort himself out. He hadn't eaten since prior to boarding the DC3 over 20 hours ago and while he'd survived longer periods without a meal, he would need to create an opportunity to eat soon because when darkness fell he knew the next meal would be at least 24 hours away.

As it turned out, an opportunity was created for him.

Lieutenant Marks was still in his office when a spotlessly clean, black Mercedes Benz W150 pulled up outside the workshop. An equally immaculately dressed Private stepped out of the car and marched smartly inside.

"Can I help you Private?" Jimmy asked, intercepting the soldier before he could knock on the office door.

"The Commandant wants Lieutenant Marks to check the exhaust system— she's rumbling rather than purring."

Never one to let a chance go begging, Jimmy wrapped an arm around the Private's shoulder and steered him back to the car.

"Tell you what, I'm waiting for some parts to be picked up from the station so why don't we kill two birds with one stone? You and I take the car for a run to the station and I can listen to the exhaust and pick up the spare parts at the same time?"

Before the Private had a chance to respond, Jimmy had sat in the driver's seat and held out his hand for the keys.

"I must protest!" the Private blustered. "I'm the only person permitted to drive the Commandant's car!"

"Your protestations are noted soldier, now give me the fucking keys!"

Jimmy had noticed a food van parked near the station when he arrived early that morning. It had been doing a brisk trade serving hot tea and snacks to the many soldiers on hand to greet the new 'deportees'. Driving the car through the entrance would also give him a chance to see how thorough the gate-house guards were; although driving the Commandant's car probably wasn't the best test.

Surprisingly, despite it being the Commandant's car, the no-nonsense guards were amazingly thorough. Both he and the Private had to provide identification while the inside of the car and the boot were searched before they were waved through.

Jimmy was in luck when they reached the station. The food van had steaming mugs of tea, albeit weak and tasteless, thick-sliced black bread spread with most likely lard and a Polish pickle. He stood to the side of the van slowly savouring the bread and tea and took the opportunity to survey the surroundings.

Fifteen minutes later, he returned to the car.

"Damn parts haven't arrived yet!" he announced to a pouting Private. "Cheer up, Private! Tell you what—why don't I sit in the back and you can drive? Just so I can hear the exhaust better," he explained.

The Private looked relieved that his charge had been returned to him and then perplexed at the thought of a lowly Sergeant sitting where the Commandant usually sat.

The guards at the gate were more relaxed on their return but this was probably due to the fact that it was extremely unlikely someone would try to sneak into a Concentration Camp.

Back at the motor transport compound, Jimmy assuaged the sulking Private by having one of the Poles check the Mercedes exhaust system. Twenty minutes later, with a hole in the tailpipe repaired, a now smiling driver returned to the car to the Commandant's office.

****

1900 hours arrived and Marks ordered the Poles back to their hut and turned to Jimmy. "Privileges of rank Sergeant; I get to go and have a hot shower while you secure the building—and don't forget to switch off the compressor. See you here at 0700 hours when we get to do it all over again."

"Do you mind if I continue working on the Kubelwagen, Lieutenant?"

"Knock yourself out."

Jan and Radek had earlier let Jimmy know that the Kubelwagen was, in fact, fully serviceable and they only continued working on it until the next vehicle arrived.

There were no idle hands in Auschwitz and if Marks had nothing for them to do, they'd be transferred to somewhere "less deserving of their talents".

Understandably, much of Lieutenant Matthias' Security Division was responsible for guarding the prisoners with only irregular patrols around the buildings occupied or controlled by the SS themselves. So when Jimmy took the Kubelwagen for a drive around the latter part of the camp on the premise of 'testing out the replacement carburettor', he wasn't really surprised that he did so unchallenged. On his way back to the MTU Compound, he stopped off at his quarters and retrieved his knapsack.

2015 hours—Part 5 begins.

Back in the workshop, Jimmy unpicked the inside seam that concealed a thin space between the back panel and the harness support board. From inside he retrieved a 1/4" thin 8"x12" green piece of plastic explosive and from the seam itself, two 2-hour delay pencil detonators. Warming the explosive in his hands, he moulded it into a ball about the size of a golf ball.

Placing all three objects in his pockets, he reboarded the Kubelwagen and drove to a brightly lit parking area near the Officer's Quarters. No point attracting suspicion parking on a dark side street.

As he climbed out he quickly scanned the area and spotted a lone soldier standing guard. Without missing a beat, he unbuttoned the left top pocket of his tunic and took out a packet of American cigarettes. He timed it perfectly to be abreast of the guard as he patted his pockets as if searching for matches.

"Evening Corporal, wouldn't have a match would you?"

"Ugh, Sergeant?" somewhat perplexed.

"At ease Corporal. A match; yes?" Jimmy tried again. The Corporal looked around the deserted car park. Satisfied they were alone, he hitched his weapon over his shoulder and took out a box of matches.

"Ah, thank you." Jimmy lit the cigarette and as he handed the matches back.

"Here, have one of these," he said, offering the soldier the small pack of Camel cigarettes. "Managed to pick up a few of these during my time in Africa."

"Thank you, Sergeant."

"Thank you for the light and keep the packet. More where those came from."

Jimmy casually walked across the car park and into the darkness and out of sight of the guard. He then quickened his pace and keeping to the shadows as much as possible, he rounded the last corner cautiously and surveilled the brightly lit building 50 yards across a deserted road.

As with the rest of the SS amenities, the building perimeter wasn't being patrolled but there were two armed guards outside the glass entry doors with another soldier seated behind a desk in the foyer.

This was the Research and Development Unit and, if the Polish Resistance Intelligence reports were correct, it contained his ultimate target.

Withdrawing into the shadows, he skirted the limits of the building lights and worked his way to the rear of the building where he knew, from the surveillance photos that he had studied religiously, were four large heating fuel tanks. Crouching down near the tanks, he removed the explosive from his pocket and worked it into the gap between the middle two tanks. Arming the detonators by crushing one end he removed the safety strips from the other and pushed each into the explosive.

Checking his watch—2050 hours—he retraced his steps back to the Officer's Mess car park where he took a second packet of Camels, this time from his right top pocket. The opened packet contained four cigarette-looking objects. Two were in fact just plain cigarettes but the others hid two small frangible glass tubes. Jimmy tore open one of the dummy cigarettes and tucked the small vial in the space between the base of the thumb and forefinger of his left hand.

Marching confidently into the Officer's Mess, he was intercepted by an immaculately dressed and perfectly coiffed Corporal with an equally spotless white napkin draped over his arm.

"Excuse me, Oberfeldwebel, may I be of assistance?"

"You may, Corporal. Would you please inform Lieutenant Matthias that Sergeant Schreiber is here to see him?"

Moments later, an off-duty and remarkably more relaxed Matthias, his tunic undone and his tie loosened, came bustling to meet him.

"Schreiber, pleased you could make it. Please come in."

He stretched out his arm signalling for Jimmy to precede him.

"After you, Lieutenant," Jimmy replied with a slight bow.

"Yes, of course. Come, come."

They meandered their way through a mostly-deserted dining room to a smoking salon that despite Hitler's no-smoking policy, was being pushed to its limit by the three current occupants.

Having three witnesses to the next part of the plan was out of the question. "Excuse me, Lieutenant, do you mind if we talk in private? Some of the information I can tell you about your uncle is for your ears only."

Matthias stopped and turned to face Jimmy. His demeanour had changed instantly and he stared suspiciously into Jimmy's eyes. As casually as possible, Jimmy leaned in close and whispered, "A man in your position surely understands that with the war in North Africa at a crucial point, any first-hand knowledge of the battles your uncle waged, remains classified?"

Matthias relaxed. "Absolutely, Schreiber. Of course, of course." He looked around the room. "Ah, the Reading Room. *Corporal*," he shouted "*two glasses of Schnapps in the Reading Room*!"

Matthias had just sat down when the Corporal knocked on the door. Still standing and with his back to Matthias, Jimmy opened the door and took hold of the tray with his right hand.

"Thank you, Corporal," and in one easy movement of his left hand, closed the door in the Corporal's face, snapped the glass vial and emptied the contents into one of the glasses.

Dropping the remains of the vial onto the carpet and grinding it with his foot, he placed the spiked drink in front of Matthias and then sat down in a leather armchair opposite and raised his glass, "In honour of the fallen and in the name of the Fatherland, Prost!"

He downed the foul-tasting liquor and was relieved to see Matthias follow suite.

Jimmy checked his watch—5 minutes for the drug to take effect; 1 hour 40 minutes until all hell broke loose. He settled back in the comfortable chair and crossed a leg over the other knee.

"So, you annoying little turd," he said to a stunned wide-eyed Matthias, "you want to know the truth about your homosexual paedophilic uncle, ja?"

"**Corporal!**" Jimmy called from the Reading Room doorway. "Give me a hand, will you? It seems the Lieutenant can't stomach cheap Schnapps."

Jimmy had an incoherent Matthias by one arm while the stunned Corporal took the other. "I have a car outside. If you help me get him into it, I'll drop him at his quarters."

The Kubelwagen wasn't known for its luxury or size and Jimmy wasn't overly careful in dumping Matthias in the front seat. "Thank you, Corporal, and not a word of this to anyone. I'm sure Lieutenant Matthias can rely on your discretion?"

"Absolutely, Sergeant."

Minus 1 hour 15 minutes.

Ever since he had surveilled the R&D building earlier, Jimmy's brain had been working overtime trying to work out how to get past the two guards outside and the one at the desk inside. Meeting Matthias that morning had provided an opportunity in regard to escaping with his intended quarry but it did little in answering his current dilemma. In the end, he had no other choice but to quickly dispose of the guards outside and then worry about the other soldier once he was inside.

He brought the Kubelwagen to a stop at the entrance to the R&D building and, concealing his silenced pistol behind his back, walked smartly up the steps to the entrance. He had almost reached the top when one of the guards started to move towards him.

"No stopping now, Jimmy," he told himself and without missing a step, he shot both guards before they had time to raise their rifles. Continuing unfalteringly, he opened the double doors and pointed the pistol at the soldier behind the desk.

"Hands on the desk, NOW!"

Jimmy stole a quick glance around the small foyer but apart from another set of solid double doors further along the hall, there were no other entry points.

"OK soldier, would you like to do this the hard way or the easy way."

"Th—th—the easy way?"

"Good choice. Now, how do I get past those doors?" Jimmy was positive opening the doors would set off an alarm unless an isolating button or switch was made.

"Y—y—you can simply push them open, Sergeant."

The 'pffft' of Jimmy's pistol and the crack as the bullet smacked into the brick wall inches from his ear caused the soldier to leap vertically a considerable distance out of his chair and grab instinctively for the said ear.

"Tut, tut, tut—and here I was thinking you had opted for the easy way," Jimmy scowled as he moved the pistol to an inch from the guard's forehead. But as he leaned over the hob at the front of the desk he couldn't help but notice the red button with the label 'Tur Freigabe'—Door Release. Jimmy had to smile at the soldier's bravery but unfortunately, he ended up in the same place as his colleagues outside.

Minus 50 minutes.

Having disarmed the doors, Jimmy's first priority was dragging the bodies of the three soldiers into the corridor behind the now disarmed doors and out of sight from the entry. While the absence of guards outside would raise eyebrows, the sight of three dead ones would make his mission impossible.

His next task was to retrieve the unconscious body of Matthias from the car, remove his uniform and then lay him down next to the other bodies.

Minus 30 minutes.

Jimmy moved quickly but silently along the corridor, stopping to glance in through the windowed doors as he passed.

All were dark but the forth, brightly lit, revealed his target—Doctor Stefan Jensen Sc Med—Doctor of Medical Sciences and a major contributor to Hitler's 'Final Solution'.

With Matthias' uniform draped over his arm, Jimmy knocked politely and then purposefully strode into the room. An annoyed Doctor Jensen barely had time to verbalise that annoyance when the butt of Jimmy's gun saw him slump unconscious to the floor.

Working quickly but unhurriedly, Jimmy removed the doctor's lab coat and dressed him in the SS Lieutenant's uniform. He had discarded the Lieutenant's riding boots—they had been a bugger to remove so there was no way he was going to get them on the unconscious doctor—and, on the spur of the moment, he purposely left off the tunic. Cutting and tearing the white lab coat into strips, he wrapped the doctor's head and hands so that they looked as if they were bandaged.

Dragging the doctor into the corridor, he gathered all the paper he could readily locate inside the laboratory, piled it in the centre of the room and set it alight. He waited outside looking through the door until he was sure the fire had taken hold and then with Jensen over his shoulder and Matthias' tunic and hat under the other arm, he returned to the Kubelwagen.

Minus 8 minutes.

Timing the finale of his getaway was crucial; if he reached the main gate after the explosive detonated, the camp would be locked down and there would be no escape. If, on the other hand, he got there too early, the guards would be suspicious of his story and want to investigate more thoroughly—something his flimsy story wouldn't hold up to.

He pulled up out of sight of the Guardhouse and checked the scientist was still unconscious. He draped Matthias' tunic around the doctor's shoulders then waited for the moment when the glow of the burning building would illuminate the sky behind him.

Minus 6 minutes.

The instructions for the use of the 2-hour pencil detonators contained the warning that the 2 hours was the mean time that had been established during testing prior to production and that in service the user should allow "minus 30 seconds and plus 120 seconds" before they fired.

Jimmy hoped like hell that the ones he was currently counting on were tending to the plus side. A moment later, he caught the first glow of the fire.

Minus 3 minutes.

Jamming the Kubelwagen into gear, he floored the accelerator and skidded to a halt, inches from the gate.

"**Contact the Commandant immediately**," he shouted at the startled guards. "**The R&D building is on fire. Lieutenant Matthias suffered major burns trying to put it out and I need to get him to a hospital as soon as possible. NOW, OPEN THE FUCKING GATE!**"

One of the guards caught site of the ever-increasing glow and started barking orders. Thankfully, Jimmy had created enough confusion that the gate was opened without anyone asking for ID—not that they could identify the bogus Lieutenant Matthias with his head swathed in the quasi-bandages even if he had it.

Minus 2 minutes.

As soon as the gate was opened far enough for the Kubelwagen to fit through, Jimmy gunned the engine and sped off in the direction of the nearest hospital in Tychy—purely for the benefit of any guards witnessing his departure.

Minus 1 minute 30 seconds.

Two hundred yards down the road, Jimmy turned the car lights off, killed the engine and pulled off the road. He climbed out of the car and jogged back down the road until he could see the flickering light of the burning laboratory.

Plus 13 seconds.

What seemed like an eternity, but turned out to be exactly 40 seconds later, a huge orange ball of fire rose into the night sky as the slightly tardy detonators ignited the explosive which in turn instantaneously ignited the tanks of kerosene – the loud 'whump' of the explosion reaching Jimmy's ears a few seconds later.

Checking that the unconscious Doctor Jensen was still breathing, Jimmy climbed back behind the wheel and with the car lights still off, he turned around and headed for the turn-off for the rendezvous with 'Curtains' and his team.

Three long bum-numbing hours later, Jimmy and the now tied and gagged Doctor Jensen, turned off the pot-holed goat track, through a humorously signed gate—**'Trespassers Welcomed—with Shotgun Pellets!'**—and into a newly mown field. Jimmy turned off the engine and drew in a large breath of the freshly cut grass.

He was about to get out when he heard a rifle being cocked just inches from his head.

"The mighty Jimmy Schreiber gets taken by surprise. This is a first."

"Come off it, Curtains. I could smell your cheap cologne a hundred yards up the road."

They both enjoyed a laugh—more from relief knowing that the mission was all but over rather than from their friendly banter.

Both of them hauled the still half-dressed Jensen from the Kubelwagen and dragged him to a waiting Junkers JU-52—kindly donated to the RAF by a defecting Luftwaffe crew some months earlier—while Victor and two of his AK pals took care of the car.

They were all too aware that German patrols would be increased once it was discovered that there had been no admission of a Lieutenant Matthias with severe burns to any of the major hospitals in the area. Hopefully, the Nazis were still extinguishing the blaze and that it would be some hours before the Commandant suspected sabotage. Hiding the Kubelwagen was simply a mandatory precaution.

"Good evening Major, Warrant Officer and unidentified guest," the pilot announced as he welcomed them aboard the aircraft. "Tonight's flight plan will take us Nor-Norwest through German airspace on our way to the coastal village of Kolobrzeg. From there we will descend to 200ft for our flight across the Baltic Sea to our final destination near Malmo, Sweden. Flight time—all going well— is about 3 hours 30 minutes so we should get you to Sweden in time for breakfast."

"And from there?" Jimmy asked.

"Ah, afraid someone would ask that" the pilot replied apologetically, "outside of my brief I'm afraid."

"Um, this is probably just a minor observation," Curtains said, "but I did notice the complete absence of runway lights!"

"That's because there's no runway, Major." And with a sly grin, he turned and made his way to the cockpit.

The flight went smoothly, so much so that Jimmy slept for most of it and true to his word, the aircraft kissed the Swedish runway 3 hours and 37 minutes later.

Once the aircraft had come to a stop and the engines shut down, the pilot reappeared from the cockpit. "Bad news and good news chaps; the bad news is we're only stopping to refuel, so no Swedish waffles for breakfast—the good news is from here we're flying direct to RAF Lossiemouth in Scotland."

After another 4 hours flight time, the aircraft bucked, sashayed and swayed its way onto a wind and rain-swept airfield. Jimmy couldn't help but notice the lines of Halifax, Wellington and Lancaster bombers and the numbers of air and ground crew scurrying in and around each one. "Don't envy the poor sods flying those buggers."

"No, course not—much rather be doing the bloody piece of cake job we're doing eh? You mad bugger!" Curtains replied.

The Junkers taxied to a remote area of the airfield and with the engines still running, stopped next to two black saloon cars. Two armed Military Police got out of one of them, opened the door to the aircraft and climbed inside.

In a loud voice, one of them announced, "*Everyone please remain seated until advised otherwise.*"

The pair of them then hauled the still-bound Doctor Jensen to his feet, placed a black bag over his head and manhandled him into the rear seat of the other car. No sooner had the door closed when the car drove off.

The Military Policeman returned to the aircraft, "Thank you gentleman, enjoy the rest of your day." With that, the aircraft door was closed and the Junkers taxied back to the main holding area and shut down.

"And just let me say that the whole country owes you a debt of gratitude, Warrant Officer Schreiber, for an absolutely heroic effort in relieving Hitler of one of his most valued scientists!" Curtains declared sarcastically.

"Ease up, Curtains. We are both fully aware that what we do will never be formally acknowledged by anyone outside SOG. Quite frankly, with some of the things I do in the name of King and country, I'm thankful they never will."

"Aye, you're right, Jimmy, but just once in a while—"

Jimmy and 'Curtains' had just unfastened their seat belts when the Junkers pilot stopped by their seats.

"I'm returning to Boscombe Down at 1100 hundred hours; Wing Commander Jessop has 'suggested' I drop you two off at RAF '*Winfield*' on my way to Wiltshire. Would you care to join me for breakfast in the Officer's Mess while the aircraft is being refuelled?"

"My first preference would be a long kip in a warm feather bed, however, a hot breakfast and a steaming hot mug of tea would definitely be a close second! What say you, Jimmy?"

"I'd say you read my mind, Curtains!"

Chapter 1

December 1956, Poplar, London

The icy winter wind, increasing in velocity as it funnelled its way down Campbell Road between the brown-grey terrace houses in London's East End, rattled its way uninvited past the poorly sealed windows and under the ill-fitting front door of number 145. A pathetically small coal fire burned fitfully in the hearth and shared its choking fumes between the chimney and the small ten feet by eight feet sitting room. The Massey family's washing hung over chair backs and Jerry-built clotheslines in an attempt to dry work clothes and school uniforms ready for tomorrow.

Nine-year-old Bobby Massey was seated on the threadbare rug in front of the fire playing with his toy cars while his parents, wearing jumpers, jackets and scarves, sat in the only two armchairs in the draughty room.

"Says here that this cold front is going to be with us for the rest of the week Mary. Better check to see if we still have any of our coal rations left," Robert Massey commented while reading the newspaper.

"What's wrong with your two legs Robert Massey?"

"Sorry, luv, didn't mean it to sound like an order; I'll check later. Hey, here's a go—have we got twenty quid in the bank?"

"You'd be joking! The rent is due on Friday so that will leave us with a fiver if we're lucky!"

"What would you say if we didn't have rationing, didn't have to pay rent, we could breathe fresh air and we wouldn't have to put on every flamin' piece of clothing we own to stay warm?"

"I'd say you've had too many pints in the 'Lord Campbell'."

"Well, just have butcher's at this!" Robert folded the newspaper in half and handed it to his wife.

Mary read the half-page advertisement that Robert had pointed out.

"You can't be serious?"

"Why not?"

"Why not! Robert, there are a hundred reasons why we can't move to Australia!"

"Such as?"

"Well, for a start, what about Mum and Dad?"

Mary was referring to her parents; neither of Robert's parents had shown any interest in maintaining contact with their son after they had divorced nearly three years ago.

"OK, I agree that will be a stumbling block, but, everything else—my work, Bobby's schooling, the 'Campbell', well, maybe not the pub—everything is available in Australia!"

Mary studied the ad once more, "Can we just talk to my parents first?"

"Of course, we can." Robert leaned over to kiss his wife, "Think of it as a once-in-a-lifetime opportunity."

Mary leaned over to respond in kind, "and a long-overdue honeymoon."

"Worry! Why on earth would we worry?" Mary's father had exclaimed when Mary had tentatively mentioned them moving to Australia.

They were all seated around the dining table, enjoying Mary's specially prepared roast beef and Yorkshire pudding dinner.

"I've only known you to make one bad decision in your life Mary and that was marrying that rogue at the other end of the table!"

"Dad!" she remonstrated but then joined in the laughter.

"I'll miss you terribly," her Mum said, placing a hand over Mary's and an arm around her grandson's shoulders, "but I think that not getting Bobby out of this cold, dark country when an opportunity to escape comes along, would be a crime. So, with our blessing, please go and explore a brand new country—but not until after Christmas!"

"Thanks, Mum."

That was all the encouragement the Massey family needed. Six weeks after completing all the necessary forms and getting all the required vaccinations, they boarded the SS *Strathaird* for the six-week voyage to Sydney, Australia.

****

Just two miles as the crow flies from the Massey residence in Campbell Road, Poplar, the West family had had a similar conversation—albeit a somewhat heated one—a few months earlier.

John West had been a sheet metal worker at the Ford Motor Company in Dagenham since completing his apprenticeship there in 1946—and he couldn't wait to get out of the place! He'd had a gutful of getting out of bed at 5:30 a.m. leaving home at 6:30, working eight hours 'making the same bleedin' panel every bleedin' day' and not getting home until 7:30 p.m. to a dried-out dinner that was heating over a steaming saucepan of water!

He had married an eighteen-year-old Brenda Simpson the same year he finished his apprenticeship when she was informed by her family doctor that she was about three months pregnant with John's child. Linda was born in 1947 to parents that were struggling to make ends meet with each blaming the other for the predicament they had found themselves in.

Then, coming home on the train one evening, John had read a similar 'Exciting New Life in an Exciting New Land'-type of advertisement that had stirred Robert Massey's imagination.

"I'm not bleedin' moving to Australia, if you want to go, then you can go on your own Johnny!" Brenda had spat when he suggested migrating.

"Come on, Bren, you're only saying that because you haven't thought about it! Here we're both working and we still don't have any money in the bank. We shove Linda off onto your Mum day and night—the poor kid is nearly ten and doesn't even know who her parents are!"

"That's unfair! She knows why we're never here! If one of us gave up work to look after her, we wouldn't be able to stay in this flat near her Nana or go to the same school or have nice clothes! Get your head out of the bleedin' clouds Johnny! I don't want to hear any more of your stupid ideas."

Two weeks later, adamant that his family would be better off in Australia, John West gave his wife an ultimatum—immigrate with him and Linda or they'd go without her.

With that, she lost her temper. Screaming, swearing and throwing everything she could lay her hands on. After she had run out of puff—and things to throw—she moved in with her mother.

Three days passed and then Brenda's mother knocked on his door.

"Hi Mrs Simpson, come in."

"'Mrs Simpson'? Ease up Johnny, I'm not here as my pig-headed daughter's deputy! Make us a cup of tea and let's talk."

"Nana!" Linda launched herself into her Nana's arms.

"Hello, Lindy-Lou!" She embraced her granddaughter warmly.

"I missed you, Nana!"

"I missed you too sweetheart!"

"Is Mum OK?"

"Nothing a dose of Cod Liver Oil wouldn't fix."

"Eww, yuk!"

"Come on, Lindy Lou, you need to be a part of this conversation too."

Sitting around the West's small kitchen table, John had laid out his plans and dreams he had for their new life on the other side of the world.

"Are you sure that the same boring job isn't waiting for you in Australia?" Mrs Simpson asked.

"No, of course not, but for ten quid I'm willing to take the chance. Nan, I know that migrating isn't going to be a magic pill that will fix my marriage or a guarantee to provide wonderful, satisfying jobs for me and Brenda. What I do know, however, is that Linda's future will be much brighter in Australia than it is in this country at the moment."

"Are you coming with us, Nana?" Linda asked excitedly, fully expecting her Nana to say 'Of course I am!'. Her Nana's answer, therefore, came as a complete shock.

"I'm afraid not, sweetheart, Australia doesn't need any old, single ladies with no more skills than your average housewife."

Linda put her hands to her face and started to cry.

"Hey, hey, no need for tears, young lady! Another couple of years and you won't be needing your Nana anymore anyway. You'll be a teenager wanting to be with your teenager girl—and boy—friends. I love you more than anything in the whole world, Lindy Lou and that's why I'm saying that you need to go with your father. You're old enough to know that if your mum and dad stay here, your family will grow further and further apart. Will migrating to a strange new world fix that—we don't know, but isn't it worth exploring the possibility?"

Linda dried her eyes with the backs of her hands.

"Nana, I love my mum and dad and want the best for them but you're a part of my 'family' and my heart is breaking knowing I might never see you again!" With that, she broke into wracking sobs and threw herself into her Nana's arms.

After a solid earbashing from her mother and her work colleagues who accused her of being insane for wanting to stay in Bethnal Green, Brenda reluctantly agreed to migrate.

The emotions of the three West family members as they stood at the guardrail of the SS *Strathaird* could not have been any more diverse; John was filled with excitement and anticipation, Brenda, still harbouring doubts about leaving England, anxious and fearful and Linda, waving goodbye to her Nana, distraught and heartbroken.

Although Linda would never forget her Nana, little did she know that somewhere on the same ship was a boy that would fulfil her Nana's prophesy.

Chapter 2

December 1957, Parliament House, Canberra, ACT

"This is Ray Garland reporting for ABC News from Canberra. Parliament House is awash in red tonight as the Australian Labor Party celebrates a resounding and, in most commentators' eyes, an unexpected victory over the Australian Liberal Party. I have with me the newly elected Member for Keating, ex-Australian Army Major—George Peterson. Major, would you agree with the comment that your Party's win was unexpected?"

"Not at all, Ray. The Labor Party has the credentials and the policies to lead Australia into the '60s. Prime Minister Fowler and his Ministry—"

"Sorry to cut you off, Major, but we are now crossing to the Main Reception Hall where the Prime Minister-elect, the Honourable Peter Fowler, is about the address the Nation."

"Congratulations, Major."

"Thank you, Mr—?"

"Forrester, John Forrester, Assistant Secretary to the Department of Foreign Affairs—but you can call me John." A wry smile accompanied an offered hand that was taken and shaken by George Peterson.

"Thank you, John, but I had to resign my Commission when I decided to contest the election, so its plain old 'George'."

"Pleased to meet you plain old George. Would you like to escape this melee for fifteen minutes? There's something I'd like to run past you and it would best be done over a single malt. I also know where the barman keeps his supply of eighteen-year-old Scotch."

"Well, I'm a sucker for single malts and I'm inquisitive enough to find out why a senior Public Servant has singled me out the moment I set foot in Canberra. So lead on Macduff!"

John Forrester, an unopened bottle of 18-year-old McCallan Scotch under his arm, led the newly elected Member of Parliament to one of the many recently vacated offices that were dotted throughout Parliament House.

"Ah, here we are! May as well see where you're going to be working for the next three years."

"'Office of the Minister for Defence'? Aren't you jumping the gun John? It will be a few days before the Labor Party Caucus nominates the new Ministry and even then, there's no guarantee that Prime Minister Fowler will allocate Defence to me?"

"George, there's Politics that they teach in Universities and there's Politics that happen inside the smoothly running machine known as the Australian Public Service. Over your time in the House, you will learn the subtle nuances that the Public Service has developed over many years of the Westminster system of government.

"While the elected members of Parliament go through their three-ring circus performances of nominally formulating, drafting and passing Bills into Law, it is the Public Service that is pulling the strings to ensure that the country runs smoothly. How do we do that? By maintaining a low as possible profile and definitely staying out of the public eye. Believe me, George, any Government, whether red, blue or brindle, would never be able to function without the 'Ringmaster' that is the Public Service. The last one tried and look how that panned out!

"Having spent the last eighteen years in the Army, you will still have khaki-coloured blood running through your veins. Working with Ministers whose only goal in life is stoking their egos and fuelling their psychopathic need for power, will come as a shock to someone with your obvious self-discipline and leadership skills. As much as I hate to admit it, we—as in the Public Service—don't cope well with your ilk. An MP with a moral compass is a rarity George and you're going to need an ally if you want to survive the next three years.

"Let me offer you some free advice; over the next three months, you will witness things that will be anathema to the principles that have been ingrained in you by the Royal Australian Army over half your lifetime—so learn to bite your tongue! Keep your maiden speech to Parliament as uncontroversial and bland as you can. Take your time in the shallow end of the pool to get accustomed to the ways of the House and to find out the strengths and weaknesses of your fellow Ministers—including those on the Opposition benches.

"If you take this advice and stay out of the newspapers, in six months you should be well on your way to cementing your place in the Ministry."

John Forrester glanced at his watch and downed the last of his Scotch.

"My apologies, George. I've taken up too much of your well-deserved celebratory party time. Remember the gist of our conversation and please, let us meet again once you're sworn in as the new Minister for Defence."

Both men stood, shook hands once more and then John Forrester left a bewildered George Peterson trying to make sense of what he'd just heard.

Five days after the election, the new Labor Party Members of Parliament gathered at Government House in Canberra.

"I, George Peterson, do swear that I will be faithful and bear true allegiance to Her Majesty Queen Elizabeth, Her heirs and successors, according to law. So help me God."

Shortly after being sworn in, George Peterson MP, Honourable Member for Keating, was allocated the Ministry of Defence portfolio.

One of his first tasks as Minister was to toast his appointment with the Assistant Secretary to the Department of Foreign Affairs, John Forrester.

"OK John, you've successfully manipulated me into the Defence portfolio; why am I there?"

"Don't be so cynical, Minister! How do you know your military experience didn't sway the PM's decision?"

"Fair point; but my money is on your, how shall I put it, 'influence'!"

"Alright, you win, I accept full responsibility—but as far as anyone else is concerned, it's a preposterous suggestion and I have no idea what you're talking about! Now that's out of the way, let's talk business. Have you heard of the 'Mau Mau Rebellion'?"

"Of course. The leader of the Kenya Land and Freedom Army was captured last October, effectively ending the uprising."

"Correct. What isn't widely known is that the KLFA rebels are still active; one of their current leaders, a General Mpoto, is reaching out to countries sympathetic to their cause, seeking military supplies to re-arm his men."

"What does any of that have to do with Australia? We certainly aren't sympathetic to their barbaric acts perpetrated in the name of 'independence'!"

"How much would it take for you to turn a blind eye to their activities?"

"For fuck sake, John! Are you serious!"

"Would one point three million US dollars in an untraceable Swiss bank account prove how serious I am?"

The Minister's eyes grew wide and he slumped back in the plush green leather arm chair.

"One point three million! Jesus!" He downed the nearly full nip of Scotch in one gulp and let the heat of the whisky settle the sudden churning in his gut.

John Forrester took a pen from his suit jacket and wrote something on the back of one of the drink coasters.

"When you get back to your office, take some time to read this file," he handed George Peterson the coaster. "Once you've read the file and worked out for yourself what hasn't been said here today, ring me to let me know whether your eyesight is failing or not."

Later that day, the phone on John Forrester's desk rang, "John Forrester."

"*John, it's George Peterson. Having read the file, I'm sorry to have to inform you that my sight is failing fast!*"

"Good man. Meet me in the Rose Garden at 1:30 p.m."

Chapter 3

3:30 p.m., Friday 8 March 1957 Barclay's Creek, NSW

March and the Australian summer was showing no sign of giving way to autumn anytime soon. A week into what should have been the start of Mother Nature's period of preparing herself for winter and the daytime temperatures were still hovering in the eighties. Everything, both animate and inanimate, was fed up with the relentless, unabating, oppressive heat.

The trees along the edges of the dirt roads, their boughs hung wearily under the weight of the ever-increasing layer of khaki dust stirred up by passing traffic, waited patiently for the quenching and cleansing rain. The normally boisterous pink and grey Galahs simply perched in the shade with their beaks agape and their wings partially open, trying to catch the slightest breeze. Even the blue-tongue lizards that usually took great delight basking in the sun, had sought relief from the heat in hollow logs or had burrowed under the thick layer of cool humus that lay beneath the spreading Lantana bushes.

Ten thousand miles away, things could not have been more different. Men and women beaten down by the privations of a country on whose doorstep, war had raged for nearly six, long, stressful years, prayed for the end of winter.

Swayed by the promise of blue skies and golden beaches, many of those men and women, queued for the spruiked opportunities that lay in a country half a world away. A country that was thirty times the size of Britain but with a population almost the same as London. A country free from the ravages of war; a country blossoming with new manufacturing industries all desperately seeking skilled workers.

If they had known then what they discovered when they arrived at one of the Migrant Hostels, a significant number of those that had come with expectations of a wonderful new life, would have chosen to stay in Britain.

As far as they were concerned, persevering with the grey skies, the weed-covered bomb-sites, food rationing and the forlorn faces of their fellow man was preferable to the hell-hole they now found themselves in.

While husbands spent their days working, eating and sleeping, it was their wives that suffered the most with the monotonous, endless summer heat, the plagues of flies during the day and mosquitoes at night, the merciless heat inside the huts, the waiting in line to use a shared laundry and a shower, and the forty-five-minute bus trip to buy the weekly groceries.

Robert and Mary Massey and their young son Bobby, had been one of many families that had fallen for the Australian Government's spiel, arriving in Barclay's Creek in mid-January 1957. As had John and Brenda West and their daughter, Linda.

Robert was a fully qualified Boilermaker which was one of the trades that the blossoming Australian manufacturing industry was eagerly seeking. He was earning nearly twice the wage he had been receiving in England, but, it came at a cost. Gone were the twilight evenings and weekends spent playing soccer with his son or taking the family down to the 'Lord Campbell' for a meal and a singalong. Now his whole life—and Mary's—was a constant juggling act based on rounds of shift work and sleeping. If wrestling with that wasn't bad enough, they had the seemingly endless summer heat to contend with as well.

The wonderful memories Mary had of hers and Robert's six-week 'cruise' from Tilbury Docks through the Suez Canal to Sydney we're still fresh in her mind. And the train trip from Sydney had been magical! 'Robert! Look! The sea—it's so blue!' she had exclaimed with excitement as the train emerged from a long tunnel to a whole new world!

The view from the bus of the Barclay's Creek Migrant Hostel as they crested a ridge overlooking the village, was the antithesis of what they had witnessed from the train.

A hot breathe of wind had touched down onto the long, straw-coloured grass covering the tree-less hill that lay behind the small township and set it rolling in a languid wave down the slope.

Then, as if sapped of energy, the 'wave' collapsed exhausted onto the pathetic excuse for green grass scattered amongst the ranks of cream-coloured corrugated-iron Nissen huts that were shimmering in the heat. Huts that were to be their homes for the foreseeable future.

The disappointment of the bus passengers was palpable. One lady summed up everyone's emotions, "My God, what have we gotten ourselves into!"

Robert and Mary had persevered for three months; Mary was philosophical, "it's not like it's forever," she would tell herself or, "We'll soon have enough saved to buy a house" and if she really wanted to convince herself, "Dad and Bobby love it here, so nose to the grindstone Mary!"

****

Three-thirty at the end of a stinking hot school day in Barclay's Creek held little pleasure for youngsters Bobby Massey and his girlfriend (he liked to think so anyway), Linda West.

Newly arrived just 6 weeks ago from an English winter, the ten-year-olds were in no hurry to get home. The Nissen huts in the Barclay's Creek Migrant Hostel their parents had been assigned on their arrival in this dry and dusty place were stifling hot and airless—school detention would have been a blessing! At least the classrooms were fitted with ceiling fans.

"Want to see if there's any water left in the creek," Bobby asked as they shuffled along the dirt road, stirring up dust as fine as talc that turned their polished black shoes a sepia brown, "might be enough to cool our feet in?"

"No thanks," Linda replied. "Mum gets angry if I get home without my shoes and socks on, she reckons I'm 'turning native'!"

Coolabah Creek ran along the bottom of a deep grass-sided gully that formed the eastern boundary of the Hostel and with its high banks, shady trees and a trickling stream, was a haven for many of the migrant children. As the gully contained the only trees on the Hostel grounds, it most likely caused some of their parents to wish they were kids again.

Many an afternoon after school, the squeals and laughter of youngsters would echo along the creek as they slid down the grass-covered slopes on large pieces of cardboard. If they failed to stop at the bottom and 'accidentally' ended up in the shallow, but cool, water? Well, they'd worry about the strife that was sure to come their way, later; at the time, it was a bonus that earned them rowdy applause and the admiration of their playmates.

"Hey, I nearly forgot, the ice man comes round on Friday afternoons. If we hurry, we might be able to grab some chips of ice off the back of the truck!"

"Bobby Massey, you're not as dumb as you look!" and without a moment's hesitation, they both forgot about the heat and ran the rest of the way in the hope of any icy treat when they arrived back at the camp.

Sure enough, no sooner had they reached the gate to the Camp when they heard the familiar bell of the ice man delivering blocks of ice for the ice chest. The ice chest was a thing of amazement to the English kids; they just couldn't work out why you needed to keep ice in a box. Not that they really cared—especially when it was 85 degrees and the by-product of the block-splitting process was free. In fact, the ice-man attracted more kids than the free movies in the Dining Hall!

Sitting in the shade of the tiny awning that protruded pathetically over the steps of the West's hut, icy water running down their arms, the young duo tossed around what they could do for the rest of the afternoon.

"You're not going anywhere young lady until you change out of your school uniform and polish your shoes ready for Monday!"

"**Yes, Mum!**" Linda shouted, then whispered, "*I'm sure she could hear a fly fart 100 feet away!*"

"What was that?" her mum shouted back.

Trying hard to suppress a giggle, Linda replied loudly, "**I said 'Yes, Mum'.**"

That was it for Bobby. Turning bright red from holding back his laughter, he took off and barely made it 50 feet before he fell to the grass in fits of laughter.

Twenty minutes later, her chores completed, Linda knocked on Bobby's door. Bobby came scurrying out. "Shhh, Dad's on night shift and he's still asleep."

"Sorry. Do you want to go to the playground?"

"Sounds good, I'll see you there in 5 minutes after I finish helping Mum fold the washing."

Linda was half-heartedly moving back and forth on a swing when Bobby joined her on its neighbour. "Want a push?" he asked.

"No thanks. I thought it might be cooler swinging through the air but I think it's actually hotter."

"Yeah, you're right. The roundabout's in the shade, I could spin you round on it."

"Ugh! Definitely not, makes me want to vomit just thinking about it!"

So, fresh out of ideas, they swayed to and fro on the swings in morbid silence until Bobby suddenly piped up excitedly, "Hey, let's go up to the old quarry! It's probably 100 degrees cooler in there and I reckon there's some gold left up there!"

"OK," Linda agreed somewhat reluctantly and then only because she couldn't come up with a viable alternative. "But we come home as soon as it starts to get dark. Deal?"

"Deal!"

Rejuvenated with the promise of adventure—and some relief from the relentless heat—the pair hurried out through the gate of the hostel and wound their way up the gravel road to the abandoned quarry, barely pausing at the narrow gap in the eight-foot-high chained gate that only caused the duo a momentary pause.

The Barclay's Creek Quarry had been in operation since the mid-19th century, supplying basalt, colloquially known as 'blue metal', for use as concrete aggregate, road base and rail ballast. Quarried ore was transported by road to a crushing plant near Shell Bay and from there it was shipped to Sydney.

The basalt deposit was small and soon exhausted so the quarry site was put up for sale and subsequently purchased by the newly formed Australian Government Department of Works.

The Department quickly surrounded the quarry with high wire-mesh fencing and similarly constructed security gates before more heavy machinery arrived. Work began at a hectic pace as soon as the security measures were in place with trucks going to and from the quarry twenty-four hours a day seven days a week.

The few families that lived in the area at the time, paid little attention to the strange goings on in the quarry or questioned the reasons for all the security measures. As far as they were concerned the 'open cut' quarrying had simply changed to underground mining.

Eighteen months later, the quarry was once more abandoned. Almost overnight, all the machinery had disappeared, the 'mine' entrance had been sealed and the gates were locked.

Neither Bobby nor Linda bothered to read the bent and faded but ominous and wordy sign mounted high on one of the gates as they squeezed through a gap between them. The sign warned that trespassers would be prosecuted and risked a heavy fine and possibly time in goal, etc., etc.—should they be unlucky enough to be caught that is.

In a small town where most of the men worked shift work and mothers with young children were too busy with the day-to-day drudgery of cleaning, cooking and washing, parental supervision of children of school age was at the bottom of their priority list. Kids, like Bobby and Linda, created their own entertainment—as long as they came home in time for dinner in the Camp cafeteria and with a minimum amount of blood escaping from them—no one really cared what mischief they got up to in the meantime.

If that included breaking some obscure law by entering the only real place for young kids to satiate their adventurous spirit in the whole district, who was going to complain?

Chapter 4

4:35 p.m., Friday 8 March 1957 Barclay's Creek, NSW

No sooner were they inside when Bobby ran eagerly over to the base of what was once the work face of the quarry to a large pile of small stones.

"Over here, Linda," he shouted. "This heap is the most likely place we'll find any gold that was left behind."

Linda, who harboured doubts that any sane miner would have left any gold laying around, ambled over to watch Bobby scrupulously studying each piece of stone only to discard it with disgust a few seconds later.

One thing Bobby was right about though, it was much cooler here than it would have been at home. Leaving Bobby to his "prospecting", Linda wandered off to see if the quarry held anything more interesting than the false hope of gold. It was while she was marvelling at the red, orange and brown colours that nature had painted on the disused mine face that she caught sight of something glittering about 6 feet up. Maybe Bobby was right after all; maybe there was gold here.

"Hey Bobby, come over here. I think I've found your gold."

Bobby scrambled down the rock pile with all the grace of a newborn giraffe and jogged over to Linda's side.

"Up there," she pointed. "Can you see it shining?"

"Yeah, you're right," Bobby gasped. "No way we can reach it from down here though." Linda thought about it for a few seconds then suggested. "What if we find some flat rocks to pile on top of each other to make some steps?"

"Hey, great idea!" Fuelled with renewed energy, they both raced off in search of the ideal stones to enable them to reach whatever it was that was beckoning them.

It was Bobby who found the cache of perfect stones—unfortunately, it was under a number of larger rocks halfway up what appeared to be the unwanted remnants of the quarrying process.

"Linda," Bobby called. "I've found some beauties but I'll need your help to get them out."

Linda trotted over and following some discussion as to whether it was safe or not—

Bobby determined, "'course it's safe, don't be a baby";

Linda cautious, "what if you fall and break your leg?"

—Bobby climbed easily to the top of the twenty-foot heap.

Not to be outdone by a boy (and forestall the inevitable "you're a big baby," jibes) Linda followed Bobby to stand beside him and decide how to clear the unwanted rocks from the flat stones.

In the end, it was simply a matter of both of them getting behind each rock and pushing it over the side.

All was going to plan until one particularly large specimen that was way heavier than its cousins refused to budge more than an inch or so despite the combined strenuous efforts of both of them. The problem, Linda discovered was that it was locked in place by a triangular wedge of stone.

Unperturbed by the situation, Linda was able to move the rock back and forth ever so slightly while Bobby—with a typical young person's *laissez-faire* attitude to his or Linda's personal safety—kicked the wedge until it was almost free.

He was prevented from freeing it totally when Linda suddenly recognising the danger, shouted, "***Wait!***"

"Why?" Bobby whined. "One more kick and it's free!"

"And what happens with this rock I'm holding once the wedge is gone?"

"Ahh, it rolls over and crushes my leg?"

"Right, so how about we both get down and work out how to remove that wedge without getting hurt?"

Bobby agreed that it was a great idea but no sooner had they reached the ground when, with a sudden grinding warning, the loosened boulder rolled off the stack and crashed to the floor inches from Linda's foot.

"Shit!" she shrieked.

"Bloody hell!" Bobby yelled. More in shock from Linda swearing than nearly being hit by a huge rock.

With masses of adrenaline now coursing through their very alert response systems, both kids acted reactively and took steps to flee the danger—very large steps! No sooner had they reached a safe distance from the mound when the whole top section also tumbled noisily to the quarry floor.

Several heart-pounding moments later, after the dust had cleared and they had recovered from the surprise of the falling rocks; Bobby and Linda found themselves staring at a small opening in the quarry wall where the top of the rock pile used to be. This was not just a natural rough hole in the wall, what they were looking at was the top of an obviously man-made tunnel.

The near-death experience from the rock fall and the exciting discovery of the tunnel instantly erased any notion of finding flat stones or determining the source of the glittering light.

"Wow!" Bobby exclaimed. "This must be the entrance to the gold mine! Let's see if we can squeeze in there?"

"No Bobby, what if there's another avalanche, besides, it's dark in there and there's probably bats and spiders and other creepy things. And the sun's going down soon and I should be going home."

"OK, but I'm just going to climb up, stick my head in the hole and see if I can see anything. If any of the rocks are loose, I'll come back down."

Bobby climbed over the rocks that were still blocking most of the entrance (and some were wobbly but he wasn't telling Linda that) and peered in through the hole. To his amazement, he could see a dull flashing red light illuminating the inside of the tunnel.

"Hey Linda, you have to see this."

"Bobby—"

"Come on. One minute—just a quick look."

"Oh, alright, but you can explain to my mum if I'm late for dinner!"

As they sat side by side watching the flashes of light bouncing off the walls of the tunnel, Linda knew exactly what Bobby was going to say next.

"No!" she said determinedly. "I am not going down into that tunnel!"

"What makes you think I was going into the tunnel?" Bobby protested.

"Because your eyes are wide and you're grinning from ear to ear, that's why."

"You must admit, it's very tempting?"

Linda wouldn't agree out of principle but she admitted to herself that, yes, it was tempting.

"Alright, Bobby Massey, but as long as you promise that soon as it starts to get dark, we get out and go home, OK?"

"OK, I promise," Bobby replied but he was already squeezing through the hole and on his way down the rock pile to the tunnel floor. With a somewhat exasperated sigh, Linda followed him down with a glance back to check that daylight was still visible through the newly formed entrance.

Chapter 5

5.20, Friday 8 March 1957 Barclay's Creek, NSW

"Phew! What's that smell?"

Bobby explained very confidently, that the air in the tunnel smelled of 'farts' because of the acid they used to extract the gold from the rock. How did he know; he knew because he'd become an expert on all things relating to gold and gold mining since reading about it in his Dad's *National Geographic* magazines.

Whatever the smell was, to the delight of both of them, the temperature was amazingly cool. While the walls of the tunnel were definitely not smooth, it was plainly obvious that it wasn't a natural formation. Some 12 feet high and the same across with a flat gravel floor, the tunnel had obviously been purpose-built to allow large vehicles to pass through.

The tunnel curved gradually and although the flashing light revealed that the tunnel was clear and the floor was flat, they both proceeded slowly and cautiously.

"Sshh, can you hear something?" Linda asked nervously. Bobby stopped and listened but apart from a low humming, he couldn't hear anything.

"No, nothing!" He wasn't about to let some angry blowflies deter him from exploring the tunnel further.

As they rounded the curve, the source of the flashes came into view.

"There," Bobby pointed to a dust-covered light fixed high up on the tunnel wall, "that's what's causing the flashes."

"But why is it red and why is it flashing?" Linda quizzed.

"Well, red is for danger," Bobby responded, "and it's flashing a warning of some sort."

"Great, so we're walking into danger and ignoring the signal that is warning us that it's dangerous?"

"No, I've seen these before at Dad's work—it's only a signal to watch out for trucks. Someone just forgot to turn this one off when the trucks stopped using the tunnel."

Unconvinced, but partially satisfied with Bobby's explanation, Linda relaxed a little but still kept an eye on the diminishing daylight still shining through their entry point.

Neither of them gave a second thought as to where the power for the light was coming from.

The red light was, in fact, a warning light that illuminated when the air quality inside the tunnel fell below a certain level. It was originally installed to warn that the facility's ventilation system had malfunctioned and all personnel should evacuate immediately.

During the construction of the tunnel complex, the engineers discovered that small amounts of sulphur dioxide gas were seeping through the rock strata.

The volume wasn't high enough to be dangerous but combined with the exhaust gases of the many trucks driving in and out of the cavern, it was enough to irritate the eyes, nose and throat.

To purge the gases, they built a rudimentary ventilation system using two electrically-powered fans that drew air through a ventilation shaft that extended from the fan room, through the rock to an intake above the facility. The inlet was housed inside, what appeared to be from the outside at least, an old ramshackle barn. The system cut in when the air quality reached a certain toxicity level and the fans simply blew the contaminated air out through the tunnel.

Although the tunnel was no longer used, the ventilation system remained operational. However, one of its safety features was that, in the unlikely event of the pressure increasing beyond a predetermined level, the compressors would cut out and wouldn't come online again until the pressure dropped to ambient or 14.7 pounds per square inch.

Unwittingly, the children had released the over-pressurised air from the tunnel when the rock pile collapsed causing the ventilation fans to automatically start up.

When the tunnel was sealed, electrical engineers modified the ventilation circuits to sound an alarm and illuminate a light on a remote monitoring control panel in a highly secure building situated in the Joint Intelligence Base, HMAS *Dolphin*, some 150 miles away in Canberra.

The pair had only gone another 50 feet or so when they both noticed that just a short distance further in, the red light was no longer reflecting off the tunnel walls and although they could make out the tunnel floor, where the walls should have been was just solid blackness.

"Bobby, I'm starting to get scared," Linda whispered.

"It's fine," Bobby replied hoping the shaking in his hands hadn't come through in his voice.

"Let's just go to the end of the tunnel where we can still see and if there's nothing there, we'll go back, OK?"

"OK Bobby, but not one step further!" she answered determinedly.

A few shaky steps further on when they could hardly make out the floor ahead, they found the reason for the vanishing tunnel walls—as their eyes adjusted to the darkness, they found themselves standing at the entrance to a huge cavern.

While the ambient light wasn't strong enough to reveal the actual size and extent of the space, it was enough for them to just make out the many stacks of dark green wooden boxes it housed.

Bobby counted ten boxes in each stack and there were five rows on either side of where they were standing. One of the boxes had fallen off its stack and had split open shedding its contents over the cavern floor. They instinctively walked over for a closer look.

"The avalanche outside must have caused it to fall," Bobby suggested.

"Well, it certainly shook me up!" Linda answered solemnly.

"There must be a hundred of those small boxes. What do you think's in them?" Bobby asked as he picked up a section of the broken box. "It's too dark to read much but there's a lot of numbers and they all have this large arrow on them," he showed the piece to Linda, pointing out the broad arrow.

"I guess that means they need to be stacked with the arrow pointing up," she said pointing to one of the stacks with all the arrows pointing skyward, "but whatever it means, I'm guessing they're not filled with gold."

Linda knelt down and gingerly picked up one of the dark green containers that had fallen free. Turning it over in her hands she could tell it was a small, lightweight hinged box—much the same size as the tin her dad's pipe tobacco came in. It didn't rattle when she shook it but it was heavy enough to have something inside.

Her curiosity piqued she stood up and walked over to where Bobby was still trying to read the contents.

"Come on, Bobby, let's take this outside for a closer look," she said and then slipped the small box into her pocket.

"Hold on, I'm going to feel my way along one of the rows just to see how many of these boxes there are," and with that, he disappeared into the darkness.

What felt like an eternity later Bobby re-emerged, "50 boxes in this row. If there are no more rows on either side, that makes 10 rows of 10 stacks of 50 boxes. That's—" after some mumbled mental arithmetic and finger counting "That's 500 boxes!"

"No Bobby, that's 5000 boxes," Linda corrected.

"Holy cow! So if there are 100 of those small boxes in each one—"

"500,000 Bobby!" Linda gasped. "Why would anyone store 500,000 thousand of anything in a cave and then forget about them?"

"Right!" she continued. "Now, we know how many there are, we really should get back and find out what's in them and whether it's buried treasure or just worthless rubbish," and with Bobby tagging along behind, Linda strode purposely back along the tunnel.

The daylight that had been streaming through the opening when they climbed into the tunnel was now a dull steely blue.

"Oh boy! Guess who's going to be in trouble when I get home?" Linda muttered as they climbed out of the tunnel into the still and steamy evening.

"Don't worry," Bobby offered, "we can tell our parents that we decided to go to soccer practice and they know that finishes as soon as it gets too dark to see the ball so we still have some time to spare."

But their adventure was about to turn into a nightmare.

Their feet had only just touched the ground at the base of the rock pile when the towering rock wall of the quarry face behind them began to pulse with bright blue light and the distant sound of a police siren echoed around the quarry.

"We're gonna!" Bobby moaned.

Linda grabbed his arm, "No wait! That police car is still coming up the hill and if we're quick, we can hide behind one of those big boulders near the entrance."

Needing no further prompting, Bobby raced after Linda and fell behind a boulder just as the flashing blue light was joined by a pair of headlights and a powerful spotlight which swept searchingly across the open area in front of the car. Thankfully for Bobby and Linda, it was a 'C'-shaped quarry and the car lights couldn't reach into the corners on either side of the entrance.

Moments later the spotlight was turned off and they heard the crackle of a 2-way radio.

Chapter 6

5:30 p.m., Friday 8 March 1957 HMAS *Dolphin*, ACT

Thirty-six-year-old Petty Officer Kevin Doyle was a 19-year Royal Australian Navy veteran and this was his last posting before he 'paid off' after 20 long years. He was looking forward to spending some quality time with his wife and son whom he'd been a husband and father to for only about half of the time he'd been married.

Recently, he thought about how his attitude to his responsibility as a married man had changed as he had gotten older. As a father of a 'terrible two-year-old', he prayed for the day the Navy posted him to a sea-going ship. He looked forward to the camaraderie and working as part of a close-knit team that kept 'their' ship sailing.

Everyone aboard knew what they had to do and when to do it. It was hard yakka twenty-four-seven but that made the downtime in foreign ports all that more enjoyable. Dealing with a two-year-old bundle of obstinate fury was definitely not part of his duty statement! It wasn't until his son started school that he realised he was missing the father/son relationship that civilian fathers enjoyed. From that day on, he started to dread his next sea posting.

He was halfway through his second and (thankfully!) last patrol of the all but abandoned Joint Intelligent Base, HMAS *Dolphin* when a sound he dreaded ever wanting to hear—and especially in the last 45 minutes of his watch on a Friday afternoon—shattered the quiet afternoon.

Casting those thoughts aside, his training snapped into action and he flattened the accelerator in the Land Rover and steered towards the source of the siren. As he rounded a corner with tyres protesting noisily, he spotted the red flashing light at the entrance to one of the disused but highly secure hangars.

Squealing to a halt outside the still locked hangar doors, he thumbed the transmit button on the 2-way.

"Control, this is Bravo Patrol, over."

"Bravo, Control go ahead, over."

"Control, I have an active alarm in Hangar 43, over."

"Bravo, please confirm building number, over."

"Control, building is Hangar 43, I repeat 4 3 Over."

"Roger Bravo. Standby."

Lieutenant Commander Jerry O'Rourke was finishing signing the last of the routine reports he, as the Commanding Officer of the base, was required to submit to the Chief of Naval Intelligence in Melbourne each Friday, when the phone rang.

"Commander O'Rourke."

"Sir, it's Lieutenant Bill English, Officer of the Day. Sir, we have an alarm sounding in Hangar 43. Petty Officer Doyle is outside the hangar awaiting further instructions."

"Christ Almighty!" not one for profanities or obscenities, this outburst by the CO meant only one thing—no one would be off duty for some time. "Tell Doyle to remain where he is. I want you to pick me up from my office in 15 minutes with the keys to the hangar."

"Aye, aye Skipper."

"And Bill, not one word of this to anyone not on the Need to Know List and close the gates and lock down the base."

"Yes, Sir."

Lieutenant Bill English hung up the phone and realised he was sweating—and it had nothing to do with the heat. The briefing he had received from the CO on his arrival some 10 months earlier, concluded with him having to sign a secrecy document.

The document contained the dire promise that if he was found guilty of contravening just one of the many clauses contained therein, he would be court-martialled and if found guilty, stripped of his commission and dishonourably discharged.

One of the clauses stated that under no circumstances were any buildings in the Red Zone to be entered without the Commanding Officer being present.

The Red Zone contained those buildings that were the subject of two routine security patrols each watch and were out of bounds to all the ship's company. The exception to this being the senior Petty Officer of the watch who was responsible for carrying out the patrols.

HMAS *Dolphin* was originally constructed as a Royal Australian Airforce Base in 1925. The Base was subsequently leased to the Royal Australian Navy when the Airforce moved its operations to Richmond on the outskirts of western Sydney. HMAS *Dolphin* was commissioned as a Fleet Air Arm establishment in 1932, however, the aircraft based there were operated by the British Royal Navy.

With the outbreak of World War II, all the aircraft returned to Britain and in 1941 *Dolphin* became a Joint Defence Services Intelligence Base with the Royal Australian Navy retaining operational command of the facility. In 1950, with the Government looking at drastically cutting spending across all Departments, it was decided that the covert and clandestine operations that were necessary during the war could no longer be justified during peacetime.

However, in their haste to shut down operations at HMAS *Dolphin* and reassign personnel, they forgot to account for the cost of dismantling the massive amounts of top-secret infrastructure. It was simply locked, sealed and secured in situ with a skeleton complement to carry out security patrols and routine maintenance.

Hangar 43 was the exception. Inside its cavernous space, that once used to house aircraft, was installed still functioning electronic equipment set up to remotely monitor the Australian Defence Department's secret storage facilities dotted around the east coast of the country.

Having closed the main gate and posted armed guards, Lieutenant English threw the main switch to the switchboard shutting down all phone links with anyone outside of the base. Donning his peaked cap, he strode out to an idling Land Rover, "Captain's office Able Seaman Lyle, on the double if you please."

Lieutenant Commander O'Rourke was in the process of removing the red 'Top Secret' file with *Operation Candy Apple* typed across the front cover from his safe when he heard the Land Rover come to a protesting stop. Hastily jamming on his cap, he hurried out to the waiting Land Rover.

"Out you hop, Able Seaman, I'll take it from here."

As the AB tumbled out of the driver's seat, the CO handed the file to Bill English, jammed the gearstick into first and shot out onto the road almost in one motion.

"Have a quick read of the 'Summary' at the back of the file Bill and pray as you've never prayed before that the scenario in the last paragraph hasn't been set in motion and that this siren is a system fault."

The 'Summary' read in part:

"—indicates a breach of a remote secret storage facility. In the unlikely event of a breach of security at any of the monitored remote facilities, it is imperative that the Designated Minister, as listed in Appendix C, is informed immediately. ***Under no circumstances is the breached remote storaghe facility to be entered without the express permission of the Designated Minister."***

If Bill English had been worried before, what he read drained the colour from his face.

"Holy crap!"

"My thoughts exactly, Bill."

They arrived at Hangar 43 a short time later to be met by Petty Officer Doyle. Kevin snapped his CO a smart salute however, the reply was totally unexpected.

"No time for military protocol I'm afraid Kevin, this siren sounding probably means that the excrement has made contact with the spinning object," and to Lieutenant English, "is there any way we can isolate that bloody siren Bill?"

"Only once we're inside, Sir," Bill replied and began searching through a large ring of keys for one with '43' etched on it.

The CO turned to PO Doyle, "Kevin, did you log the time you first heard the siren?"

"No Sir, but Control would have logged the time I called it in, so it would have only started sounding 10, 20 seconds before that at the most."

"Roughly?"

"I'd say 1715, Sir."

"OK, thanks, Kevin."

"Got it!" Bill English announced as he located the key.

"Great, let's get inside and stop that incessant racket! Kevin, log the time of entry please."

"Aye Sir. 1732, Sir."

"Right. Let's see what all the fuss is about," and the trio entered the hornet's nest.

Bill English quickly located the alarm isolating switch and they collectively sighed with an appreciation of the silence.

"Right," the CO said. "Knowing the security protocols in regards to entering any 'Red Zone' buildings, this is probably a stupid question but have either of you been in here before and know the layout of the building?"

"No sir, but if it's a standard hangar configuration, all the office spaces are located on both sides with any workshop spaces situated where the aircraft would be stored if this was an air base," Kevin responded.

"OK. Kevin, you search the port side spaces, Bill you check the workshop area and I'll start looking in the spaces on this side. What we're looking for is a console with a blinking red light. Let's go gentlemen!"

Less than 10 minutes later Bill English called out, "Found it! Over here in the centre of the hangar." Commander O'Rourke and Petty Officer Doyle joined him seconds later.

"Log the time please, Kevin. When the dust settles after all this, we'll need a very precise account of what followed in the wake of that alarm sounding."

As they arrived, the CO opened the Top Secret file and unfolded a large diagram of the console before them. The diagram had arrows pointing to the various buttons, switches and dials with each arrow numbered. On the side of the diagram was a table describing the function of each numbered object.

The actual panel on the console with the flashing red light was labelled 'Remote Storage Sites'; the numbered arrow corresponding to the light in the table was titled 'Barclay's Creek NBC'.

"That's all we bloody need someone breaking into a site designated 'Nuclear, Biological and Chemical' storage! OK, most importantly, where the fucking hell is Barclay's Creek?" the CO asked—more out of hope than anything else.

"There's a large map in the Superintendent's office over on the port side, Sir," PO Doyle offered.

"Of course there would be. Bloody boffins wouldn't know how to find their own arse without a compass and a slide rule!"

They hurried over to inspect the map and sure enough, each of the storage sites was marked with a red sticker; not only that but a strand of red string connected each site to a photograph of the actual site.

The CO grinned, "Well, well, well, those boffins weren't such a bunch of useless gits after all. Bill, leave the hangar keys with Petty Officer Doyle and get back up to the switch room and connect my office phone to the outside world, please. I need to get a broom up someone's arse in Barclay's Creek pretty damned quick."

As Bill hurried outside, the CO turned to PO Doyle, "Kevin, I'm going to have to leave you to secure the building and find your own way back. Try reactivating the alarm on your way out but if it begins to wail again, isolate it, however, we'll need to detail someone off to monitor that console in case any more sites are compromised. And log the exact time you lock up," the last order given as he strode purposely back to the Land Rover.

"Aye, Aye Sir," Kevin replied to the now vacant space and with a rueful sigh resigned himself to the fact he'd probably be on duty for the rest of the night.

Arriving back in his office Lieutenant Commander O'Rourke was pleased to find he had a ringtone on his phone and seconds later he was speaking to Assistant Commission Andy Duncombe, Head of the Special Operations Branch of the Australian Federal Police.

"Andy, Jerry O'Rourke, CO HMAS *Dolphin*."

"Hello Jerry, haven't heard from you since you attended one of my security lectures late last year. What prompted this call?"

"Andy, sorry I can't go into the why, but I need you to make an urgent call to the Barclay's Creek Police Station and have them investigate a possible break-and-enter at one of our secret storage sites."

"Coming from you I can appreciate the secrecy so no apology required or expected. Now, whereabouts in Barclay's Creek is this storage site situated?"

Chapter 7

6.35, Friday 8 March 1957 Barclay's Creek, NSW

"Car 58 to base, over."

"Base, is that you, Steve? Over."

"Yeah, good one, Phil; who else gets the bogus B&E's on a stinking hot evening? Over."

"Sorry, mate, force of habit. Are you on-site? Over."

"That's an affirmative. Is Vic there? Over."

The Barclay's Creek Police Station was the standard New South Wales buff-coloured weatherboard with green corrugated iron roof building with a covered veranda running along the front. The grass-green panelled wooden front door opened into a small vestibule with a counter delineating it from the rest of the station. Behind the counter, there was an open office space large enough for three tables and a radio operator's desk.

The Station Officer in Charge had his own office; a hallway running along the front of it led to a single holding cell, a kitchenette, a store room and bathroom facilities. For all intents and purposes, the Station outwardly resembled a normal country dwelling; except for the large white and blue 'Police' sign hanging from a post just inside the front white picket fence and the obligatory flag pole in the centre of the garden.

The Officer in Charge was Sergeant Vic Rogers. The other police officers at the Station were Senior Constable Tim Masters and Constables Steve Ahearn and Phil Cummins the radio operator.

Sergeant Vic Rogers method of policing was termed by his young charges as 'old school'. He demonstrated just how 'old school' his methods were, when a call came from an Australian Federal Police Commissioner directly to Vic Roger's office, strongly advising that the Barclay's Creek police immediately—

if not sooner—get someone out to the Barclay's Creek Quarry to investigate a suspected break and enter.

He never gave a second thought as to why a Commissioner from the AFP would be ringing about a B&E in Barclay's Creek; he simply shouted through the office for Constable Ahearn to '*Get your head out of that porno magazine Ahearn and get your arse over to the old quarry tout suite! That's NOW, Constable!*'

Victor Reginald Rogers was born in 1915 in a two-bedroom flat above his parent's hardware store backing onto the busy Sutherland to Central rail line in Rockdale. He was always big for his age and was the first picked in any schoolyard rugby league game.

Despite his height and weight advantage over many of the other kids at Rockdale Primary School, he never used his size to bully or intimidate.

Truth be told, it was Victor that was the discouraging factor to those that did try to bully or intimidate. Surprisingly though, he never made any true friends. Most of the time he would walk home alone, get changed out of his school uniform and help out in his parent's shop rather than kick a footy around on the nearby oval with the other kids in the neighbourhood.

This trend continued through High School. Despite being a loner, he became a great all-round sportsman winning the Rockdale Amateur Middleweight Boxing competition twice; played in the second row for the Rockdale Bulls— winning the Best and Fairest medal in the Under 21's and also excelled at basketball. All before he turned eighteen.

He joined the New South Wales Police Force in 1936 on his twenty-first birthday. Much to his father's displeasure.

"You're throwing your life away boy!" Vic knew when he was in trouble when his father stopped calling him 'Victor' and started referring to him simply as 'boy'. "With your talent, you could have been as great a league player as 'Snowy' Justice or as famous as 'Les' Darcy, but no, you choose the worst-paid job in Australia! You must have custard for brains boy!"

Despite not receiving his father's well wishes, Victor had discovered his calling; revelling in the physical training and achieving top grades in academic subjects. He graduated as a Probationary Constable in 1939 and was assigned to the Darlinghurst Police Station where he remained for the next seven years.

Here he had learned the 'art of community policing', as described by his Sergeant and mentor, "you don't arrest anyone in our patch if a kick up the arse will suffice." He failed this lesson only once. He had attempted to arrest an individual on a minor charge. A charge that if it had been brought before a Magistrate, would have been 'embarrassing' for the individual's Boss, "and we never, ever, want to embarrass the Boss, do we, Constable?"

His Sergeant later explained to him that it wasn't simply a matter of applying the written law but also considering what the best outcome was for the community as a whole.

"Constable, what's the point of cutting the tail off a sleeping snake when all that's going to happen is you piss it off."

It was advice that had ensured he survived those seven years and had resulted in him being promoted quickly through the ranks to Sergeant and a posting as Officer in Charge, Barclay's Creek.

Senior Constable Tim "The Master" Masters gained his nickname by being conspicuously unavailable when any job that he considered to be below his capabilities required investigating. A break and enter into an abandoned quarry positively and unequivocally was too menial for him, however, it was the perfect opportunity for a young constable to gain some invaluable knowledge.

His theory—although others saw it more of an excuse—was that in a town where the single police cell was used exclusively for the storage of 'confiscated' items, inexperienced Constables needed all the 'real' cases that came their way.

Twenty minutes after dispatching Constable Ahearn to the scene of the alleged break and enter, Constable Phil Cummins yelled from behind the 2-way radio desk.

"Boss, Constable Ahearn—"

"No need to shout, Constable."

Phil jumped as the large, hairy and muscled arm of Vic Rogers reached over his shoulder and deftly plucked the microphone from his hand.

"Constable, Ahearn, what took you so long? You didn't stop off for a beer on the way did you?" A 2-second pause. "Cat got your tongue Constable?"

"*Sorry Boss, waiting for you to say 'over', over.*"

"For fuck sake! Over!"

"Right. Arrived on scene 1835 and immediately surveyed the area. Gates were found locked and secured with no signs of attempted forced entry. Do you want me to use the emergency lock release system (police euphemism for bolt cutters) and search the entire area? Over."

"May as well make yourself useful while you're there Constable. And turn that blue beacon off, you'll have everyone in the town wondering what all the fuss is about. Over."

"How the bloody hell did you know the blue—?"

"Yes, Boss. On it. Over and out."

As the radio conversation ended and the blue light was extinguished, Linda pulled Bobby close.

"The policeman is going to search the quarry," she whispered, "that means he'll have to open the gates to get inside. Once he's inside and over by the rock fall, we'll sneak out quietly and run home. OK?"

"OK," Bobby managed. "But what if he searches behind this boulder first?" He had never been as scared as he was now. If he was caught by the police, his dad would beat the living daylights out of him. Not that his dad was a violent man but his son being a criminal would definitely change that real fast.

They watched from the cover of the boulder as Constable Ahearn cut the chain and opened the gate. A torch beam came on and moved carefully around the edges of the quarry passing over the boulder they were hiding behind in its travels.

Thankfully, the policeman's torch beam moved further into the quarry leaving their escape route open. When the torch was no longer visible, as silently as they could on loose gravel, Linda and then Bobby walked slowly through the gate and past the police car. They had just cleared the rear of the police car when suddenly the 2-way radio squawked into life scaring both of them into a flat-out sprint back to the Migrant Camp entrance.

"Base to Car 58, over," PC Ahearn had just rounded the corner of the quarry with his torch picking out the large mound of rocks where Bobby and Linda had scrambled down minutes before, when he heard the radio call.

"Base to Car 58, over."

"Car 58, over."

"Ahearn, Sergeant Rogers. Belay entering quarry, I repeat, do not enter the quarry. Over."

67

"Uh, a bit late for that Boss! Over."

"Bloody hell, Ahearn! Why is it that the only time you comply with an order immediately is when you shouldn't have? OK, can't put the egg back in the shell. Close the gates, park the car across the entrance and await further instructions. Understood? Over."

"Car 58, Understood Boss. Over."

"Base, Over and out."

Steve Ahearn knew from the tone in the Boss's voice that something monumental had or was about to, happen.

It was now fully dark when Bobby and Linda raced through the Camp entrance but even though they knew they would both be in for an ear bashing when they got home, they collapsed onto the grass and burst into fits of laughter as the threat of capture disappeared and the excess adrenaline slowly abated.

The small box in Linda's pocket lay momentarily forgotten in all the excitement.

As the laughter subsided, Linda stood and extended a hand to the still-prone Bobby. "Up you get lazy bones, let's get home and cleaned up before our parents get really angry."

Bobby accepted Linda's outstretched hand, "Thanks, Linda. Sorry for nearly getting us arrested!"

"OK, but next time we might stick to checking out the creek eh?"

"Deal! See you in the cafeteria for dinner?"

"Sure, see you then."

Later that evening, their ears still burning from the anticipated tongue lashing from their parents, Bobby found Linda in the Dining Hall seated at a table separate from her mum but still within "steely-eyed-glare" range. The glare changed to an "if-looks-could-kill" directly aimed at Bobby as he began to sit down next to Linda.

"Hi, Mrs West," he tried feebly.

"Don't you 'Hi' me, Bobby Massey! The next time you go to soccer practice you make sure my Linda gets home before dark. You hear me?"

Bobby was relieved to hear that Linda had remembered their cover story.

"Yes, Mrs West. Sorry, Mrs West," the confidence in his reply exposing his relief. Even so, he decided to avoid eye contact and quickly moved to sit opposite Linda with his back to her mum.

Bobby had escaped relatively unpunished. Thankfully, his dad was on night shift and truth be known his mum was grateful that Bobby wasn't "getting under her feet" or constantly having to remind him to be quiet while dad was sleeping.

Linda lowered her head under the pretext of eating her dinner. "Meet me round the back of your hut after you finished dinner," she whispered. "We need to work out what to do with the box we stole."

Bobby simply nodded his agreement and then replied, "I'm going to leave now. I don't like meatloaf and creamed spinach anyway. See you when you're ready." Bobby dumped his largely uneaten dinner in the bin—earning him another glare, but this time from the cafeteria supervisor—and hurried out to await Linda in the now cool evening.

Chapter 8

7:30 p.m., Friday 8 March 1957 Barclay's Creek, NSW

Bobby lay on the grass between the rows of huts and thought hard about their adventure and the discovery of the cavern with its mysterious contents. He couldn't for the life of him find any logical answer to the questions raised as they had stood in the darkness of the cave—what did the boxes contain, why were there so many and why were they stashed away in a sealed cavern?

He was no closer to finding the answer to any of them when Linda lay on the grass beside him.

"I think we're in big trouble." She said as she placed her hands behind her head and gazed up at the stars. Bobby turned and propped himself up on one elbow.

"Not if we don't tell anyone. OK, the cops scared the hell out of us but we weren't caught so no one knows we were there. What I can't work out though is; if no one knew we were there, who called the cops?"

Linda, let Bobby's question go unanswered—it didn't bear thinking about!

"Keeping a secret from our parents and friends is easy—I'm not so sure I could keep quiet if the cops arrested me though," Linda countered.

"Why would they arrest us? What are they going to do—arrest the whole of Barclay's Creek?"

"No, 'course not, but—"

"But what?"

"What if, that red light in the tunnel really was a warning of something really bad? What if, whatever is in the box that's in my pocket is really dangerous?"

"Do you think we should open it and see?"

"Absolutely not!"

Bobby lay back down. "Then we need to get rid of it."

After they had lain in silence for several minutes, both deep in thought, Linda sat up. "I don't think we can get rid of it Bobby. We can't return it to the cave or hand it to the police without getting into trouble and, if it is dangerous, we simply can't throw it away and risk some other kids finding it. No, we're stuck with it. We just have to figure out how and where the safest place is to hide it."

"You know, for a girl, you're pretty smart. Ow! That hurt!" he yelped as Linda landed a hefty punch on his arm.

She smiled and replied, "You know, for a boy, you're a bit of a wimp."

The next morning, Linda answered a knock on the door to a grinning Bobby. "I have the perfect hiding place," he declared.

"Are you sure?" Linda had asked after Bobby had laid out his plan.

"Absolutely."

The plan sounded simple enough. Bobby had received a 'Revell' model ship kit from his parents for Christmas and had started building it but soon left it on the shelf unfinished. His primary source of fun lay outside the stuffy confines of a hot Nissen hut. But that was going to change.

"So the box will be sealed inside the ship?"

"That's right! I had already glued the two halves of the hull together before I got bored and stuck it back in the carton; all I have to do is place the box inside the hull and glue on the top deck. Mum and Dad will be pleased I've started building the ship again, so no questions asked there and once it's finished, they'll be so proud of my efforts, they'll be afraid to touch it in case it breaks! What do you think?"

Linda reached out and hugged him—which caused Bobby all sorts of weird, but wonderful, new sensations to surge through his body. Linda suddenly let go and stepped back, "Ugh, sorry about that, but you're a genius, Bobby Massey!"

Bobby blushed furiously, both from the unexpected hug and from being called a genius.

"Ugh, thanks Linda." He managed sheepishly.

Linda produced the little green box from her pocket and held it in front of her face. "Well, I can't say it's been fun but you certainly created a very memorable moment in my life." (Bobby had to agree with the 'memorable moment' bit, but it had nothing to do with the small box) "I do hope we don't see each other again." And with that, she passed it to Bobby.

Chapter 9

7:30 a.m., Saturday 9 March 1957 Barclay's Creek, NSW

"Car 63 to base, over."

"Base, go ahead Car 63. Over."

"Base, this is Senior Constable Masters for Sergeant Rogers. Over."

"Silly prick!" Phil Cummins thought out loud, "must think he's in a station of 300!"

"What was that, Constable?"

"Uh, nothing Boss. The Mast—um, Senior Constable Masters on the 2-way for you."

"Yes, Masters, go ahead," Vic said into the mike after he had ambled from his office, obviously reluctant to engage the over-officious Senior Constable.

"Sergeant, my watch ended at 0700 hours and there's still no sign of my replacement. Over," the Senior Constable unable to mask his displeasure at having to work shifts—and over the bloody weekend!

"That's because your replacement is currently carrying out a higher priority task on my orders Senior Constable." Phil Cummins smiled broadly—the 'higher priority task' was in fact, making the tea and frying the bacon and eggs for the Sergeant's breakfast. "But you can rest assured that Constable Ahearn will relieve you well in time for 'smoko'. Over."

'The Master's' groan was audible through the speaker.

"I'm sorry Senior Constable, I missed that. Say again. Over," with a wink to Phil Cummins.

"Uh, nothing Sergeant. Just clearing my throat. Over."

"Yes, I thought as much. Over and out." He handed the mike back to Phil and then leaned down ominously. "I very much frown on insubordination in my Station Constable, so although 'The Master' is indeed a prick, you will afford him the respect his rank demands. Is that clear, Constable?"

Phil swallowed the lump that had formed in his throat and managed a squeaky, "Yes Boss, absolutely Boss!"

"Good man. Now, go give Ahearn a hand making my breakfast."

Chapter 10

7:30 a.m., Saturday 9 March 1957 HMAS *Dolphin,* ACT

Commander O'Rourke sat expectantly behind his desk trying hard to distract himself from what had happened yesterday afternoon. The saving grace—if there was one—was that no other alarms had sounded and the console that was foremost in his mind, was still flashing only one warning light.

He snatched up the handset almost before the phone rang.

"Commander O'Rourke."

"Good morning, Jerry."

Jerry recognised Captain Peter Fleming's voice immediately. He and the Captain had gone through the Officer's College together and were firm friends up until the start of their final semester.

Jeremiah Aloysius O'Rourke had been born and raised in the upper-class Sydney suburb of Hunters Hill. The only son of wealthy parents—both were partners in a Macquarie Street law firm—Jerry attended the prestigious St Ignatius College for boys in Riverwood, just a short ferry ride over Tarban Creek from his home. With Hunters Hill situated on a promontory separating the beautiful waters of Tarban Creek and the Parramatta River, it was natural that Jerry would spend much of his leisure time either sailing his own single-person 'Cadet' dinghy or helping to sail his father's yacht.

Being accepted into the Royal Australian Navy's Officer's College seemed to be the obvious progression for his enormous natural talents and unrealised leadership potential.

The Officer's College was basically a private university with the addition of various navy-specific subjects. Like Universities, the College recognised academic achievement but it also awarded those that excelled in the various sporting activities offered by the college.

All three arms of the Australian Defence Forces believed it was on sporting fields where the skills absolutely necessary for the Force's future leaders; teamwork and leadership, were learned.

While it was never documented or openly discussed, all Officer Cadets were keenly aware that if you failed on the sports field, you would never be awarded Dux even though you may have been outstanding academically.

Peter Fleming was the exception.

Jerry was ticking both boxes—he was a brilliant scholar and a superb athlete. He was captain of the College rugby team that had won the local rugby competition two years running, he had represented the Navy in the Tri-Service basketball competition and had yacht skippers scrambling for his sailing skills in regattas up and down the coast.

Unfortunately, his father wasn't Vice Admiral Fleming.

Jerry was philosophical. He knew from the get-go that once they joined the fleet as fully-fledged Naval Officers, Peter was always going to get the best postings and the earliest promotion. However, while they were both cadets—for whatever reason—they became friends.

That friendship counted for nothing though come the start of that final semester. That was when, rather than an experienced seaman branch Petty Officer or Chief Petty Officer acting as their mentor and class leader, one of their own was appointed. While his class believed Jerry was the only choice, Officer Cadet Peter Fleming was appointed 'Class Captain' together with a shiny gold (not yellow, definitely not yellow!) stripe added to his epaulettes.

While Jerry took the rebuff in his stride, it was obvious that Peter now saw their friendship as a hindrance to his leadership of the group.

In fact, it seemed he went out of his way to distance himself from their friendship at every opportunity, ranging from assigning Jerry the most difficult and/or demanding tasks his team were given, to the plain petty such as not approving leave for Jerry to attend Rugby training.

Jerry had endured all the crap Peter had thrown at him over the last six months. The final straw, however, came when Officer Cadet Fleming was awarded Dux of the intake.

The bitter pill was sweetened somewhat when, following the presentation ceremony, the Chief Petty Officer who had been their class mentor for the first two years, shook his hand and said, "The true test of a Naval Officer, O'Rourke, is how they handle defeat and not the way they gloat over victories."

Then to rub salt into his wounds, Midshipman Fleming was posted to HMAS *Anzac*, a new Battle Class destroyer while Midshipman O'Rourke was posted to HMAS *Katoomba*, an ageing Bathurst Class corvette on mine clearing duties based in Cairns, Queensland.

The two had never spoken since that day—until now.

"Captain Fleming, given the gravity of the situation, I was expecting this call last night."

"Come now, Commander, you know how the system works. As you rightly point out, this is a grave situation. So much so that the protocol demands that I contact the Minister directly. Unfortunately, unlike Senior Naval Officers, Ministers are not always readily available."

Jerry regretted the figurative bouncer he'd bowled as soon as he'd said it but, give the Captain his due, he had easily deflected it through the slips cordon.

"Yes sir, my apologies. It's been a long night. Do you have any updates on the situation?"

"Understood Commander. Thankfully, at this early stage, it appears the alarm was triggered by a rockfall—yes, you heard correctly—that uncovered the entrance to the storage facility. The local police found the gates still chained and locked at 1835 and have had an officer guarding the entrance since then. The police are under strict instructions not to enter the quarry and maintain the guard until you arrive onsite."

"Me, sir?" Jerry answered incredulously.

"Affirmative. You are to team up with Sergeant Rogers of the Barclay's Creek Police. You two will be the only persons allowed on-site at the quarry and you alone are permitted to enter the facility itself. Is that clear?"

"Yes, sir."

"You will liaise directly with me and I expect an update each morning at 0800 in time for me to brief the Minister."

"Am I to be briefed on what exactly the facility contains?"

"I'm afraid not Commander. There are currently only three people who know what is stored in that cavern and I'm not one of them nor do I know the names of the other two—assuming the Minister for Defence is one of them that is.

"What I can tell you," he continued, *"is that the contents pose no danger if the packaging remains sealed and normal 'Fragile' handling techniques are applied. I will also send you a plan of the site by courier tomorrow so you know*

the layout. As far as I'm aware, our concern lies in the large storage section only, but while you're there you can have a scout around the rest of the facility to see if anything was damaged or vandalised."

"Understood, Captain. When am I expected to be on-site?"

"0730 tomorrow—I understand Sergeant Rogers is arranging your accommodation and is expecting you for breakfast—in his office."

"In his—? Aye, aye, sir."

Well, that didn't go too bad, Jerry told himself. Fleming must be mellowing in his old age.

Chapter 11

7:30 a.m., Sunday 10 March 1957 Barclay's Creek, NSW

Having set out from Canberra at 3:00 a.m., Jerry opened the main entrance door to the Barclay's Creek Police Station to be assaulted by the mouth-watering aroma of bacon frying.

A police constable greeted him from behind the counter facing the small linoleum-covered foyer.

"Welcome, Commander. See you found the place without any dramas." Jerry wondered if he meant the police station or Barclay's Creek itself. Hedging his bets, he simply replied, "Yes, thank you."

"Constable Phil Cummins, the station radio operator and recently promoted sometime sentry of Barclay's Creek Quarry," he announced and stretched out a hand.

"Jerry O'Rourke," he replied, shaking the constable's hand, "and please dispense with the 'Commander'."

"Pleased to make your acquaintance Comm—uh, Sir."

"Likewise, Constable. Now, before I salivate all over your desk, can you please lead me to the source of that delightful smell!"

Phil knocked on his boss' door and then held it open for Jerry to enter.

"Commander Jerry O'Rourke, boss."

"Ah, Commander, please come in. Park your ar—backside on the lounge there while I let Constable Ahearn know that breakfast can now be served." Vic walked to the doorway and shouted, "*Ahearn, get your bloody finger out. Two of us will die of starvation you take much longer!*"

"Yes boss, on its way boss," came the plaintive reply.

Vic closed the door and the welcome/meeting ritual was repeated but this time Jerry had to check he had been left with the four fingers he had offered the Sergeant.

"More tea, Jerry?"

"Don't mind if I do thanks, Vic."

"*Ahearn, two teas—today!*" And then in a normal voice, "Got to keep the buggers on their toes eh?"

"Oh, absolutely, Sergeant," and then he and Vic had a quiet laugh.

"Right, what's the plan—if there is one," Vic asked after PC Ahearn had cleared the breakfast crockery from the office.

"To tell you the truth, Vic, I have no idea what I'm here to investigate. My orders were to get to Barclay's Creek, team up with you and investigate a suspected break-in at an abandoned quarry."

"OK, first of all," Vic leaned on his desk and stared intently at the Commander "if you and I are going to work together, you need to be up-front with me. I've been in this game long enough to know bullshit when I tread in it. The fact that I get a call from a Federal Police Commissioner no less, ordering me to investigate a suspected B&E at an abandoned quarry 150 miles from his office in Canberra, makes this whole thing smell fishier than a dunny door on a prawn trawler! So what the fuck is going on!?"

Jerry smiled at the Sergeant's forthrightness, "Vic, I understand your annoyance. Yes, you're correct, something is definitely not right. But, what I said earlier is true—I'm in the dark almost as much as you. I say almost because there are certain things that because of the Secrecy Act, I obviously can't disclose. What I can brief you on is the background to why it's me sitting here and not a Military Police Officer."

Over the next 20 minutes, without breaching Navy security protocols, Jerry gave a condensed timeline of events starting with the alarm sounding in one of their secure locations and ending by letting Vic know that he, in his capacity as CO of the base, was the person who asked for the AFP Assistant Commissioner to ring Vic.

"Thanks for that, Jerry. So, like three blind mice, you, me and PC Ahearn better go and have a shufti at this damn quarry.

"*Ahearn, grab your hat, we're doing policing!*"

The trio arrived at the quarry gates just as a rather dishevelled Senior Constable Masters, rubbing sleep from his eyes, almost fell out of the police car in his haste to greet, what he hoped was, his relief.

"Senior Constable," Vic said as he came to a looming stop, inches from Tim Masters face. "Hope we didn't disturb you, Senior Constable?"

"No sir, I mean, Boss. I was just—"

"Save it. But when we get back to the station you and I are going to have a little chat. Now, be a good lad and open the gate for our guest. Commander O'Rourke, Senior Constable Masters."

Jerry shook the man's hand, "Senior Constable."

"Sir," from an extremely sheepish Tim Masters.

Vic led the way followed by Jerry who was about to be followed by the two constables when Jerry put up his hand. "Sorry chaps, but my orders are that only the Sergeant and I are allowed inside the quarry—at this early stage of the investigation anyway."

If Tim Master's sulk was low after his dressing-down from his boss, it was now painfully pitiful.

"Yes Sir, understand Sir."

"I have absolutely no idea how he ever managed to get that second stripe." Vic muttered as soon as they were out of earshot, "he's almost as good as two men short."

"Had a few of those in my time," Jerry replied, "but the Navy has a solution; we promote them out of harm's way."

Once inside the quarry, Jerry did a quick 360-degree scan of the whole area. The first thing he noted was that the security gates were next to useless and much of the wire safety mesh fencing around the lip of the quarry was in a state of disrepair and in several places, had fallen over completely.

There were no buildings or remains of mining machinery laying around so unless someone knew of the existence of the cavern, there was absolutely no reason why anyone would want to break in.

"Kids," Vic said.

"Sorry?"

"You're wondering why anyone would want to illegally enter an abandoned quarry with nothing in it of any value other than the odd piece of quartz. Did you notice the Migrant Hostel we passed as we drove up?"

"Yes, I feel sorry for the buggers; I don't envy them one little bit having to live in those tin sheds!"

"That's the source of your 'criminals'." Vic continued, "Most of the migrants are young families with Primary School-age children. The Government needs workers to man the ever-expanding manufacturing industry, so it pays for male foreigners to come to the "land of opportunity" to cover the shortfall—the by-product of that scheme are the wives and kids. Poor sods. Stuck in that place—dads working shift work, mums going off their nut wanting to go back to the old country and the kids are left to fend for themselves. Now, put yourself in the shoes of those nine, ten, and eleven-year-olds." Vic opened his arms and swivelled around, "isn't this just the perfect place for an adventure?"

Jerry agreed—what Vic said made perfect sense. What didn't make sense, was how did they break into the cavern. A short time later, he concluded that they didn't.

"Up there," Vic pointed to the small opening to the tunnel. "I guess that's the reason you're here?"

"That would be it, but it raises more questions than answers."

"Mind if I hypothesise?" Vic asked.

"Please, hypothesise away."

"OK. Would I be correct in assuming that an alarm has sounded somewhere in secret squirrel land, set off by the uncovering of the tunnel entrance?"

"Correct."

"As we're not in an earthquake zone and there were no reports of an explosion, kids, quantity unknown, enter the quarry—through a poorly secured gate—and climb up the rock pile that was intentionally placed—rather amateurishly I suggest—to seal the tunnel. Somehow, miraculously without death or injury to themselves—as far as we know at this stage—they cause a minor rock fall that uncovers the tunnel. How am I doing?"

"Sergeant, I do believe that was the finest example of a police investigation I've ever had the pleasure of witnessing."

"But that's not the reason you're here is it, Commander?"

"No Vic, it isn't. Unfortunately, I don't give a big rat's arse what occurred outside the tunnel, my problem arises if any of those kids entered that tunnel."

"I've got news for you sunshine," Vic said as Jerry started walking towards the base of the rock pile "there's no way I'm going to squeeze my finely sculptured physique through that little hole."

"That's fine Vic, because I'm the only person authorised to go in there anyway. Not that I'll be going anywhere until I get a plan of the facility from Canberra."

"Well, now we've got some spare time, how about we get your accommodation sorted? I'd offer you a bed at my place, but unless you're deaf as a post, you'd never get any sleep. A snore loud enough to rattle the tiles off a roof—or so I'm told! You have a choice of the Barclay's Creek Travelodge Motel or the Lakeside Inn. If it were me, I'd choose the latter. It's not as quiet as the Travelodge but breakfast is included—and you won't want lunch if you have their breakfast I can tell you!"

"You've convinced me; the Lakeside it is. If you drive me back to my car, I'll go and book a room and you can ring me when the courier has delivered the plan?"

"Done."

Chapter 12

11:00 a.m., Sunday 10 March 1957 Barclay's Creek, NSW

The courier arrived just after 'Smoko'.

Armed with the facility layout in one hand and a powerful torch—that Bobby and Linda would've given a week's pocket money for—in the other, Jerry climbed carefully to the top of the rock pile and shone the torch into the tunnel. The first thing he noticed was the air softly blowing into his face had a smell of sulphur. Scanning the tunnel floor for any signs of recent footprints, drew a blank.

The floor was compacted gravel road base; a herd of elephants would have been hard-pressed to leave evidence of their passing. It would have been nice if the floor was covered in wet red paint with the footprints of the intruder/s clearly visible. Then he had a subsequent thought; or better yet, it would also reveal if no one had entered the tunnel and save him from investigating further.

Jerry passed under the still-flashing red light and assumed it was somehow connected to the console in the hangar at HMAS *Dolphin* back in Canberra. He had only gone another twenty or thirty feet when the torch beam picked out the stacks of Army Olive Drab boxes. He whistled in amazement as he entered the cavern proper and saw just how big it was and the number of boxes it contained.

He directed the torch at the nearest stack and walked over hoping to read what the boxes contained and was just as disappointed as Bobby had been when he saw it was only a mass of numbers. He was just about to move on when the light picked up a small smudged handprint in the layer of fine dust that covered everything. Checking the immediate vicinity of the handprint, Jerry noticed that whoever made the print had trailed their fingers along the whole row, twice. Why twice, he puzzled?

And then with the speed of deduction to match Vic Rogers, he came up with the answer.

"You didn't do it twice; you didn't have a light so you felt your way up the row and back again," another pondering pause. "Counting; you were counting how many boxes are in the row. Why?"

Despite tossing this thought around, he couldn't find a logical reason why a child would want to know how many boxes there were. In the end, he concluded it was simply childlike curiosity.

Walking to the far end of the same row Bobby had walked down, Jerry caught the humming sound of a generator. He moved the torch beam across the floor and found, what appeared to be, a rudimentary plywood-clad structure some 80 to 100 feet away. Set into the centre of the wall were a set of glass-panelled double doors.

The cavern floor was obstacle-free so he made a bee-line for the doors. It was only when he was up close that he realised how thick and sturdy the whole structure was—the doors alone were at least three inches thick! He also noticed that there was a pneumatic rubber seal around the edges of the doors.

"You'd better have a butchers at these plans before you go through those doors me old mate," he told himself and unfolded the document on the floor. "You do realise that you should have done this before entering the complex?"

The plan contained a dearth of information. Where he was at the moment was the 'Storage Area', the tunnel he entered by was labelled 'Heavy Vehicle Access Tunnel' and beyond the doors, 'Administration Offices'.

"Well, thank you Captain Fleming for the exhaustive facility layout!"

The one thing that was surprising came from the colour coding of the spaces; the tunnel and cavern were red while beyond the double doors was green. At the bottom of the diagram was the explanation—the red sections were ventilated while the green wasn't.

"Now, why on earth would you need to ventilate a storage area? 'Curiouser and curiouser thought Alice'."

Jerry tested the doors to see if they were locked by pushing against each one—they didn't budge. He was about to turn back when he realised that if the cavern was pressurised by the ventilation system, it would force the doors closed. He tried them again but this time pulling and they opened slowly but smoothly.

Walking through the doorway, he entered a long corridor flanked on either side by six wooden doors. At the far end of the corridor, were a pair of bright blue steel doors with 'Machinery Space' stencilled on them. It was through these doors that the sound of a generator was coming from.

He was just about to set off for the first office door when the edge of the torch beam picked out a panel on the wall to his right; 'Switchboard'. Inside we're numerous labelled switches. Jerry switched them all on and the whole place lit up like a Christmas tree. Extinguishing the torch he then turned off any switch that wasn't a light—the last thing he needed was to turn on something that resulted in burning the place down!

"So, I wonder who's getting the electricity bill for this then?" he mused.

None of the offices was locked and a single glance in each had been enough to determine they hadn't been entered. Only furniture remained and everything was covered in a layer of talc-like dust.

Lastly, he opened the steel door at the end of the corridor and found that it wasn't a generator that had been humming but an electric motor driving a large shrouded fan that was blowing ducted air through the ceiling into the cavern.

"Of course, the ventilation system!" To the right of the fan was a single blue steel door with 'Emergency Exit' written on it. Jerry cracked open the door and found a small tunnel disappearing into the distance. "No, definitely not going down there."

As he turned from the 'Emergency Exit' he had cause to stop dead in his stride, "What the—?"

Hanging on the wall behind the open entry door was a row of ten bright yellow, full-body protection suits with built-in hoods. Sitting on the floor under each suit was a small black oxygen cylinder and breathing mask. It took Jerry about half a second to realise that whatever was contained in the stacks of boxes out in the cavern was highly toxic.

"Maybe taking the Emergency Exit isn't such a bad idea after all!"

If Jerry had decided to exit via the tunnel, he would have discovered something even more 'Alice in Wonderland'-like.

The tunnel, high enough for his 6' 3" frame to walk upright in, exited through a plain white interior door into the garage of a typical suburban 3-bedroom house on the opposite side of the hill to the quarry.

"Right, Jerry, back to the cavern and a stocktake."

Pausing to switch off all the lights, he walked back into the storage area.

Starting from the end of the row nearest the offices, he counted the number of boxes in that row. Reaching the tunnel end, he was in the process of counting the number of rows when his torch lit up the broken box with its contents spilling from it.

"Oh shit!" With the vision of the protection suits still fresh in his mind, Jerry hoped like hell that none of the containers had broken open. "Bit late for worrying about that old son! Let's see what we've got?"

Casting the beam of the torch over the contents, he could see that the broken box contained numerous tobacco tin-size boxes. Thankfully, they were all still sealed. Moving the broken box so he could read the numbers stencilled on its end, he found the one he was looking for '100ea', meaning that there should be 100 matchbox-size containers. He lifted one of the intact boxes off its stack to use as a stool and began counting.

"Ninety fucking nine!" he swore vehemently. "Now, the shit really hits the fan!"

Sweeping the torch beam across the complete floor area in the vicinity of the broken box for any sign of the missing container proved fruitless so he returned his temporary seat to its stack and trudged heavily back down the tunnel.

"Bad news then?" Vic asked as he stepped onto the quarry floor.

"If you can imagine a worst-case scenario—this is worse than that," Jerry replied forlornly.

"Well, what is it they say 'Plan for the worse; hope for the best'."

"Vic, in this situation, I'd be strongly inclined to replace 'hope' with 'pray'— and I'm not a religious man!"

Chapter 13

1:30 p.m., Sunday 10 March 1957 Barclay's Creek, NSW

"*Captain Fleming.*"

"Captain, it's Lieutenant Commander O'Rourke. Bad news I'm afraid."

Jerry had been sitting alone in Vic's office in the Barclay's Creek Police Station for ten minutes, steeling himself for the phone call he was about to make.

While Jerry hadn't been able to fill in the finer details, he and Vic had tossed around how to approach the children of Barclay's Creek and coax out of them an admission that they had been in the quarry on Friday afternoon—the tunnel, under no circumstances, could not and would not be mentioned.

"*Isn't that line supposed to be accompanied with 'but there is some good news'?*"

"I'm afraid not at this stage, Sir."

"*What are we looking at Commander?*"

"As you can understand Sir, some of this is pure assumption, but, backed up by physical evidence found inside the tunnel, the Sergeant and I have pieced together a pretty strong scenario."

Over the next twenty minutes, Jerry outlined the scenario to Captain Peter Fleming, Chief of Naval Intelligence.

After bouncing theories and suppositions back and forth, the Captain reached the same conclusion Jerry had—they were in deep shit! Although the Captain did describe it more eloquently.

"*How do you plan to proceed from here Commander?*"

"The presence of a police car outside the quarry gates won't have gone unnoticed. Sergeant Rogers is on the phone with the local radio station, as we speak, setting up a plausible story for the local news along the lines of an anonymous caller reporting a loud rumble coming from the quarry around 5:30 p.m. on Friday.

"Police went to investigate and found that a large unstable pile of rocks had partially collapsed. Fearing children may be injured if they enter the quarry, a police guard has been posted until the gates can be repaired and securely locked.

"Sergeant Rogers will also have one of his Constables visit the Primary School first thing tomorrow morning and ask if any of the children had been playing in the quarry on Friday afternoon. We are using the old 'a substantial reward for any information' incentive to see if we get any witnesses."

"*Commander, you mentioned a Migrant Hostel where most of the children are located, might be an idea to carry out a door-to-door through there to see if the parents can recall where their children were at that time.*"

"Yes Sir, I'll recommend that to Sergeant Rogers." This had already been organised by Vic who would be assisted in the task by some constables from a neighbouring command, but, Jerry was disinclined to steel the Captain's thunder.

"*I'll brief the Minister on the latest developments. It's probably pointless for you to brief me tomorrow morning but I'll expect a call at 0800 on Tuesday.*"

"Aye, aye, Sir."

Chapter 14

8:45 a.m., Monday 11 March 1957 Barclay's Creek, NSW

Constable Steve Ahearn—shirt ironed, uniform pressed and shoes spit polished—was on his way to the Barclay's Creek Public School in a freshly washed 'Black Maria' police van when he noticed a young boy hitchhiking further up the road.

The boy, seeing a police car heading towards him, quickly darted into some bushes lining the road.

Steve pulled onto the grass verge alongside the boy's hiding place.

"Good morning, Barry. Can I give you a lift to school?"

Barry Thompson had originally planned on spending the day at the Public Baths and had no intention of going to school. He emerged from the bushes.

"Umm, good morning, Sir," he managed.

"No school uniform today, Barry?"

"No sir, Mum forgot to wash my shirt."

"And no school case either. Are you sure you were going to school? I think you were intending to wag school and were trying to hitchhike to the Pool for the day, isn't that right Mr Thompson?"

"No sir! Absolutely not, sir! I was hitchhiking so I wouldn't be late for assembly, sir!

"Well Barry, you're in luck because that's just where I'm headed." Steve reached over and opened the door, "Come on, hop in and can I suggest next time you try wagging school, carry your towel in a bag, not over your shoulder."

The school bell rang at precisely 9.00 a.m. The children gathered in the quadrangle outside the Headmaster's Office, lined up in their respective class groups.

The Kindergarten, First Class and Second Class children had to hold the hand of the child next to them but the 'senior' classes were saved this embarrassment—much to Bobby's displeasure. He could think of no better way of suffering the agony of Assembly, than by holding Linda West's hand for 15 minutes.

The final recorded (thankfully!) strains of *God Save the Queen* faded away and the booming voice of Mr Ring, the Headmaster, echoed around the square, "Good Morning staff and Good Morning children."

"Good morning, Mr Ring," came the united sing-song reply.

It was during the headmaster's greeting that Linda noticed the policeman walking to the front of the gathering with a rather forlorn-looking Barry Thompson in his grasp.

She grabbed a startled, but pleasantly surprised, Bobby's hand and when she had his attention, nodded in the policeman's direction. He gasped audibly.

"Stay calm," Linda urged, "he's probably just caught Barry wagging again."

Pausing to allow the stirring to stop, the Headmaster continued, "This morning's normal Assembly has been suspended due to the local police having a special announcement. Children, please welcome Constable Ahearn."

"Good morning, Constable Ahearn," came the same sing-song reply.

Steve Ahearn cleared his throat.

"Ahem, thank you, Headmaster. Good morning boys and girls. You may have heard the news on the radio about a rockfall inside the old abandoned quarry."

Linda's grip on Bobby's hand tightened. "Thankfully, no one was injured. Now everyone knows that the quarry is a magnet for adventurous children like yourselves but, I can't stress enough, the pain and anguish that your parents and friends would suffer if any one of you was injured or worse. Unfortunately, as the gates have signs strictly forbidding entry, the police have been tasked to determine the cause of the rockfall. The reason I'm here today is to ask if any of you were in the quarry around 5.30 last Friday afternoon?"

Almost as one, the children looked around to see if any hands were raised. Bobby had the impression they were looking at him and Linda. After a few seconds and no raised hands, Steve continued.

"So no one was at the quarry; did any of you see someone going to or coming from the quarry at that time."

Again, the heads swivelled round and Linda's grip became frantic; an arm was raised! It was Barry Thompson.

"Yes, Mr Thompson, you saw someone at the quarry?"

"Yes, sir."

"Are you able to identify that person or persons?"

"Yes, sir."

"Are they present at this assembly?"

"Absolutely, sir."

"And can you tell me who that person is?"

"Yes, sir."

"Well?"

"It was you, sir, I saw your flashing blue light and saw you at the quarry."

"Yes, thank you, Mr Thompson. How very observant of you." That will teach you to pick up hitchhikers; sometimes policing is best left undone he thought.

The children had erupted into muffled giggles and Bobby started breathing again as he massaged his crushed fingers.

"Alright children, quiet please. Constable Ahearn, please continue."

"Thank you, Headmaster. Children, please think hard about what you were doing on Friday afternoon. Even if you didn't see anyone—apart from me—at the quarry, you may have seen someone heading to or from the quarry around that time.

"If you can remember anything, the Barclay's Creek Police are offering a substantial reward for any information that may help us determine what caused that pile of rocks to collapse."

"Thank you, Constable Ahearn. Children, please do as the Officer requests but for now, you need to concentrate on your schoolwork. Teachers, please take charge of your classes. Assembly, dismissed."

Bobby couldn't keep the smile from his face and looking at Linda, he could tell just how relieved she was too.

As the days turned into weeks, there were no more visits from the police and, apart from not visiting the quarry, life returned to normal for Bobby and Linda.

Bobby had finished the model ship and his mum was so proud of his skill, she placed it with her 'special' things in a glass display cabinet.

The small olive drab box was all but forgotten.

Chapter 15

8:00 a.m., Tuesday 12 March 1957 Barclay's Creek, NSW

"Absolutely nothing Sir," was Jerry's answer to Captain Fleming's question as to whether any information had come to light in regard to the investigation. "The story has been on the news for over 48 hours with no response. The door-to-door of the Migrant Camp and the houses close to the quarry proved fruitless and none of the school children admitted being in the quarry nor seeing anyone going to or coming from the quarry that evening. I'm afraid it's a dead end, Sir."

"*Very well, I'll advise the Minister that we're closing the file on the case. Meanwhile, I've organised for the Army Engineers to seal the tunnel more substantially and for the rock pile to be replaced on completion. I want you to remain in Barclay's Creek and be the OIC of the Engineers until the work is done.*

"*Basically, you're there to ensure no army personnel decide to explore the tunnel before it's sealed.*

"*It will be impossible to deny the existence of the tunnel but once it's sealed and if the need arises, we'll release the story that it was once an armaments storage site. Hence the security.*

"*The Minister has also miraculously found some money in the Defence budget to be spent on, quote, 'the long overdue modernisation of facilities at HMAS Dolphin'.*

"*Read this to mean the building of a more secure facility to house the storage site monitoring equipment and the removal of most of the disbanded facilities in the 'Red Zone'.*

"*Unfortunately, once that is completed, Dolphin will be decommissioned. How do you feel about that?*"

"To tell you the truth, Captain, it should have happened years ago."

"*I agree. So unless there are any developments in regard to the missing canister, I can't see the need for any further briefings. As of now, you are officially seconded to the Royal Australian Engineers. Your orders will be mailed to you care of the Barclay's Creek Police Station. Take care, Commander."*

"Thank you, sir."

Over the next three weeks, Jerry spent his days divided between the quarry, the Barclay's Creek Police Station and the local golf course.

Captain Fleming's concerns regarding any unauthorised entry into the tunnel by inquisitive army personnel took all of four days to resolve. The remaining rock pile had been cleared from the tunnel entrance on day one, the wooden formwork for the concrete pour was completed in the afternoon of day three and the concrete was poured the following day.

By the end of the third week, Jerry and Vic Rogers leaned on the bonnet of Vic's police car and admired the now fully secure quarry.

There was no sign of the plugged tunnel entrance, hidden by a towering pile of rocks and boulders; the fallen down perimeter fencing had been replaced with eight-foot high barbed wire topped mesh fencing and the mesh wire gates had been replaced by padlocked heavy-duty steel beam framed gates that were also topped with barbed wire.

"Bit of an overkill if you ask me," Vic commented.

"I agree, but at least you can sleep easy knowing that Barclay's Creek will never have another break-and-enter into its abandoned quarry," Jerry replied.

"Yes, there's that. Now, I'll just lose sleep wondering how much my taxes will go up to pay for the bloody thing! Another *Flag Ale* Commander?"

"Don't mind if I do, Cheers Vic."

"Cheers, Jerry."

The following week, Lieutenant Commander O'Rourke was back at the helm of HMAS *Dolphin*.

Over the next 3 years, he witnessed the construction of a state-of-the-art, high-security building, purpose-built to house the equipment used to remotely monitor the security of the secret storage sites; he oversaw the long-overdue dismantling of the 'Red Zone' infrastructure and he took the final salute at the decommissioning ceremony of HMAS *Dolphin*.

Now, as he sat in his office for the final time, staring at the blank walls where his memories once hung and the now open empty safe that kept so many secrets secure, he pondered whatever had happened to the mysterious little green box that had set the wheels in motion that led to the demise of HMAS *Dolphin*?

During that same three-year period, Vic Rogers was promoted to Senior Sergeant and his complement grew by two. A Probationary Constable fresh out of the Police College joined the team as did an experienced Sergeant from Wollongbar command. Constable Ahearn had been promoted to Senior Constable with Senior Constable Masters promoted to Sergeant and then promptly posted to a small station in the far west of New South Wales.

The additional manpower was still only just managing Vic's workload as more and more migrants took up residence in the hostel and the level of misdemeanours and petty crimes increased.

In 1959, Linda's family moved into a small, three-bedroom, fibrous cement NSW Housing Commission residence about a half mile from the Migrant Hostel. Linda was struggling in her first year at Barclay's Creek High School. Life at home was becoming unbearable. Her mum was constantly bitching about why they should have stayed in England. Her dad was staying longer at the club and coming home drunk and then the shouting match would start.

While the problems at home didn't help, the truth was, she missed Bobby. Not that she would admit that to anyone! But they had become close friends soon after he had arrived on the hostel and the incident in the quarry had drawn them even closer. She missed his teasing and his laughter, his casual outlook and his adventurous spirit. Her world had become mundane and boring without him.

After finishing High School with above-average marks, Linda applied for and was accepted into Sydney University to undertake a Bachelor's degree in Physiotherapy in the Faculty of Medicine. She moved out of home and into a room on campus and said a somewhat relieved goodbye to her parents and Barclay's Creek.

By the end of her first year of studies, she had settled into the University rhythm, had made lots of new friends and was firmly rooted in the vibrant, pulsating, cosmopolitan lifestyle that Sydney had become in the '60s. But as the Uni slowly wound down for the year, she found herself looking for the slightest excuse not to go home for the Christmas break. The decision was made for her when she received a letter from her father.

"Dear Linda,
Sorry that my first letter to you is a sad one.

Your mother has withdrawn all our savings from the bank and flown home to England. I'm moving out of the house and into a unit in Wollongbar. I had to sell most of the furniture so all your old stuff is gone. You'll have to find somewhere to stay in the unlikely event of you deciding to come down for Christmas.

Don't worry about me; I should have seen the writing on the wall years ago. Love, Dad."

No phone number or address was included so she guessed he didn't want her sympathy, but, Linda could have told them that all the whinging, drinking and fighting wouldn't end well. Now her mother was back in London, Linda wondered how long it would take for her to realise Australia wasn't such a bad place after all.

Linda re-read her father's letter and was surprised that she didn't feel the sadness that he presumed she would. "You survived living in the same house as them Linda and that's all it was; survival."

She sighed heavily, then with great care refolded the letter, replaced it in the envelope it had arrived in and tore it into as many pieces as she could.

"OK, Linda, where's the first Christmas party!"

Mid-way through her second year, she was visited by two uniformed police officers. Her heart fell and her stomach heaved.

"Miss Linda West?" the Senior Constable Policewoman asked.

"Yes, that's me," trying hard to stay relaxed.

"Do you mind if we come in?"

Not here to arrest her then.

"No, please," she held the door open for them to enter her room. "Can I ask what this is about?"

"You might like to sit down first."

'*Oh shit!*' she thought as she slumped onto the small sofa.

"Miss West, I have the sad duty of having to inform you that your father was killed in a motor vehicle accident at 11.03 p.m. last night. His car was involved in a head-on collision with a fully laden coal truck on the Griffin Road between Wollongbar and Griffin. He would have died instantly."

Linda sobbed into her hands and the policewoman sat beside her and placed her arm around her shoulders.

"Is there anything we can do while we're here? Is there anyone we can contact to be with you at this time?"

"No, no thank you—?"

"Gillian, Gillian Williams."

"No thank you, Gillian. Truth is I've been estranged from my parents ever since we arrived in Australia nearly ten years ago. My mother returned to England last year with all their life savings without even saying goodbye and with the amount my father was drinking, he was probably living on borrowed time. Was anybody else hurt in the crash?"

"No, your father was the only fatality."

Linda was spared the gruesome details of her father's remains; suffice to say, the cremation urn wasn't exactly full. She had organised with a Wollongbar funeral home by phone to collect and cremate his remains with his ashes to be spread over the crematorium's gardens.

Bobby's life changed dramatically in those three years. His dad had bought a house in the beachside town of Shell Bay where Bobby discovered heaven in the form of Shell Bay Beach. Every spare moment he had was spent either body surfing or simply exploring the wind-swept sand dunes looking for freshly uncovered treasure. At first, he had been devastated at the thought of not being close to Linda, but it hadn't taken long for the delights of the beach to push the memory of her to the back of his mind.

None of them could have foreseen how the now largely unforgotten spoils of a youthful adventure into a secret tunnel would again draw them together with drastic consequences.

Chapter 16

9:00 a.m., Wednesday 13 March 1957, Office of the Minister for Defence, Parliament House, Canberra, ACT

George Peterson MP and Minister for Defence hung up the phone and leaned back in his plush leather office chair. He removed his glasses and pinched the bridge of his nose.

"Bugger!"

Several seconds later, he leaned forward and pressed the intercom button on his phone connecting him to his Private Secretary.

"Yes Minister?" Henry Edwards was a long-serving member of the Australian Public Service. Starting his career in the Parliament House Mail Room, Henry had risen through the ranks until he became the Private Secretary to the Minister for Defence. So far, George Peterson was the third Defence Minister he'd served.

"Henry, would you ask the Assistant Secretary of the Department of Foreign Affairs to ring me on my private line please?"

"Certainly Minister."

John Forrester had come through the same Public Service system as Henry Edwards, only ten years earlier. Now in his early forties and never married, he had a reputation in the Service as being a hard-nosed, fastidious bastard; it was a reputation he fought hard to maintain.

"Good morning Minister; to what do I owe the pleasure?"
"I hear the Rose Garden is especially magnificent this time of the year!"
"10.30!"

At precisely 10:30 a.m. John Forrester sat down next to the Minister for Defence on a bench in the centre of the Parliament House Rose Gardens. The bench had a clear line of sight 50 metres to their left and right.

"I assume that this meeting isn't to discuss the roses George?"

"Unfortunately, John, I wish it were! One of our saleable assets has gone missing."

John Forrester stared straight ahead and said nothing for a significant length of time. When he finally spoke, George Peterson could almost taste the venom in the solitary. "How?"

"Early reports suggest at least one child, between the ages of ten and thirteen caused a landslide on the rock pile that was concealing the tunnel entrance. The child has then entered the cavern and taken one of the containers that had spilled from a broken crate.

"An investigation was undertaken by a Navy Commander, under the command of the Naval Intelligence Branch and the local Barclay's Creek Police. They found nothing and a door-to-door failed to produce any witnesses of children either in or going to or coming from the quarry last Friday evening.

"At this stage, there has been no increase in hospitalisations so it's safe to assume, the container is still sealed. The normal inquisitiveness of a child would have resulted in it being opened as soon as they were able. My theory is that when they found there was nothing of any value in the box, they threw it in the nearest garbage bin."

"And what pray tell, am I supposed to tell the 'client'?"

"Nothing! Why give him cause for concern when there is absolutely nothing to suggest anything has changed? The Army Engineers have permanently sealed the tunnel, beefed up the security fencing and installed heavy-duty gates at the quarry entrance so our remaining assets are more secure than ever!"

"I assume you are actively seeking the whereabouts of the missing item?"

"Correct. The position of Chief of Naval Intelligence, currently held by Captain Peter Fleming, is responsible for maintaining the security of all the Australian Defence Force's secret storage facilities. Having read Captain Fleming's file, I believe he will see the break-in and theft as a personal failure and he will do everything in his power to redress that failure. With the resources available to him, I fully expect that if there is even a whiff of information regarding the whereabouts of our asset, he will pursue it at all costs.

"The beauty is—you and I and our other partner keep our hands clean and are insulated from any subsequent fallout!"

"I wish I shared your confidence! Regarding the shipment of the goods; are we any closer to drafting the 'Removal of Contaminated Waste Bill'?"

"Come on, John, you of all people should know how slowly the wheels of Government turn! The biggest stumbling block is trying to overcome the differences between my department and the Department of Works. Thankfully, both have finally agreed on the composition of the joint Bill drafting committee, but, how far off is a draft Bill is anyone's guess.

"I understand your frustration but we all knew that the only way we were ever going to get the goods from the quarry to the client was with the Government's blessing. Unfortunately, creating that 'blessing' takes time. My concern is whether the General will still be interested in proceeding with the purchase knowing the delays are out of our control?"

"George, General Mpoto joined the KLFA when he was twelve and has been fighting for the 'freedom' of his people for over twenty years. While they no longer enjoy the support of certain Eastern Bloc countries, they still believe their country deserves a better Government than the one it is currently suffering under. So in answer to your question; the General is, if nothing else, a very patient man and he is fully aware of how slowly the wheels of an Imperial Government turn.

"As long as I can keep giving him positive updates, he will bide his time and honour his commitment. Your job George is to ensure the updates stay positive."

Chapter 17

10:00 a.m., Friday 8 September 1967 Shell Bay, NSW

Following what is now considered to be a contrived event involving the USS *Maddox* in the Gulf of Tonkin in 1964, America became militarily involved in the decade-long conflict between North and South Vietnam.

That same year, the Australian Government passed the *National Service Act* that resulted in the selective conscription of Australian males whose twentieth birthday fell on specific dates. A National Ballot was conducted bi-annually to determine those dates.

10:00 a.m., Friday 8 September 1967 was the time and date Bobby's number came up.

The number that ensured his life as he knew it and any dreams he had of the future, were about to disappear forever.

The number that was drawn in a ballot conducted by the Department of Labour and National Service which ultimately resulted in a letter being sent to Mr Robert Massey, currently residing in Shell Bay, NSW. The letter stated that he was required to report to the Sydney District Employment Office, York Street, Sydney, for the purpose of determining his suitability *for various postings in the Army*.

Bobby had been happily cruising through life up until then. He had become a tanned, sun-bleached, long-haired 'surfer' (he never caught the surfboarding craze), he was just out of his teens and life was good.

He had left school at the end of '63 with a mediocre pass in the Intermediate Certificate and immediately joined the ranks of the employed as an apprentice Fitter and Turner. The pay wasn't that crash hot but his parents were understanding and only charged him a mediocre amount for board.

His weekends were spent either hanging out with his mates at Shell Bay Beach, playing pool in the Shell Bay Hotel or catching a concert and dance at the Workers Club. Many a large, cold glass of beer and the obligatory cigarettes accompanied all these activities.

Being forcibly enlisted into the Australian Army was definitely not on Bobby's agenda. However, despite some 'dummy spitting'—including the odd 'Fuck the Prime Minister!'—on receiving the call-up notice, he never gave a second thought to not turning up for his recruitment interview.

Having been declared fit for service, Bobby spent twelve gruelling weeks undergoing military training at the Army Recruit Training Battalion at Kapooka in Southwestern New South Wales. On completion, he was posted to the 3rd Battalion, Royal Australian Regiment and in December 1967 he and several hundred other fresh-faced young Australian males found themselves aboard the 'Vung Tau Ferry'—HMAS *Sydney*—bound for Nui Dat in Phouc Tuy Province, South Vietnam.

While his Platoon carried out routine patrols, reconnaissance and security missions, in and around Nui Dat, Bobby hadn't fired his rifle in anger during the four months he had been there. In fact, apart from the B-52 bombers and the F4 *Phantom* and A4 *Skyhawk* jet fighters taking off and landing, he could have sworn the war was a myth! However, in April 1968 all that changed when his Company was moved to 3RAR's Fire Support Base *Balmoral*, near the hamlet of Lai Khe, approximately 50km from Saigon and 115km from Nui Dat.

On 26 May, the North Vietnamese Army launched an assault on the FSB. Bobby's platoon was defending their position against a heavy and prolonged attack by the enemy when Bobby sustained a gunshot wound to his upper right leg that shattered his femur. After spending three weeks in the 1st Australian Field Hospital in Nui Dat, Bobby was airlifted back to Sydney where surgeons at the Royal Prince Alfred Hospital reconstructed the shattered bone in his leg.

Four weeks later he was transferred to the Concord Repatriation Hospital where he began the long and painful task of learning to walk again.

Chapter 18

1:30 p.m., Monday 15 July 1968, Concord Repatriation Hospital, Sydney, NSW

Bobby was propped up in bed finishing his corned beef and mash lunch when a voice, with a very bad Humphrey Bogart impression, came from the door to the 4-bed ward.

"Of all the hospitals, in all the towns, in all the world, Bobby Massey ends up in mine."

Even though it hurt like hell, Bobby swung his legs over the side of the bed and reached for his crutches, a broad, yet strained, smile spreading across his face.

"Wow, I bet that's the fastest you've moved in years," Linda said as she hurried to catch him before he fell flat on his face.

As he regained his balance, Bobby asked, "I was going to ask why you're here, but it says on your name tag 'Linda West, Physiotherapist'. Does that mean you're—I mean, are you—"

"Yes, Bobby, you are now officially one of my patients."

Linda had undertaken three years of full-time study at Sydney University and was now completing her fourth-year undergraduate study in the hospital under the supervision of Doctor Jeanette Barber, the Head of Applied Sciences.

Bobby couldn't hold back any longer and with the will of Samson, he dropped the crutches and embraced Linda in a mix of grapple and hold-me-up-before-I-collapse sort of hug.

"Easy soldier, you need to learn to walk before we start dancing!" Linda said half-heartedly. She had a strong desire to match Bobby's hug, but two of them falling down would just be too embarrassing.

Maintaining the hug, Bobby allowed Linda to guide him down into his wheelchair before she collapsed into the visitor's chair next to his bed.

Linda reached for his hand. "It's good to see you again, Bobby Massey."

"I have absolutely no idea who this woman is!" Bobby proclaimed loudly to the smiling occupants of the other three beds.

Then placing his free hand over Linda's, he said softly, "And it's absolutely wonderful to see you again Linda West. Now, take all the time in the world and tell me how you came to be sitting in front of me today."

Bobby was going to say, '*tell me how the most beautiful woman in the whole Universe came to be sitting in front of me*', but he thought that might sound a little bit creepy, so he substituted that with a stupid grin instead—way to go, Bobby!

"I have a better idea," Linda replied with a smile, "rather than bore these other poor soldiers," She waved in their direction, "how about we get you walking again, then you can come to my flat just down the road in Mortlake I'll tell you everything over a medium-rare T-bone steak and a glass of Claret?"

If Bobby had needed any external motivation for getting out of his wheelchair, it was seated in front of him, but the promise of steak did help a little.

****

"OK, one more try then we'll call it quits for the week," Linda calm and encouraging.

"I fucking can't for Christ's sake!" Bobby yelled, both frustrated and dispirited.

The first week of Bobby's rehab had gone remarkably well considering he had been completely immobile when Linda first arrived.

He had managed to stagger the length of the parallel bars without assistance from 'Doctor Banner'—Bobby's nickname for the male nurse who he reckoned was the size of the Incredible Hulk—and had progressed to a shuffling stagger with the aid of crutches.

Though in obvious pain, Bobby wanted to impress Linda and be walking normally as soon as possible. He was buoyed with enthusiasm at the start of the second week.

But that enthusiasm came crashing back to earth, along with Bobby—several times. Each time he fell, he was gently picked up and they would start again and again and again. While he was adamant he could do it, Linda was afraid that he would re-injure his reconstructed leg and convinced him to return to the parallel bars.

"You need to build up more muscle strength not only in your legs but your upper body also. At the moment, even with the crutches, you're not able to support yourself when the right leg collapses.

While you are managing to take some unsteady steps, you need to be able to automatically shift the weight from your right to your left side when you feel the right leg start to collapse."

"Yes, Mum," at least he still has his sense of humour. She bent down and kissed his forehead.

"That's a good boy" and as she stood, she ruffled his hair.

But that was then.

Halfway through the third week, Bobby had finally crossed the length of the room on two crutches and by week's end had, although rather slowly, unsteadily and with a lot of sweat, gone the same distance using only one crutch.

With newfound confidence, he proclaimed adamantly, "Right, next week, we ditch the training wheels. Time to rejoin the land of the bipeds. Wadda ya say, doc?"

"I'd say that may be premature and my recommendation is that we try a device called a 'walking frame' first." Which Bobby did. In fact, by the Wednesday he was finding it easier to use than the crutches. Linda, suitably impressed then agreed he could attempt to walk unaided. That's when it all came crashing back to earth.

No matter how much he tried, as soon as the full weight of his body came onto his right leg, the pain that shot through his thigh into his back was too much and he fell to the floor like a sack of spuds.

Then Bobby had reached the end of his tether.

"I fucking can't for Christ's sake!" he sobbed dispiritedly. Linda knew there was nothing she could do.

"Marco, (Hulk's real name) please help Bobby back to the ward."

Linda was troubled. According to the post-operation X-rays, Bobby's leg was healing well. So there was really no reason why he shouldn't be walking unaided by now.

As she passed the Nurse's Station, she had a thought; backtracking to the desk, she asked, "Hi Julie, can you tell me if there's still an Orthopaedic Surgeon in the hospital?"

The nurse picked up the phone and several minutes later turned to Linda, "You're in luck, Doctor Ramsay is still in theatre on the 2nd floor. The duty nurse should be able to give you an approximate time he'll be finished."

"Thanks Julie. Oh, can you give me Bobby Massey's X-rays please?"

An hour and twenty minutes later, Doctor Ramsay emerged from the Operating Theatre.

"Excuse me, Doctor Ramsay?"

"Yes?"

"Sorry for disturbing you, but can you spare me 15 minutes?"

"So Miss West, what's this all about."

They were sitting in Doctor Ramsay's plush office with magnificent views over one of the many secluded tree-lined bays on the south side of Sydney Harbour.

"Thank you for seeing me, I know how busy you are these days and please, it's 'Linda'."

"'David', now, how can I be of assistance?"

Linda gave the surgeon a summary of Bobby's history, explained how he wasn't responding to his therapy as expected and was hoping that David would please cast an expert eye over Bobby's post-operative X-rays.

"You do realise that you should be speaking to Mr Massey's doctor?"

"Yes, I apologise Doctor Ramsay. I'll talk to—" she had started to rise from her chair.

"Hold on, hold on. Although it's against my better judgement, I can see that you have more than a therapist/patient relationship with Mr Massey."

"It's that obvious, is it?"

He smiled. "My dear girl, it couldn't be more obvious if you had it tattooed on your forehead! Now, let's have a gander at those pictures."

"Ah yes, nasty. Unlucky, but still nasty. An inch to the left and the bullet would have passed through muscle and out the other side. In Mr Massey's case, it fragmented the bone just below the hip joint. I must say the surgeons did a marvellous job of reconstructing the bone as well as they did. But unfortunately, they missed this little shard of bone. See here?"

Doctor Ramsay used his pen to point to an almost invisible smudge on the X-ray, "that, my dear, is why your soldier is finding it difficult to walk. In fact, I'd say he would find it hard to stand without it causing him grief."

Linda put her hand to her mouth to muffle the sob, "Bobby Massey, you're a stupid, stubborn idiot!" She sank back into her chair and broke down in tears.

"Here, drink this, Doctor Ramsay's cure for the blues." Linda took the small glass and downed the contents. Thankfully, she already had a handkerchief out so she managed to muffle the coughing that followed.

"I was going to say 'sip it slowly', but that obviously works just as well."

Doctor Ramsay resumed his seat and handed the X-rays back.

"Mr Massey will need another operation to remove the bone fragment. What you need to do is explain to him that he should tell his doctor that he is suffering excruciating pain when standing—which I expect is not so far from the truth."

"The doctor should review these," he tapped the X-rays, "and if he's worth the money he's charging, he'll come to the same conclusion I've just outlined to you.

Under no circumstances, however, will you reveal to Mr Massey or anyone else the content of this conversation. Is that clear?"

"Yes David, absolutely. Thank you so much, Doctor Ramsay!"

"Easy, Miss West, I haven't reached deity status—yet!" He smiled, stood and extended a hand, "Good luck Linda. Come and see me once Mr Massey is walking again and we'll toast the event—slowly!"

Chapter 19

8:00 a.m., Monday 18 August 1968, Concord Repatriation Hospital, Sydney, NSW

"Good morning, Bobby."

"Hmph."

"Oh, wadda madda widdle baby?" Linda sooked, "Did the bad nursey wursey take away your dummy?"

"Cut it out Linda, I'm not in the mood for your silliness!"

"'Silliness', you call that silliness! I'll tell you what fucking silliness is Bobby Massey—silliness is pretending to be a fucking hero and trying to walk when the pain is nearly killing you!"

Bobby covered his face with the bed sheet and mumbled something unintelligible.

Linda yanked the sheet from his face, "***What was that***!" She snapped angrily.

Bobby grinned, "I love it when you talk dirty!"

She couldn't help but crack up. She thumped his arm. "You bastard!" she laughed.

"Ow! Is that the way to treat a wounded war hero?" and then he too burst into laughter.

Linda could only shake her head. After they had stared into each other's eyes for a few seconds longer than was necessary, she realised that she wanted to be with this infuriating bastard for the rest of her life and the longing look reflected in his eyes said that he had similar feelings for her. She reached for his hand that was already seeking hers and when they touched, she knew it was true.

She released his hand, bent down and kissed him passionately. His arms closed gently around her back and pulled her on top of him—to a round of applause and wolf-whistles from the other three patients in the room.

A throat-clearing cough came from the doorway, "Will you be needing any help with Mr Massey this morning, Miss West?" Which elicited another round of applause, whistling, several rude comments and a burst of laughter from Bobby. Linda just managed to keep a straight face, "No thank you, Marco. Mr Massey will not be needing either of our services for a few days."

Linda disentangled herself from a perplexed-looking Bobby and sat in the chair next to his bed.

"Bobby, I'm going to say something that you don't want to hear, but, I'm asking you not to interrupt until I'm finished, OK?"

"Yes, Mum."

"Over the last four weeks, you have been trying valiantly to impress me by desperately forcing the pain in your leg to the back of your mind. You've endured extreme pain but drove yourself through it. Most of the time it worked—when you could transfer all your body weight onto your left leg. You even convinced yourself that if you really, really tried hard, you could block out the pain completely and walk unaided across that room.

"In the end, the pain won. The tantrum you threw last Friday when you cried that you couldn't do it, wasn't because you couldn't walk unaided, it was because you couldn't overcome the pain.

"The fight you're having with the pain ends today Bobby. Your doctor will be seeing you sometime this morning and when he asks *And how are we feeling today Mr Massey?*, you're going to tell him the truth. All of it Bobby. OK?"

"Yes, Mum."

"I'm serious, Bobby!"

"Sorry. You're right, of course, the pain is horrendous most of the time and gets worse when I put the slightest weight on it. I was so pleased to see you when you first arrived that the only thought I've had since that moment, is being able to walk into your office and ask you out. That thought and that thought alone was what drove me through the pain—until I just couldn't. Yes, you're right when you say I couldn't overcome the pain, but the hardest thing to swallow was the thought that I was going to end up in a wheelchair and never be able to *walk* into your office to ask you out!"

Linda stood up then leaned down and hugged him. "Yeah, you're right, I'd never date a man in a wheelchair. Especially one from Shell Bay! You're an idiot, Bobby Massey. Now, talk to your doctor. I'll come and see you tomorrow to get an update." She kissed him, stroked his cheek and left him grinning like the Cheshire cat.

Chapter 20

6:00 a.m., Monday 15 September 1968, Concord Repatriation Hospital, Sydney

"Off home, are we?" Inquired the patient in the bed opposite.

"Yes mate and not before time either." Bobby replied as he was packing his belongings, "You in for long?"

"Bloody hope not, the food's terrible, the nurses wake you up all hours and you can't get a bed pan when you need it! You got far to go?"

"'bout three hours on the train and another hour on the bus, should get me home for lunch."

"And where do you call 'home'?"

"Shell Bay."

"Beautiful spot! Great fishing off the Point! Anyway, you have a great day!"

"Thanks mate, you too." Bobby gave a wave to the other patients, picked up his duffle bag and walking stick and headed to Linda's office.

"It's open," she called out to the knock on her door.

Bobby opened the door, dropped his duffle bag and stick by the door and stood at Linda's desk.

"If I could be so impertinent my lady," and he gave a bow Sir Walter Raleigh would have been envious of "would the indubitably beautiful and impossibly desirable Miss West be so inclined to partake in a walk to the omnibus stop with her humble servant, Mr Bobby Massey!" another deep bow which he held.

"Arise, Sir Crapalot," she responded walking around the desk. "Although you are so, so impertinent, I am indeed inclined to accompany you to the omnibus stop—only if it's to ensure you get on the bloody thing!"

They fell into each other's arms and just held on.

"I have to do this Linda," he said softly into her dark hair.

"Hey, I understand completely," she lied. She had no idea why he had to go home. "It's not like it's going to be forever!"

Three months! Three agonisingly long months! In the end, she could see the logic in Bobby's plan—she didn't like it but she did understand.

Bobby had given himself three months in which to do all the things that would sever the invisible umbilical cord that was tying him to Shell Bay. Twelve weeks to hand in his notice at work, find a new job in Sydney, buy a car, find a place to stay, say goodbye to his mates and the hardest part—move out of home. He was never a 'mummy's boy', but, being an only child, he knew his mum would be upset.

As it turned out, everything went better than expected!

With the assistance provided by the Australian Government's Repatriation Department, Bobby found a job with a small manufacturing company in Lidcombe and a two-bedroom apartment a short walk from Strathfield railway station.

The clincher came late one Saturday morning as he was sleeping off a hangover; a consequence of enjoying yet another prolonged farewell party in the Shell Bay pub with his mates.

He was woken by a knock on his bedroom door.

"Yes?"

His father stuck his head inside the opened door, "You awake?"

"I am now—but I wish I wasn't!"

"I'm in the process of cooking Robert Massey's famous 'Shell Bay Sure-Fire Hangover Cure'—tinned tomatoes on toast with runny poached eggs. I strongly suggest you get your arse into gear, get showered and come out for breakfast. You've got fifteen minutes, so rise and shine son o' mine!"

"Uhh, thanks Dad—I think?"

"That's the way—upward and onward!"

"I've got the message; you can leave now!"

Fourteen minutes and two Alka Seltzers later, Bobby was sitting at the kitchen table listening to his father whistling some unidentifiable tune while buttering toast.

"You sound very cheerful this morning; you win the Lottery or something?"

"Why wouldn't I be happy—it's Saturday, the sun is shining, and my son is going to mow my lawns while I lay on my banana lounge and watch him—what more could a man ask for?"

Bobby hung his aching head in his hands and let out a pained groan. "Ugh! Forgot all about the lawns!"

"Here you go." Bobby's dad placed the tomatoes and poached eggs in front of him, "Get that little lot into you and you'll feel like a new man!"

He had to give his father his due; his stomach had settled and while the aspirin had almost stilled the pounding in his head, he almost felt human again. He was enjoying a cup of coffee when his dad said mysteriously, "When you've finished your cuppa and before you start on the lawns, there's something I need to show you."

Intrigued, Bobby quickly finished his coffee, "Right then, let's go!"

Robert Massey, a knowing grin creasing his face, led his son through the house to the front door. "After you son," he said standing aside as he opened the door.

No sooner had Bobby stepped out onto the porch when his body slumped against the wall.

"No fuc—sorry, I mean, bloody hell! Is that—Is she—"

"Yes Bobby, she's all yours!"

Bobby flung his arms around his dad in a hearty embrace.

"Thank you, thank you, thank you."

Sitting in the driveway, with his mum standing by the passenger door, was a gleaming second-hand 1965 metallic British Racing Green Ford GT Cortina.

"Think of it as a belated twenty-first birthday present."

"I am truly lost for words! Did you know about this, Mum?"

"Of course, I did! Why do you think I've been out here for the last forty-five minutes? Me crying with joy would have given the game away! Come on Robert, you'd better take us for a spin around the block." Bobby's headache was instantly forgotten.

In his haste to start learning how to drive, his father's lawn looked like it had been mown by a blind person. Robert Massey chuckled to himself 'don't dampen the boy's exuberance Robert—you were twenty-one once.'

Six weeks later, Bobby, recently the very proud owner of a Provisional Driver's Licence, fixed the red and white plastic 'P' plates to the front of his Cortina.

Moving out of the family home was also easier than he expected. His Mum had been visibly upset when he'd told her his plan to move to Sydney, but as the weeks passed and his belongings had disappeared into packing boxes, she slowly accepted the inevitable.

All his concerns about moving out were washed away over dinner one evening. His dad had just finished his meal, lay his cutlery purposefully on the empty plate, made a show of wiping his mouth with his napkin and cleared his throat.

"Ahem—Mary, I know you're upset that our son is leaving home. To tell you the truth, I'm a bit apprehensive as well, but, twelve months ago, our long-haired boy went to fight someone else's war in a country we'd never heard of. That boy never came home—the person sitting eating with us tonight is Bobby Massey, the man.

A man that has made a decision that you and I, no matter how we personally feel, must accept.

Bobby, I respect your judgement, but, please know that this house will always be your home and should things not turn out the way you've planned, we'll welcome you back with open arms."

Bobby, who had never heard his father string two sentences together in his life, managed a choked, "Thanks, Dad."

His mum, lace-frilled handkerchief dabbing her eyes, came around the table and gave Bobby a long, wet hug. "Doesn't mean I'm not going to fret about you!"

Four weeks later, Bobby moved into his new apartment.

Chapter 21

May 1969, Strathfield, Sydney, NSW

Three months after settling in Sydney, the nightmares started. They had begun benignly enough; Bobby would wake with a start, laugh it off and promptly go back to sleep. Then they became more regular and darker until Bobby was awake longer than he was asleep.

He jokingly mentioned them to Linda, who took it more seriously than Bobby and she suggested he see a doctor.

Bobby had made a conscious effort to get into a comfortable routine the moment he arrived in Sydney. On weekdays he was up at 5:30 walking and doing the exercises Linda had given him to strengthen his right thigh muscles, catching the 7:30 train to work, working from 8:30 to 5:00 p.m. and arriving back home about 6:30 p.m.

Linda was working long, irregular hours but when she managed to knock off early, she and Bobby would meet somewhere for dinner and a glass of wine before heading back to their respective apartments.

Most weeknights though, Bobby cooked himself a simple meal washed down with a couple of cans of beer and a 'Bex' headache powder.

Once the nightmares began, all that changed. He would forego cooking himself a meal and have two 'Bex' washed down with half a dozen beers instead. Linda noticed him drifting off and staring into space on several occasions but Bobby laughed it off.

"Sorry. Just been a long day."

In the end, he admitted to her that he wasn't sleeping well due to some 'weird' nightmares.

Knowing Linda was right about seeking help, he went to see his local GP who prescribed him 10mg of Valium twice a day. For a while, they seemed to do the job. The nightmares were less frequent which enabled Bobby to resume his normal routine.

And then came the migraine headaches.

Then the paranoia.

Then the night sweats.

In the end, Bobby cracked. He drank until he fell over, then smashed everything he could lay his hands on.

Two hours later, summoned by an angry neighbour, police officers kicked open his door and found Bobby lying unconscious in a pool of his own vomit.

Three days later, his stomach pumped, an intravenous drip in his arm and wires hanging off him everywhere, he awoke to the rhythmic 'beep' of a heart monitor next to his bed. As his eyes regained focus he looked around to see his mum sitting next to the bed holding his hand.

"He's awake!" she called out and then his dad and Linda were standing with her.

Chapter 22

June 1969, Strathfield, Sydney, NSW

"Wow! Who let the herd of elephants in here!" Linda exclaimed as she wheeled a semi-comatose Bobby into his apartment.

Bobby was still heavily sedated. They had released him from the hospital reluctantly and then only after Linda and his parents had agreed to remain with him twenty-four hours a day.

"In his current state, I should be committing him to a Psychiatric Ward," the Repatriation Department Psychiatrist had told them. "However, as long as he continues with the medication, he shouldn't be a danger to himself—or anyone else!"

Bobby had been diagnosed with, what was commonly termed "shell shock" or clinically, "war neurosis". The prognosis wasn't good. While the illness could be identified, the cure was still hit and miss. Each individual presented with varying symptoms which meant medications and their dosage had to be tailored to the patient. Finding that out was purely a matter of monitoring his behaviour and adjusting the type and amount until Bobby could function with relative normality.

At Linda's insistence, Bobby's parents were staying at Linda's apartment until Bobby's had been cleaned up and a more permanent solution to managing Bobby's condition was found.

Linda wheeled Bobby in front of the TV.

"Any particular channel you want to watch?"

Bobby lifted his head and stared blankly at her. She knelt in front of the wheelchair and took hold of his hands.

"We'll work through this, Bobby. You don't have to suffer on your own."

"Thanks, Linda," she could see he was struggling with the effects of the drugs he was on, "but—but there's something—wrong with my head—I—I don't—know you can—hel—help me!"

She gripped his hands tighter.

"You're right on both accounts; there is something wrong with your head and I have absolutely no idea of how to fix that. I do know that you admitting there's something wrong, is a big step on the road to you helping yourself. What I and your mum and dad are here for, is to hold your hand while you walk that road and to give you a nudge if it looks like you're losing your way. Is that OK?"

Bobby reached out and placed his hand on her cheek, "Tha…t's very—OK!"

She kissed his hand and stood, "Right, my original question—what channel?"

Bobby looked at his watch, "Chan…nel S…even. The 'Thr…ee Stoo…ges' are on."

"You big kid!"

With Bobby watching TV, Linda began the task of tidying up the mess he had created in his fit of rage.

It was while she was sweeping up that she found the broken model sailing ship and the little olive drab box lying nearby.

Chapter 23

September 1969, Concord Repatriation Hospital, Sydney, NSW

It had been nearly three months since Bobby's breakdown. Although he could carry on a normal conversation, the drugs he was taking had extinguished the zest for life that used to sparkle in his eyes.

His parents had made the hard decision to have him committed to a psychiatric hospital when it became patently clear that he was never going to return to his old self. After two weeks, Bobby's dad had exhausted his leave credits and returned to Shell Bay leaving Mary and Linda to tend to Bobby.

A week later, Mary broke down in tears and admitted to Linda that she couldn't bear to see her son in his current state. The deciding factor came when the doctors couldn't give a guarantee that he wouldn't suffer another meltdown. The following week Bobby found himself in a private room in the Cumberland Lunatic Asylum in Parramatta.

Linda was gifted with a beaming smile each time she entered his room and the hugs were heartfelt but the warmth had gone from both. Every time she said goodbye and closed his door, she sat in Bobby's car and cried.

Now, as she sat at her desk, pondering the shitty luck befalling Bobby from having a 20th birth date that saw him wounded in Vietnam and, ultimately, resulted in him being committed to a Lunatic Asylum, her mind drifted back to the abandoned quarry in Barclay's Creek. Reaching into the back of the bottom drawer in her desk, she retrieved the still-sealed box that she had rediscovered in Bobby's apartment.

"So my little green friend, we meet again. The question is; what am I going to do with you?"

Chapter 24

September 1969, Cumberland Lunatic Asylum, Sydney, NSW

"Ian, it's Gordon Wright, Mr Robert Massey's psychiatrist, I think you should listen to the recording from my hypnotherapy session with him this morning. Are you in your office?"

"Yes, Gordon; come on up."

Ian Garland was the Head of Psychiatry at The Cumberland Lunatic Asylum. Since the end of the Second World War, the Asylum had been the main depository of ex-servicemen suffering from 'war neurosis'. As well as the usual medication and therapy regimen, the psychiatric team had found that hypnosis had benefited some patients. Bobby Massey was one of those patients.

Doctor Wright had just completed his third hypnotherapy session with Bobby and the reason he had called Doctor Garland was because he was puzzled by what Bobby had revealed. He pressed the 'Play' button on the tape recorder.

"Good morning, Bobby."

"Good Morning, Doctor."

"How are you feeling today?"

"Good!"

"Are you comfortable?"

"Yes, Doctor."

"Bobby, can you remember what we talked about last time?"

"We talked about Vietnam."

"That's right! Today, I would like to take you back to before you went to Vietnam. Is that OK?"

"Yes."

Doctor Wright then proceeded to probe Bobby's life as a teenager to see if there was anything of any consequence that may be causing the breakdowns.

Apart from concealing the fact that he had smoked a joint from his parents, his teenage years were very ordinary. But when he asked Bobby if they could go back before he turned thirteen, Bobby's demeanour changed instantly. He clenched his fists and shook his head from side to side.

"You don't want to talk about it?"
"No!"
"Can you tell me why?"
"It's a secret."
"Did you hurt somebody Bobby? Is that why you can't tell me?"
"No!"
"Bobby, I don't want to know your secret, but can you tell me how old you were when this thing happened."
"We were ten."
"There's someone with you?"
"It's a secret. It's all my fault!"

Doctor Wright knew he risked ruining the progress he had made but whatever the secret was that had Bobby so agitated, could be the key that was causing his psychosis.

"Bobby, do you remember me telling you that I'm forbidden from revealing anything you tell me to anyone else, don't you?"
"Yes, I understand, Doctor."

He was treading on thin ice here. While it was true that he was bound not to reveal their conversation, there was a caveat that allowed Doctor Wright's replacement to review all material associated with the case.

"Bobby, I get the impression that you want to tell me your secret, but you don't want to get the other person into trouble. Would that be correct?"
"Yes."
"OK, so how about you forget the other person is with you and just tell me what your secret is?"
"Yes—It's hot, I'm playing in a quarry—"

"What are you thinking?" Doctor Wright asked.

Doctor Ian Garland was laying back in his plush office chair, obviously deep in thought after listening to Bobby describing how he had broken into a secret tunnel that was filled with dark green boxes with arrows painted on them. Both doctors knew that the arrows and the colour identified the boxes as being the property of the Department of Defence.

Gordon was about to repeat the question when Doctor Garland pinched the bridge of his nose between his thumb and forefinger and sat upright. He let out a huge sigh and said, "I really don't think we have any other option than to call Colonel Muir."

Colonel Muir was the Army Liaison Officer for the Asylum. While a fully qualified Psychologist, his main role was advising the Repatriation Department in Canberra on the health and well-being of the many returned servicemen that were undergoing treatment in the Asylum.

What the Asylum didn't know, however, was that the Colonel was also a member of Army Intelligence. While the Army was genuinely concerned about their returned servicemen's welfare, the last thing it needed was a psychotic soldier spouting classified information for all the world to hear. It was Colonel Muir's job to ensure that never happened.

"How are you planning on side-tracking the ethics issues?" Gordon asked.

"Bit late to start worrying about crossing that line, isn't it Gordon?"

"That's true, but I was hoping you would take on Mr Massey's case to relieve me of that problem?"

"Ah, right." Doctor Garland stroked his chin, then said, "OK, so as of now, Mr Massey is my patient."

"Thank you."

"Don't thank me yet, you haven't heard the rest of the plan!"

Twenty minutes later, after they had tossed around every possible scenario, Doctor Garland picked up the phone. "Lucy, would you ask Colonel Muir to come to my office at his earliest convenience? Thanks."

Chapter 25

September 1969, Cumberland Lunatic Asylum, Sydney, NSW

Doctor Garland's intercom buzzed a short time later.

"Yes Lucy?"

"Colonel Muir's here Doctor."

"Thanks Lucy, send him in, please. And would you be so kind as to make us a pot of tea please?"

"Certainly Doctor."

Having completed the mandatory small talk over their cups of tea, Doctor Garland placed his cup and saucer on the coffee table between them and addressed the Colonel.

"Colonel, as you know, we have been using hypnotherapy on those patients that are both receptive to hypnosis and who respond positively to the treatment. One of those patients is Mr Robert Massey."

"Ah yes, the young Sapper that was shot in the thigh. How is Bobby?"

"Physically, he's in great shape. He now walks without a cane—limping, but walking. Mentally—not so well. His first two hypnotherapy sessions went surprisingly well. He was able to describe the attack on the Fire Support Base—with a lot of careful coaxing mind you—in only his second session but, unlike other patients, while he can now verbalise the events of that night, his psychosis remains.

"It wasn't until we took him further back into his childhood, that we found, what we now believe, is the root cause of his terrors. Colonel, I've agonised over what to do with the information that Bobby revealed during that last session. Ethically, I can't reveal anything one of my patients discloses whilst under hypnosis, so, unfortunately—even though I believe our National Security may be at risk—I can't under any circumstances release the transcript of that session," he said as he tapped the file that lay between them.

"You'll have to forgive me, Colonel, but I need to wander down the hall. Bloody tea goes straight through me!"

"I understand completely, Doctor Garland. Do you mind if I help myself— to another cup of tea that is?"

"Please do."

Doctor Garland returned some ten minutes later.

"Excuse me, Doctor?"

"Yes, Lucy?"

"Colonel Muir had an urgent meeting he needed to attend. He said to tell you that he was pleased with the outcome of your meeting."

"Thank you, Lucy, that is good news!"

Once back in his own office, Colonel Muir quickly wrote a cryptic message to Brigadier Martin, Head of Army Intelligence in Canberra marked 'Secret', it read *Ten-year-old child discovers hidden treasure in abandoned quarry.*

The 'Secret' telex was received by the Signals Office, sealed in a red envelope marked 'Secret' and hand-delivered to Brigadier Martin. The Brigadier immediately picked up his phone, "Get Commodore Fleming on the blower for me please."

Commodore Peter Fleming hung up the phone and leaned back in his chair, a smile crossing his face, "Well, well, well—after all these years, the chickens are coming home to roost!"

Commodore Fleming grabbed his cap and strode purposefully out of the building and directly to the office of the Minister for Defence.

"Evening, Commodore. I'm assuming it's not a 'good' evening, otherwise, you'd ring to make an appointment?"

"Actually Minister, it's a very good evening. Does the title *Operation Candy Apple* ring any bells?"

The Minister repeated the title a couple of times, "No, never heard of it. Why?"

"I suggest you look in your safe for a sealed Top Secret file of that name with *For the Minister's eyes only* stamped across the front. I'll wait in the ante room. You may wish to cancel any appointments you have for the next few hours. Buzz me through when you're ready."

Forty minutes later, the Minister's secretary advised the Commodore he could go back in.

"I notice that you're not on the 'Need to Know' list Peter. I would have thought that the position you hold would have ensured a place on it?"

"I suspect that when the list was created, my position would not have existed. Now it does, there hasn't been the need to review who is privy to the file's contents and quite frankly Minister, I don't really want to know. My job is to ensure and maintain the security of all Defence facilities. What those facilities do or contain is out of my purview."

"Having now read the file, I'm wishing my name wasn't on the bloody thing either! Cutting to the chase—why are you here, Peter?"

"As you have read, twelve years ago we had a security breach at one of our storage facilities in the small town of Barclay's Creek. Although our investigation didn't lead to the apprehension of the perpetrator/s, we did establish that one or more of them was a young child.

"While we could have closed the investigation as kids taking advantage of a fortuitous rock fall, the shit hit the fan when we found one of the containers, which had been sealed in the cavern, was missing.

"Despite the best efforts of the local police and our own investigator, those responsible were never found. That has now changed with the hypnosis-induced confession of one of our wounded Vietnam veterans.

"The reason I'm here is to request the Minister's written authorisation to re-open the investigation?"

Chapter 26

October 1969, Canberra, ACT

Having received the Minister's signed authorisation to re-open the investigation into the break-in of the Barclay's Creek quarry over twelve years ago, Commodore Fleming picked up the phone.

"*Hume Pest Control, how can I help you?*"

"Terry, Commodore Fleming."

"*Morning sir, been a while since we last spoke.*"

"Yes, indeed it has. Terry, I have a very bad infestation of cockroaches that I need you to deal with. Is your company still in the business of pest eradication?"

"*We most certainly are, Commodore. When would you like us to come out; I'm assuming you're still at the old address?*"

"Yes, still there. I'm busy for the remainder of today; will you be available tomorrow say, 1030 hours?"

"*Certainly, sir. We'll have a schedule and a quote ready for you when you arrive.*"

"Thank you. See you tomorrow."

The Commodore was all too aware of the 'Reds under our beds' paranoia that was still gripping the halls of the Federal Government following the Petrov affair in the '50s and the more recent Skripov operation. 'Always assume your phone conversations are being monitored' was the advice he gave all his operatives.

Contacting Terry was one call he certainly wanted to remain under the radar!

At 0930 the following morning, the Commodore emerged from his office in an everyday dark suit and tie, much to the surprise of his Adjutant.

It was very unusual to see his boss dressed in this manner.

Yes, he did play golf regularly with the Defence Forces Golfing Association, but, other than that, he was always immaculately dressed in his uniform.

One of the reasons the young Lieutenant had been chosen for the position, was because of his absolute discretion concerning the Commodore's, shall we say, 'unconventional' methods. He knew instinctively not to ask his boss where he was headed or why he was dressed the way he was; the Commodore would tell him—if he needed to know that is.

"I'll be out of the office all afternoon, Andrew—for your ears only."

"Understood, Sir."

Peter Fleming donned a pair of dark sunglasses, adjusted the brim of his dark grey Fedora low over his eyes and descended the fire stairs to the lower basement car park. Checking through the glass-panelled door that no one was in the immediate vicinity, he exited the stairwell and headed for a run-of-the-mill light blue 1968 VE Chrysler Valiant registered in NSW to a Mr Peter Fordham.

Peter Fordham actually existed—on paper anyway—and in the unlikely event of anyone checking, they would find that he owned a house in Bankstown and looked exactly like Commodore Fleming.

"Peter? Yes, quiet bloke, never see him much. Travelling salesman I believe," would be his neighbour's response.

The Commodore drove a circuitous route through the city centre—on the off chance he was being followed—to a nondescript red brick building near the Canberra Airport that was surrounded on the sides and back by carefully manicured six-foot high *Photinia Robusta* hedges. The doors to an apparent ramshackle garage opened smoothly as he turned into the driveway and were closed as soon as the car was inside.

"Afternoon, sir."

"Afternoon, Terry. Is your team here?"

"Yes, sir, all in the lounge room."

The three members of Terry's team rose as one and snapped to attention as the pair entered the room.

"At ease. Please, sit.

"Gentlemen, all the missions you've undertaken since we employed you, have been against known foreign agents or their sympathisers. The operation I'm now assigning you is a completely different kettle of fish.

"Your target isn't some scum-bag Commie trying to steal National secrets, the focus of the operation is a young man who is an Australian Vietnam Veteran. The young man is a Sapper Robert 'Bobby' Massey who fought for our freedom from the spread of Communism and was wounded for his efforts.

"Do we owe him a debt of gratitude? Absolutely! But—and it's a big 'but'—this young man stole something from an Australian Government secret storage facility. Something so lethal that if it falls into the wrong hands, would severely threaten our National security.

"Your job is to retrieve what was stolen—by whatever means necessary.

"I'm not here to tell you how to suck eggs, but, taking into consideration the fact that in the eyes of the general public, this man is a war hero, your methods will be, 'limited' to suit. Terry will have overall control of the operation and will be briefed on what those 'limitations' are."

Commodore Fleming had no idea what the box contained, but he wasn't going to tell these men that. All he knew was that Bobby fucking Massey was the reason for the thorn that had been pricking his ego for nearly twelve fucking years! 'Well, guess what you arsehole, your time is up!' he said to himself.

"Is that all, Sir?"

The Commodore started, "Sorry, Terry, caught up in the moment. Yes, that's all, carry on. Terry, a word in private if you please."

Terry followed the Commodore back out to the garage. He waited while his boss retrieved a black leather folio case from the front passenger seat.

"In there are your 'official' orders which authorise you to carry out covert surveillance of Mr Massey only.

"You understand that these are for my protection should you get captured." A statement, not a question.

"There is also a signed document that gives you access to a Departmental car that lends weight to those orders and a 'get out of jail free' card should the New South Wales police try to book you for any traffic offence.

"Any questions?"

"Not really a question, sir, more of an informed observation. The search of Mr Massey's apartment poses no problems whatsoever, however, should we need to move to plan B—you do realise that the time frame we've been given to come up with a result, requires—shall I say, a little less finesse than our normal methods usually entail?"

"Yes and I make no apologies for that. My reasons for setting the short mission phase are twofold; one—Mr Massey is a young wounded conscript, not a trained or campaign-hardened soldier so his defences to your methods will consequently, not be high. Secondly, it's police policy not to register a missing person until 72 hours have passed since he or she was last seen. Once the 72 hours have lapsed, the media will be all over the story of a 'missing war hero' like bees to a honeypot.

"Anything else?"

"Yes, sir, about the car; wouldn't we be better driving something a little less conspicuous?"

"No. Your team is on an 'official', Department-authorised surveillance operation so why do we need to hide the fact? If we need to implement Part B of the plan, I suspect you will be using the 'Hole' in which case, a Government registered vehicle will blend in very well with all the others in the carpark. Now, is there anything else?"

"No, sir. I'll brief you as events unfold."

The Commodore offered his hand, "Three days from when he's released Terry, after that the Police and the Press will start looking for him—assuming that someone reports him missing in the first place?"

Terry shook the offered hand, "Understood, Sir."

Forty minutes later, 'Peter Fordham' parked his Valiant in the basement car park of the Office of Naval Intelligence building and entered the stairwell leading to the fourth floor and the office of a smiling Commodore Peter Fleming.

Terry put on his suit jacket, straightened his tie, donned his hat, activated the house alarm and headed out to the car idling out the front of the house.

"Drop me outside the Navy Intelligence building then sanitise and dump the car. I'll pick up our transport and meet you all in the Lounge of the Ainslie Hotel at 1800 hundred hours. It's too late to drive to Sydney tonight and get 'the Hole' ready; 'Debra', book us two suites."

"Yes Boss. Uh, one thing before we start this venture."

"Go on."

"Boss, we've been on about six missions together and not once have I questioned anything we've had to do, but, going after a soldier that was wounded in battle—I'm afraid my ethics don't abide that. I'm opting out of this one."

"OK, disappointing but I understand. You do realise you're missing out on a substantial slice of pie?"

"Yes sir, but my heart wouldn't be in it and that may put the rest of the team at risk."

"Right then. You live in Sydney so how about staying with us until we get the 'Hole' organised?"

"Will do."

"Good man!"

Chapter 27

October 1969, Parliament House, Canberra, ACT

"Yes, Henry?"

"Mr Forrester on line one, Minister," Henry Edwards, the Minister for Defence's Private Secretary, pressed the button on his phone to connect John Forrester, the Assistant Secretary of the Department of Foreign Affairs.

"Well, that didn't take long!" George Peterson thought out loud then, resigned to the inevitable, lifted the handset and pressed the red blinking light on his phone.

"Good evening, John, to what do I owe the pleasure?"

"*Rose Garden, ten minutes.*"

"Thank you John, we'll have to chat like this more often!" he said to a dead line.

"Sit!"

"Now you listen to me, you—!"

"George, shut the fuck up and sit down! Now, as you can probably tell, my anxiety level is at 110%! What the fuck is going on George? And don't even think about putting on your politician's hat!"

George Peterson sighed and sat down on the bench.

"Peter Fleming has located the person who stole one of our items."

Silence.

Then, with an extremely calm and calculated voice, John Forrester simply said, "George, do you recall our conversation following your Party's narrow re-election win just two short years ago? The one in which you promised to stay the course as long as you retained the Defence portfolio?"

"I do and I haven't strayed from that promise?"

"You also swore over 12 years ago, that the missing item would never be located. You guaranteed our client that only the three of us in Government—

sorry, four, since we had to include another Minister following the Cabinet reshuffle—knew of the contents of those items."

He twisted his body around on the bench and stared icily at the Minister for Defence, "Now, would I be correct in assuming you fucking lied?"

"Ah now, I have to correct you there John; at no time did I swear that the container would never be found. What I believe I said was that without any evidence suggesting that the box had been opened, the most probable theory was that it had been discarded! Twelve year's John! Twelve years and nothing! How much more of a guarantee do you need?" George Peterson was fumbling; he knew that he'd stuffed up but the pragmatist in him—or maybe the greed—had weighed up the possibility of the box being found against the promise of his share of $US4,000,000—the reward won hands down.

John Forrester turned back to face the roses, "What are the odds that Peter Fleming will recover the lost item?"

"Knowing the team he contracts and the methods they employ, combined with the vulnerability of the subject, I'd say the odds are in our favour."

"How soon could you arrange the transfer of the goods?"

"Jesus, John! We're not talking about transporting a piece of furniture here, it will take at least a dozen heavy vehicles to shift all those cartons! I think that might just get someone's attention!

"We have to stick to the original plan and unfortunately, that means we are at the mercy of the Senate. The 'Removal of Contaminated Waste' Bill is before the Senate as we speak. Once it passes—and, if I'm to believe you, it will—then we can proceed as planned. In fact, I already have a removal crew on standby."

"What if Fleming's team fails?"

"It won't. Either we retrieve our property or the thief will never tell anyone else its location—in which case, we'll be in a better position than we have been!"

"Why don't I feel assured?"

"Look, John, I apologise for giving assurances when I wasn't one hundred percent sure of the facts, but, I've read the British Ministry of Defence reports on how effective the contents of those containers is. Believe me, if anyone had tampered with the contents, the resulting disaster would have been headline news the world over for months!"

"You do realise that I need to apprise our client of the situation?"

"Yes."

"Do you also understand that it's possible that his offer may be substantially reduced and if I can't convince him that the goods will still be available, cancelled altogether?"

"Yes, but he knows he's getting a fantastic deal; crushing the Government forces is his ultimate goal and he doesn't have the money to start a civil war. Four million US dollars wouldn't buy him one MIG-21 let alone the munitions to arm it and he knows it! Besides, if he reneges, we could always strike a deal with his opposition?"

"You're in the wrong business George." John Forrester stood, turned up his collar and pulled his hat low on his brow. "Keep me informed of developments as they happen!"

"Yes, John."

George Peterson returned to his office, ducking Henry's question as to whether he was feeling OK, closed the door and with a shaking hand, poured himself a large Scotch.

A short time later, he realised he needed to formulate an escape plan.

Chapter 28

October 1969, Concord Repatriation Hospital, Sydney, NSW

"George, it's Linda West."

"*Hello Linda, haven't spoken to you in a while!*" George Fielding, Senior Laboratory Technician, Sydney Chemical Testing Laboratories, replied.

"Are you free for lunch, George?"

"*Are you paying?*"

"When was the last time I didn't?"

"*Umm, let me think—that would probably be never?*"

"Sammy's Sushi, 12:30?"

"*You sure know how to capture a man's heart. See you then.*"

"What's this all about then?"

"Can't a girl buy an old friend lunch without there being an ulterior motive?"

"Linda, I can count on one hand the number of times we've done lunch since you graduated. Now, I love you dearly so stop ducking the obvious and lead me by the nose into why we're here."

George Fielding was a wild-eyed Scotsman with long bright copper-red hair and a scruffy beard to match. Linda first encountered George when she attended a debate in the University's auditorium. He was the captain of the Sydney Uni debating team in the last year of his science degree while Linda was in her first year.

She had sat captivated as the kilt-clad Scot marched up and down the front of the stage, stopping every now and then to lean on the opposition's table and stab the air between them, loudly and emphatically stating his case, his voice echoing around the walls of the auditorium. When his time was up and he stood down from the rostrum, everyone in the audience rose as one and gave him a standing ovation.

Did his team win the debate? No one really cared; they had witnessed pure live theatre and had rejoiced in its magnificence!

Linda was fascinated by George Fielding and introduced herself to him in the student bar one Friday afternoon. They hit it off immediately and would sit for hours just talking rubbish mainly and simply enjoying each other's company.

George left Uni the following year but they kept in touch until, like many Uni friendships, they didn't—unless Linda needed something. Like now.

"George, what I'm about to tell you will sound like something I read in a spy novel, but, every word is true. Before I begin, I want your solemn promise that you will not repeat anything to anyone!"

"Being a bit melodramatic, aren't you?"

"I'm deadly serious, George. Please promise!"

"OK, I promise," he reached out and held her hand, "even so, are you sure you want to tell me?"

"No, I'm not sure, but, I'm at the end of my tether!"

Linda spent the next fifteen minutes giving a précised version of events that had led to Bobby's kidnapping.

"—and the black car with a drugged Bobby in the back disappeared."

George, not one to be normally lost for words, stared silently into Linda's eyes.

"Well Stanley, it's another fine mess you've gotten me into!"

"Groucho Marx?"

"Oliver & Hardy you ignorant Sassenach! I'm sorry lassie, but while I am the oracle and fount of all knowledge, I'm not sure how Uncle George can help with this one?"

"There was one teensy, weeny bit of the saga I left out." With that, she checked that no one in the restaurant was looking in their direction, reached into her bag and lay the green box down in front of him.

"Ah, and here layeth the crux of the problem!"

"You do realise that I'm not only risking my job if I get found out but my life!?"

"Come on George, you always said life was boring and that you wanted to go out with a bang! Well, here's your opportunity."

"I'm guessing you need to know yesterday?"

"Please."

"OK, but if I survive, I get to choose the restaurant you take me to next time!"

"Deal."

"It's Sunday so the lab should be deserted. I'll call you this evening."

"Bad news my dear, nothing conclusive so what I'm about to tell you is pure calculated conjecture. The box itself is a brass, commercially available container. Inside was a double-sided rubber moulded, shock-absorbing insert with two impressions that held two small glass tubes. The tubes were sealed, single-use type, which means that after testing, standard laboratory protocol calls for the remaining contents and their containers to be incinerated.

"Now to the interesting bit; neither of the contents matched any compounds—known to this lab. I stress the last bit as we are a 'general/commercial/industrial testing lab' and not a medical testing facility. I can emphatically say that neither tested positive to any known illicit drugs so unfortunately, I can rule out a secret stash of marijuana or cocaine.

"What was intriguing was that while one tube contained an apparent inert substance, the second contained what appeared to be dead bacteria suspended in some sort of carrier agent. The interesting part came when I mixed a tiny sample of each—not only were the bacteria cells 'revived' they multiplied at a phenomenal rate. So much so that they literally 'overpopulated' the minuscule sample and died within seconds. Suffice it to say, everything that was used to open and test the contents has also been incinerated.

"I can return the box though. A memento of your misadventures shall we say?"

"Thank you so very much for doing that for me George, but—"

"Here we go! Well come on then, I've climbed the gallows, may as well put me noggin in the noose!"

"George, I've got a feeling that no one is supposed to know what was in that box."

"Well lassie, your safe—because we'll never know for certain now!"

"But whoever owns the remainder of the cache of boxes doesn't know that we don't know. That's why I need some 'insurance'. George, I want you to write a report exactly as you would with any other customer's analysis request."

"Whoa! Linda, I do that, I may as well kiss my career goodbye!"

"I know it's asking a lot George, but I swear to you that the report will not be released until it's absolutely necessary and as a last resort. It would also be heavily redacted to conceal yours and your laboratory's involvement—I promise!"

"*You know how to sweet talk a fella! OK, the report and the box will be mailed to you by Registered Mail tomorrow. Now, I'm hanging up before you talk me into assassinating the Prime Minister.*"

"Hey yeah!, how about—"

"*Goodnight, Linda!*"

"Goodnight, George, I love you, you know!"

"*Yeah, yeah, yeah!*"

Chapter 29

November 1969, Strathfield, Sydney, NSW

At two-twenty in the morning, a Commonwealth-registered black MkIV Humber Super Snipe, its lights off, glided silently to a stop two houses away from its occupant's destination. Three men, dressed from head to toe in black, woollen beanies pulled low on their heads, silently exited the vehicle. Without a word spoken, the doors were closed gently and while two of them crossed the road and headed for the apartment block, the other remained in the shadows.

Two minutes later, the 2-way radio in the Humber squawked once and the third man followed his colleagues into the building and the target's apartment.

Once inside the apartment, the three men split up and then quietly and methodically, searched every square inch of Bobby's home. Pillows, cushions and mattresses were slashed, drawers and containers were upturned and cupboards and wardrobes were systematically emptied. Even the toilet cistern cover was removed.

Eight minutes later, the men relocked Bobby's door, exited the building, got back into their vehicle and with its lights remaining off, the car very quietly drove off.

"Nothing, sir."

Commodore Fleming stopped himself from asking if the caller was sure there was nothing. He knew he could rely on his team to find the proverbial needle in a haystack, on a moonless night, blindfolded.

"*That's a shame. Right, Plan B it is then. Your team up to the challenge?*" Covert surveillance and clandestine searches were one thing, kidnapping and torture were a completely different story.

"If everything goes according to plan, then we're completely capable and comfortable with it, so, yes sir, we're up to it!"

"*Report back to me once the asset's 'relocated'.*"

"Aye, aye sir!"

****

Bobby awoke, sat up with a start and looked around the room, puzzled; it took him a whole second to realise what the cause of his consternation was.

"No headache! And, bugger me, its bloody daylight outside!"

He couldn't remember the last time he had slept the whole night without waking at least once shaking uncontrollably and drenched in sweat. He checked the time; 0630. The nurse would be around at 0700 to give him his meds.

"May as well shit, shave and shampoo Massey. Give the poor nurse fifty fits when she sees you up and about!"

Later that morning, Doctor Garland was standing next to his bed checking his blood pressure. What is it with doctors, Bobby mused, the nurse had given Bobby the full driveway service less than two hours ago and entered all his vitals on his record that was hanging on the end of his bed! Probably needed to prove he could use the stethoscope permanently hung around his neck!

"How are we feeling this morning, Bobby?"

"Don't know about you, Doc, but I could eat the ar—, back end out of a horse!"

"Umm, that good eh? Well, your blood pressure is only slightly high but your pulse rate is way too fast, so how about we settle for—" He checked the hospital lunch menu, "the veggie soup with an unbuttered bread roll?"

"Bobby," he continued, "I'm afraid that this feeling of euphoria won't last. Your heart is racing because the meds you're currently taking are at the high end of the recommended dosage rate. My job now is to reduce those rates while constantly monitoring your condition with the aim of weaning you off completely. Unfortunately, many patients are never entirely drug-free, in which case, we'll get you to the stage where you are free from psychotic attacks but can still carry on a relatively normal life.

"In the meantime, please keep attending the group therapy sessions; if not for yourself, then to inspire others in the group to realise that recovery isn't a hopeless cause. Enjoy your lunch!" And he signed off with a wink and a wry grin.

Two weeks later, his mum was hugging him and crying while his dad shook his hand and said, "Welcome back, son."

It was their first visit since Bobby had been committed. He didn't blame them for sending him here and later he would come to thank them for intervening when they did.

"When are you coming home?" his mum asked.

"Right at this precise moment, I feel right as rain, but, even without Doctor Garland's diagnosis, I know I'm not right in the head—yet.

"I'm gradually coming off the anti-hallucinatory drugs but the dosage of Valium I'm on means I'm not allowed to drive or operate machinery. So, sorry dad, I can't take on mowing lawns!"

"Has Linda been to see you?"

"No, Mum. She was coming nearly every day but I could see it was breaking her heart so I told her I didn't want her to visit."

"Bobby Massey, you are such an idiot! Are you sure you didn't leave your brains in Vietnam instead of half your leg!"

"Easy Mum!"

"No, I won't go easy! You need to listen very carefully; do you think that poor girl was coming to see you out of a sense of duty or because she felt sorry for you? No, you dope—it was because she loves you! You telling her not to visit would have been akin to a slap in the face!

The one thing that may save the most precious thing in your life right now, is for you to get down on your knees and beg for her forgiveness or better yet, you can tell her you love her and care about her more than your own sorry arse!"

"Mary!"

"I'm sorry, but sometimes he truly is your son!"

Then she collapsed into Bobby's arms with a fresh round of tears—and then Bobby joined her.

****

"Target is being released next week."

"Very good. Accommodation is ready for his arrival."

Chapter 30

5:30 p.m., Friday 5 December 1969, Cumberland Lunatic Asylum, Sydney

"Mr Massey, how do you feel about re-joining society, with all the pressures that the average person experiences in their day-to-day lives?" This comment was from Doctor Garland. As head of Psychiatric Services, he had the casting vote if the Review Panel was deadlocked.

The other members of the Review Panel were Colonel Muir, on behalf of the Repatriation Department and the Head of Medical Services, Doctor Harold Chambers.

"Honestly, to say I'm totally relaxed about facing the world again, would be a lie. Will I need to keep taking my meds, absolutely, but, am I likely to suffer another meltdown; no! My mind hasn't been this clear since leaving Barclay's Creek over twelve years ago—and I have you, gentlemen, to thank for that."

The review lasted another twenty minutes with routine questions such as; did he have a place to stay, was there someone that would regularly check on him, what was the name of his GP, etc.

Then after Doctor Garland had asked if Bobby had any questions, he said, "Thank you for that, Mr Massey. The panel will now deliberate and vote on your case so would you please wait outside while we do so."

A short while later, Bobby used the pay phone in the foyer to ring his parents. "These bloody psyches haven't a clue!"

"*I'm so sorry Bobby, maybe next time eh?*" his dad said sympathetically.

"What are you talking about, the dopey buggers released me! I'm out of here as soon as I pack my bag!"

His mum and dad were still laughing and whooping it up when he hung up several minutes later.

Picking up his bag, he gave a final look around the room that had been his home for the last three months and with a newly found spring in his step, Bobby walked out of the Asylum into the twilight of a summer's evening.

A choked sob caught in his throat as descended the steps from the Asylum's main entrance. Parked at the kerb directly in front of him and bathed in the soft amber glow from the street light, was a sparkling waxed and polished, dark metallic green, MkI 1965 Ford Cortina GT. But that wasn't why he was choked—leaning on the front quarter panel was the most beautiful woman he had ever seen.

Dressed in a lime-green pants suit, a white beret at a jaunty angle on her glossy-black hair that flowed freely over her shoulders, and one platform-shoe propped backwards onto the front wheel, was Linda West.

She pushed herself away from the car and sashayed exaggeratingly to stand directly in front of Bobby. Sliding her large framed sunglasses down her nose, she casually draped her arms around Bobby's neck, stared into his eyes and whispered huskily, "Going my way, sailor?"

Then, when she couldn't hold a straight face any longer, burst into laughter. "Careful, Bobby, you'll trip over your jaw if it drops any further!"

Bobby couldn't hold back his tears of joy; he dropped his bag and lifted her in an embrace, whispering repeatedly, "I love you, I love you—"

****

"Abort, abort!"

"Shit, who the fuck is that?"

Instead of pulling into the kerb, the Humber accelerated past the 'Patient Pick Up' area and merged back into the traffic on Bridge Road. A short time later, the car pulled over next to a telephone box.

"It appears that Mr Massey has a girlfriend, sir."

"Will that be a problem?"

"We do know from the search of his apartment that she's not living with him. We'll stake out Mr Massey's apartment and take him from there. The delay will alter our schedule somewhat but the outcome is still achievable."

"The problem will come if his girlfriend believes he needs some close personal care after his stay in hospital and decides to move in with him—we don't have the necessary resources to abduct the pair of them."

"Any chance you'd recognise the girl if you saw her again?"

"No, she had her back to us and was wearing a cap and sunglasses. The only feature I did notice was that she had long black hair. She was driving Mr Massey's car so we can't even run the registration to get her name and address."

"Leave it with me. I'll see if our Colonel can shed any light on her identity. I'll contact you if I discover anything."

"Yes, sir."

****

Bobby adjusted the bucket seat, realigned the rear-view mirror and squiggled his rear-end into the bucket seat.

"Are you going to drive this thing or make love to it?"

"Do you know how long it's been since I drove this supreme example of British engineering?"

"You're right Bobby," Linda replied undoing her seatbelt. "Come on, hop out and let me drive."

"Ha, bloody ha! You and 'The Hulk'…"—Linda's assistant, Marco, at the Concord Repatriation Hospital—"couldn't pry me out of this seat!"

Twenty minutes later, Bobby drove into a parking bay beneath his apartment block. With his bag in one hand and Linda's hand in the other, they climbed the stairs to his apartment. Stopping outside his door, he took Linda in his arms.

"My last memory of this place is not a good one and I wasn't that keen on returning to be honest. But now you're here with me, I can't wait to get inside!"

Linda smiled, gently touched his cheek and kissed him.

"And I can't wait for you to be inside."

The wonderful churning emotions that were flying around inside him all came crashing back to earth as soon as they opened the door.

"What the f—"

"Oh, Bobby!" Linda sobbed as she clutched his arm.

****

"Bobby, I think you should call the police."

"I would but the telephone's not working. I checked it when I picked it off the floor—probably because I haven't paid the bill."

They were sat on the floor, their backs against the ripped and cushion-less sofa, sipping their second can of beer. At least the electricity hadn't been disconnected.

Linda placed her can of beer on the floor and then stood. "You stay here, I'll go and find a telephone box and ring the police. Better not have any more grog before they've done what they're going to do."

Linda walked out of the apartment and turned towards the main road where a telephone box was more likely to be located. As she turned from Bobby's building, her eyes moved instinctively over a sleek black car parked some fifty feet away on the other side of the road and she was sure that she saw cigarette smoke drift out of the driver's window.

Suddenly the hair on the back of her neck were standing on end and with her heart in her mouth, she forced herself to carry on walking. To stop herself from looking directly at the car, she rummaged in her bag as if searching for something.

Safely out of sight from the mystery black car, Linda stopped and, from the shadows of a large Moreton Bay fig tree, looked back up the street.

****

"Do we take the two of them?"

"No, we're not set up to handle both of them at the same time. The good thing is, we now know what the girlfriend looks like. I do want to know where the girl is going though; 'Daphne', take the handset and follow her."

Linda saw a black-clad figure emerge from the back of the car and head in her direction. She ran a short distance to make it appear that she hadn't stopped then resumed her walk to find a telephone box.

"*She's making a phone call.*"

"Most likely to the police to report the 'break in'. Get back here and we'll wait."

****

"Are you OK, miss!"

"Just shook up over this," she replied to the young female constable's concerned inquiry.

"Apart from a 'stress relieving' beer, nothing else has been touched?" asked the Senior Constable.

"No, sir," Bobby answered.

"And the door was locked when you entered?"

"Yes."

"Nothing of value stolen?"

"Not that there was much of anything of value to steal, apart from the Marantz Hi-Fi system, but no, nothing was stolen."

"Does anyone other than yourself have keys to the apartment?"

"No—yes! The landlord would have a spare key."

"Would your landlord have any reason to trash your apartment?"

"Seeing that my 'landlord' is the Repat Department, I don't think so."

"OK. So, as there is no sign of a forced entry, which rules out *Break* and Enter and there's nothing stolen, there isn't anything the police can do Mr Massey. If—once you've cleared up the mess—you do find anything of value missing, please give the Station a call and we'll investigate it further.

"Goodnight Miss West, Mr Massey."

Linda was a nervous wreck. While the police were looking around, the penny had dropped. She now knew why the mysterious black car with its black-clad occupants was parked outside. They had been the men responsible for trashing Bobby's apartment in a vain search for the green box that was now in her desk at work. This meant that Bobby had, intentionally or by accident, revealed his part in their discovery of the hidden tunnel in Barclay's Creek. The question was, had he revealed her involvement?

What she was absolutely certain about was that she couldn't tell Bobby any of this. If he knew that he was responsible for any of it, there was every likelihood that he would relapse into his previous psychotic state. Linda prayed like hell that he had no recollection of revealing their secret.

She found Bobby just about to open another can of beer. She placed her hand on his arm, "How about we straighten the bedroom and I'll show you how much I've missed you?"

Bobby put down the unopened can and took Linda in his arms, "Do you know how long I've waited to hear those words? But right now—well, let's just say I wouldn't be operating on all six cylinders." He kissed the top of her head then held her at arm's length, "But if the offer to help clean the place is still open—?"

Linda punched his arm, "And who said romance is dead?"

By two in the morning, they had managed to move all the unsalvageable items into the lounge room and anything worth saving was moved to the bedroom.

"Do you want to come back to my place? Today's Saturday so we can sleep in and then go and buy you some new furniture—especially a bed!"

"No Thanks Linda, my mattress is still useable so I'll kip here—if that's OK." Bobby noticed the look of concern on Linda's face. "Don't worry, I'll take my meds and you can take the rest of the beers with you. You take the car home and come and pick me up about ten-thirty."

What Bobby didn't realise was that Linda's concern was sitting in a black car outside of his apartment block, but apart from knocking him out and carrying him to the car, she could see no other way of getting him out of harm's way.

In the end, she decided to watch the watchers.

"Shit! Do we follow the girl to find out where she lives or do we stick to the original plan and grab Mr Massey?" Terry thought out loud, "Fuck it! We stay on track! Right, let's do it!"

Linda parked the Cortina a block away and around the corner away from any street lights and carefully walked back to the shelter of the large fig tree. "We'll have to stop meeting like this," she told the tree in her best Groucho Marx voice.

Three minutes after she reached the tree, three men emerged from the apartment block, an obviously drugged Bobby draped limply between two of them. Bobby was bundled into the back seat and the Humber moved silently towards her. Linda quickly memorised the number plate and then ducked back against the tree as the headlights came on and the car picked up speed to disappear into the night.

Chapter 31

9:00 a.m., Sunday 7 December 1969, Location Unknown

"He's waking up, sir."

"Very good. I'll be right down."

Bobby woke up with the biggest hangover he had ever experienced! It was when he tried to clutch his throbbing temples that he discovered he was tied to an extremely uncomfortable wire-sprung bed frame tilted at a forty-five-degree angle to the wet concrete floor. Managing to focus his bleary eyes, he took in his surroundings. He had just spotted the two figures standing at the foot of his 'bed' when a voice came from behind him.

"Good morning, Mr Massey—well, not really good for you at the moment, is it?"

Bobby didn't answer, he was still studying the balaclava-clad men—their physique indicating that they were in fact men—and trying hard to work out what the fuck he was doing here.

"You're probably wondering how you come to be tied up in this cold, damp hole? It's simple enough, you have some very important information that I'd like you to share with me—you tell me what happened to the small container you stole from a Government facility twelve years ago and I'll set you free. Fair deal?"

No answer from Bobby.

"What do you think gentlemen, is that a fair deal or what?"

"Very fair, I reckon, Boss," said one.

"Couldn't be any fairer, Boss," replied the other.

"It seems Mr Massey is still making up his mind. Perhaps we can help him come to a decision. Daphne if you please?"

"Certainly, Boss."

'Daphne' picked up a bucket of water and threw it over Bobby. He then walked over to what looked very much like an electric arc welding machine and flicked a switch.

Bobby's back arched off the bed until he thought his spine would snap and his jaw clenched shut so tightly, he thought his teeth would shatter. Then the power was switched off and he collapsed panting and shaking uncontrollably onto the frame.

"Now Daphne, that was a bit naughty—I specifically asked you to start on the lowest setting!"

"Ugh, sorry, Boss. I'll try harder next time!"

"I'm awfully sorry, Bobby—is it OK if I call you, Bobby?—it's so hard to find good torturers these days! So, where was I?"

"You were asking Mr Massey about a small container, Boss."

"So I was, thank you 'Doris'. Bobby, I know for a fact—you know what a 'fact' is, don't you? A fact is something that's 100% true! Well, I know with a solid gold 100% guarantee, that you broke into a secure Government facility and took something that doesn't belong to you. That's break, enter and robbery Bobby. All of them criminal offences. Stealing something from the Australian Government carries double the penalty you could expect in this State.

"Now, I'm going to do you a favour—you tell me where to find that box and I won't hand you over to the Federal Police. What do you say to that, Bobby? Do we have a deal?"

"I have no idea what you're talking about, but, if I had what you were after, I'd gladly hand it over if for nothing else than to shut you up!"

"Oh dear, it seems Mr Massey didn't get the message the last time. Tell you what, let's start over and see if 'Doris' can do better than 'Daphne' at loosening your tongue. 'Doris', if you please—?"

Bobby wasn't sure what he hated most, the grating voice of the man behind him or the electric shocks. In the end, the shocks won and he thankfully passed out.

"I do believe Mr Massey will let himself fry before he tells us anything. Throw him in the dark room and let's try sleep deprivation."

Bobby woke with a start as The Beatles' *A Hard Day's Night* blasted from the speakers eight feet above the floor where he found himself lying. Then a bank of extremely bright lights, also in the ceiling, came on. Even with his hands pressed firmly against his ears, which deadened the sound to some extent, the music was so loud he could feel the sound waves vibrating in his chest.

"Wakey, wakey sunshine, breakfast is served," the steel door swung open and a bowl of something was pushed inside—it looked and smelled exactly like urine.

The noise/lights routine went on for an indeterminate time and after the fourth or tenth time—Bobby didn't have a clue—the steel door clanged open forcibly, a bag was placed over his head and he was dragged back to the wire frame bed.

This process was repeated until it reached the stage where Bobby was unresponsive and ranting incoherently.

"What is it with this arsehole! Anybody would think I was asking him to reveal Winston Churchill's battle plans for bloody D-day or something! Right, let's try the 'nice guy' routine. Put him in the furnished 'room' and let him sleep and then shower and then serve him a full breakfast. Have him back here in," the 'Boss' checked his watch, "five hours and I'll try again. Meantime, I need to make a phone call."

****

"Give him his due, tougher men than him would have cracked by now."

"*He's said nothing? Not even some expletive-ridden invective?*"

"Nothing, sir."

"*You do understand that time is money?*"

The 'Boss' knew exactly what that meant—it was their time and his money.

"I understand sir, but I can't get the information out of a corpse and that's where we'll end up if I continue down the physical torture route. I'm trying the 'nice guy' treatment tonight but after that we'll have to resort to the 'whoopie juice' together with its inherent dangers—if you know what I mean?"

"*Understood. I do have some good news for you; Mr Massey's girlfriend is one Linda West. Miss West is a Physiotherapist at Concord Repatriation Hospital but spent much of her spare time visiting Mr Massey in the Asylum. I have an address for her—do you have a pen handy?*"

"Yes sir, go ahead."

"She has an apartment at 4/28 Livingstone Terrace, Mortlake. I'm not authorising your team to carry out any action against Miss West, but, if you need 'leverage' to extract the information I need then I believe your orders are sufficiently clear, are they not?"

"Your orders are crystal clear, sir!"

****

Bobby woke to the pain shooting through his injured right leg, "Well we can rule out shock treatment to heal a wounded leg," he groaned silently.

Carefully opening his swollen eyes and moving his head very slowly he could just make out that he was in a room with at least a table and a chair. He then came to the realisation that he was lying on a mattress on a real bed.

He knew exactly what his captors were doing. It hadn't been that long since his army training at the Kapooka Barracks where the recruits had undertaken a two-day exercise in torture techniques to gain an insight into what they could expect if captured by the enemy—but with a difference!

They didn't just sit in the classroom and listen to an explanation of various torture techniques—they had experienced them first hand. Not to quite this extent, but enough for him to know what to expect. The kidnappers had tried the physical torture phase and failed—the soft mattress and furniture were the start of the mental phase and was called the 'nice guy' routine.

Bobby had no idea of the time, but he wasn't going to let this thin but ever so comfortable mattress go to waste and with the thought of being woken with a hot breakfast, he quickly lapsed into a dreamless sleep.

"'Daphne', 'Doris', change of plans. We now know the name and address of Mr Massey's girlfriend. We all grab a couple of hours sleep then we recommence the program with Mr Massey as planned. If,—and I fully expect this will be the case—if, Mr Massey still fails to give us the information, we stick him back in the 'Light and Sound' suite. At 0700 hundred hours tomorrow morning 'Doris' and I will pay Miss Linda West a visit. 'Daphne', I want you to stay here and babysit our guest."

Chapter 32

8:30 p.m., Sunday 7 December 1969, Linda's Apartment, Mortlake, Sydney

Linda knew that whoever took Bobby was going to interrogate him to find out firstly; what had he done with the stolen box and secondly; was anyone else with him and what is the identity of him or her? If Bobby did admit that someone was with him, it wouldn't take them long to put two and two together and search for the girl they saw driving Bobby's Cortina.

"So thinking cap on girl, what's your next step?"

In the end, she decided that first off, she needed to ring Bobby's parents.

"Hello, Robert?"

"*Yes?*"

"Robert, it's Linda West."

"*Oh, hello Linda. Mary and I were expecting a call from Bobby; I guess you two were out celebrating his release from* the Asylum?"

"Robert, what I'm about to tell you will come as a shock to you both, but, I need a sworn promise that you won't tell another soul?"

Robert uttered a small nervous laugh, "*What's this all about, Linda? Why the secrecy?*"

"Please, Robert, swear you won't tell anyone!"

"*OK, but now you have me worried! Is Bobby hurt? Has he suffered a relapse? Has he been in an accident—?*"

"No, none of those things. You'd better sit down and I'll tell you what's going on."

"*My God, after all this time? I can't believe anyone would kidnap Bobby for such a small thing!*"

"The 'small thing' obviously means a great deal to whoever has Bobby. Robert, I've decided to ask a policeman to help me. Now I know that goes against everything I've asked you not to do, but, I sense that this particular policeman will help us find Bobby without alerting the whole NSW Police Force which in turn may alert the kidnappers. Don't ask me how I know this—maybe it's what my Nana called 'women's intuition'.

"I'm driving down to Barclay's Creek tonight as soon as I finish talking to you. When and if I have any news on Bobby, I'll call you, OK?"

"*OK, Linda, but, just to let you know—my intuition tells me to ignore everything you've asked me to do and ring the police. I've made a promise, so I won't—yet!*"

"I understand. I'll talk to you later, OK?"

"*OK. Bye, Linda and good luck!*"

"Thanks, Robert. Bye."

****

"*Barclay's Creek Police Station, how may I help you?*"

"Hello, is Constable Ahearn there please?"

"*It's Senior Constable Ahearn and who may I say is calling?*"

"Can you just tell him it's a former pupil of Barclay's Creek Primary School ringing about the quarry."

"Boss."

"Yes Steve," in Senior Sergeant Vic Roger's eyes, Senior Constables had earned the right to be addressed by their first name.

"I think you need to hear this." Steve walked around Vic's desk pressed the flashing button and placed the call on 'Speaker'

"*Senior Constable Ahearn.*"

"Hello, I'm ringing about the break-in at the old quarry in 1957. Do you remember you came to the school looking for information?"

"*Yes, I remember. Can you give me your name Miss?*"

"No—not at this stage anyway. Is it possible to speak to someone in charge please?"

"*Not without providing—*"

"*Miss*," Vic cut in and held up a hand to belay any protests from Steve "*my name is Senior Sergeant Rogers, Vic Rogers. You are obviously troubled with something Miss, if you give us all the information you have, it may relieve the burden you've carried all these years.*"

"Nice try, Sergeant!" and she hung up the phone.

"What now, girl," she asked herself. "Time to talk to the seagulls."

Linda's apartment was a stone's throw from the Parramatta River foreshore. On work days and when the weather was fine, she would walk along the river to the Concord Repat Hospital just 3 kilometres away. Walking along the quiet track was peaceful and relaxing and it freed her mind from the garbage of everyday living and working. Along the way, she would be joined by a flock of ever-hopeful seagulls looking for a free feed.

Grabbing a couple of slices of bread—"sorry, fellas, no chips today"—she headed over to a shady spot on the other side of Yaralla Bay and, over the next thirty minutes, had a long consultation with a flock of gulls.

"Yes, you're right, of course—"

"Well, there is that, but—"

"OK, say we go down that path, what if—"

"Are you sure?"

"Right then! Let's do it!"

Breaking up the remaining scraps of bread, she scattered it across the grass and with purpose in her stride, she headed back home—to probably put her head in the proverbial noose!

She checked her watch; 8:30 p.m. This time on a Sunday night, traffic wouldn't be a problem—two hours should have her in Barclay's Creek easily.

The traffic heading out of Sydney along King Georges Road was, as she expected, light. Once she hit the highway, it was non-existent. With no traffic lights to slow her down, Linda opened the twin throttles in the Weber carburettor and the Cortina responded with a hearty growl.

One hour and fifty-four minutes later ("I wonder if Bobby knows the Cortina can do 120kph?"), Linda was standing in a telephone box in Barclay's Creek, looking in the phone book for the home address of 'Mr Rogers, V'. Ten minutes later she knocked on his front door.

"Yes? Can I help you, Miss?" A slightly annoyed Vic Rogers asked.

"Sergeant Rogers, my name's Linda West. I spoke to you on the phone the other day."

"Miss West, its Sunday night, I've had a long day at the end of a shitty week and all I want is a cold beer, a hot shower and a warm bed. Now please, pi…go away and come and see me at the station tomorrow when I'll be in a much nicer frame of mind." He started to close the door.

"My boyfriend may be dead by then!"

The door remained half closed, then with a rueful sigh, "You'd better come in then."

Linda had managed to hold her emotions at bay—right up until she described seeing the men shove Bobby in the back of the car and then it all came crashing down.

Vic had listened carefully while she went through the whole sad tale. Now as she sat quietly sobbing into her handkerchief, he got up and went to the kitchen to make a pot of tea. One good thing he had learned from the Poms; in times of crisis; make a pot of tea!

Linda followed him into the kitchen a few minutes later, "Sorry about that."

"Nothing to be sorry for. My dear departed mum used to say *You hold too much inside, Victor. One day you're going to burst!* But with a real Romanian accent. Since then, I don't—much to the annoyance of the young police officers at the Station. Come on back to the lounge room. We'll drink our tea and figure out our next move."

"Steve, its Vic Rogers. I think I'm coming down with that bug you and your poxy mates brought into the office." Linda heard Steve Ahearn laugh at the good-natured jibe, "I'm going to stay home and drink copious amounts of vitamin C-laden Bundy rum to hasten its departure. Can you mind the shop for a couple of days? Good lad!"

"Now, the next step you're not going to completely agree with," he said to Linda as he hung up the phone, "but this gentleman and I have been mates ever since both of us were responsible for investigating your Quarry case. Commander Jerry O'Rourke is a straight shooter and I reckon we can trust him. OK?"

"Won't his sense of duty see him report everything to his superiors?"

"Yes, of course. Your job, young lady, is to convince him, the way you convinced me, to delay that duty until after we find where they're holding Bobby."

"OK."

"Jerry, its Vic Rogers—yeah, I know it's past my bedtime—sorry mate, as much as I enjoy shooting the breeze with you, this isn't a social call. I have a desperate young lady sitting in my lounge room and we are in need of your expert advice."

After a quick summary of what Linda had told him, Jerry agreed to provide as much help as he could. Vic jotted down an address and then ended the call.

"You're in luck, Jerry is currently billeted at HMAS *Kuttabul* near the Garden Island dockyard while his ship is undergoing maintenance. He has agreed to meet with us tomorrow morning. I suggest you go and grab some shuteye in the spare room while I go and have a long-overdue shower! Up at sparrow's fart tomorrow morning!"

Linda was woken by Senior Sergeant Rogers at 4:30 a.m.

"Here you go, sunshine," he said as he placed a hot cup of tea on the small bedside table. "The bathroom is down the hall on the left. If you need a change of clothes, there are some girls' clothes in the wardrobe that might fit you. We need to be on the road by 5:45 if we're to meet Jerry by 8:30."

Linda decided to leave her tea until after she had grabbed a quick shower. She was back in her room twenty minutes later and drank her—cold—tea while she dried and brushed her long hair. The shirt she was wearing last night was creased and a bit on the nose so she took Vic's advice and rummaged through the clothes in the wardrobe. Whoever owned the clothes had a larger bra size and a smaller waist than Linda but she did find a T-shirt that fitted loosely.

"Now, why would a single man have a wardrobe full of young lady's clothes?" she asked herself. Thinking the worst, Linda decided it was probably safer not to ask.

The drive to Sydney was proceeding in silence; Linda worrying about Bobby's fate and Vic, knowing what she was going through, let her be. He glanced in her direction and noticed for the first time that she was wearing one of the T-shirts that had been hanging in the spare bedroom wardrobe.

"Diane," he said.

"Sorry, what was that?"

"Diane, the name of the young lady whose T-shirt you're wearing."

"Vic, you don't have to tell me your family secrets. I'm just grateful that you don't have to put up with the pong of my BO!"

"She wasn't family or any other relative. She was a beautiful-looking sixteen-year-old prostitute being exploited by some very bad men in a port town not far from Barclay's Creek. 'Rosey' was apprehended soliciting in our patch so I arrested her and put her in a cell.

153

"I received a call at 2.15 a.m. the following morning from Constable—as he was then—Masters telling me that 'Rosey' had tried to hang herself in her cell and had been rushed to the Emergency ward in Wollongbar Hospital.

"For some reason, that I still can't get my thick head around, I rushed to the hospital and sat by her bedside until she woke up."

"A daughter you wished you had?"

"Maybe. Probably. I honestly don't know, but one thing I swore to myself as I watched her sleeping, was that she would never go back to the life she had.

"Her real name was Diane Beasley, mother and father deceased, left in the care—uncaring, more like—of foster parents, she was urged to drop out of school and earn some 'real money' working for the local crime Boss.

"Nearly ten months she lived with me. I found her a job working in our local news agency and she settled into her new life well.

"Then the bad guys found her again. The bastards beat her up so badly that she never regained consciousness and died three days later.

"You know the thing that eats me up the most, is the fact that if I'd have let sleeping dogs lie, she may have been alive today. That's the reason her clothes are still in the spare room—just going in there brings back the guilt." With that, he stopped talking and stared out of the passenger door window.

"Vic, if that had been me, right now I'd been looking down on you and saying; Vic Rogers, those ten months living with you were 100 percent better than a lifetime prostituting myself for those bastards!"

"Yeah, you're probably right," he replied half-heartedly.

Chapter 33

8:30 a.m., Monday 7 December 1969, Sydney City

Vic and Linda had arrived in the city at 7.45 a.m. and had spent 30 minutes searching for a parking spot.

"What is it with city Councils?" Vic opined, obviously uncomfortable in a city environment. "They approve all these flamin' high-rise buildings without any thought as to where the people who live or work in them are going to park their bleedin' cars!"

They finally found a space two blocks from their agreed rendezvous with Jerry. Unfortunately, Vic's mood became even darker as they now had to weave and dodge the throngs of pedestrians hurrying to work. Fifteen minutes later, with Vic complaining all the way about the relentless hustle and bustle of Sydney, they were all seated in a small a wrap-around, red vinyl and black Formica booth in 'Theo's Greek Restaurant' in Macleay Street—a favourite haunt of sailors and dock-workers.

'Theo's' was only a short walk up the hill from HMAS *Kuttabul,* where Jerry was billeted, and the Garden Island dockyard. Linda sat on one side of the booth with Vic and Jerry crammed together on the opposite side.

"Before we get started, I'd better use the phone box outside and let the hospital know I won't be in today."

Linda rang the hospital and asked to be put through to Doctor Jeanette Barber, her boss at the Concord Repatriation Hospital.

"Good morning, Linda, not coming in today?"

"Jeanette Barber, are you clairvoyant?"

Doctor Barber chuckled. "Linda, I can't remember the last time you weren't at your desk, beavering away by the time I got to work! So, whatever is keeping you away this morning, must be vitally important. Will I see you tomorrow?"

"Jeanette, I can't go into details; suffice to say Bobby Massey is in trouble and needs my help. I might need two days?"

"Gosh! I hope he's OK! Please take all the time you need and good luck! Oh, I nearly forgot! There were two gentlemen at the desk this morning asking for you."

"Did they say what they wanted or leave a message?"

"No, nothing. They were very 'official' looking; black suits, and Fedora hats. They didn't show any ID, but my guess is they were from the police. Would they have anything to do with the trouble Mr Massey is in?"

Linda had to swallow the lump that had suddenly formed in her throat, "No, I shouldn't think so—it's not that sort of 'trouble'."

"Oh, that's alright then," Jeanette said, relieved. "Well, you take care!"

"Thanks, Jeanette."

Two minutes later, she resumed her seat.

"They've found me!"

"Who's found you?" Jerry asked with concern.

"There were two men in suits and hats asking for me at the hospital this morning. They didn't show any ID but my boss said they looked like 'policemen'!"

"Bobby must have given the kidnappers your name," Jerry remarked.

"Don't be so sure," Vic countered. "These blokes are professionals and wouldn't waste their time trying to extract information out of Bobby that would be easy to obtain by other means. My professional opinion is that someone—probably one of the doctors at the Lunatic Asylum—has leaked information given confidentially by Bobby, including his release details, during his treatment there. It wouldn't have taken the informant long to check the names in the Visitor's Book that probably has in flashing neon lights 'Miss Linda West visiting Mr Bobby Massey in Room 45 at 5:00 p.m.'"

"So what do I do now?"

"Nothing." Vic continued, "If they visited your place of work, they probably searched your apartment as well. They've shown their hand and fortunately for us we now know they're looking for you—unfortunately for them, they don't know we're with you. Even if they did, they're certainly not going to try taking out the three of us! My recommendation is that we carry on as planned."

"I think I need a Greek coffee!" Linda sighed heavily.

"What's that when it's at home?" Jerry asked.

"A double-shot espresso with a slug of Ouzo in it!"

Linda settled for a double espresso without the Ouzo and then with a huge sigh, she grasped the hand of each of the men opposite her.

"Can I just say that I'm extremely grateful to you two gentlemen for dropping everything to help me? Especially, when it was my stupid fault that ended up with Bobby being kidnapped!"

She held up a hand to stop them when they both began to speak, "Now, I know you're both going to say that anyone would have done what you are doing—quite frankly, that's cod's wallop!

"If I had gone to any other police officer with my story, they would have either brushed me off completely or passed me from pillar to post hoping I'd give up and go home.

"Regardless of whether we find Bobby—" she paused and choked back a sob. "Whether we find him or not, I can never repay your wonderful generosity and kindness. But, I insist on buying you breakfast!"

Vic and Jerry both smiled and nodded that they understood what she was going through.

"I should bloody well hope so too!" Vic said after a short pause, "I'll have a full English—with Black Pudding—and a pot of Darjeeling! Please."

Jerry turned to him, "'Black Pudding'? In a Greek cafe, you'll be lucky!" Then to Linda, "I had breakfast in the Officer's Mess earlier, but I will have a long black coffee with a slice of their excellent Baklava, please, Linda."

Linda realised that she was famished and also ordered the full English breakfast but without the Black Pudding thank you very much!

Much to everyone's surprise—even Vic, his two sausage, baked beans, grilled tomato, three rashers of bacon, two fried eggs, sautéed mushrooms and two slices of buttered toast—did come with two slices of fried black pudding!

The trio was an interesting mix; twenty-two-year-old Linda West in jeans and a borrowed Rolling Stones t-shirt, beautifully clear olive complexion, brown almond-shaped eyes and long black hair tied back in a ponytail; Jerry in his thirties and obviously awkward in 'civvies', his short back and sides haircut an obvious sign of his military service and the large, well-muscled six feet three-inch form of Vic with his remaining blond hair all but hanging on for grim life and piercing green eyes that were difficult to look into without confessing to something you may or may not have done at some stage in your life!

The waitress had cleared their table and delivered another round of tea and coffees when Jerry leaned over the table and asked incredulously, "So the box was concealed in a plastic model ship for twelve years? Weren't either of you curious as to what was inside the box?" Jerry asked incredulously.

"Of course, we thought about it but once Constable Ahearn's police car arrived at the quarry, we both knew that we hadn't simply stolen a box of sweets. The other thing was, we'd had the living daylights scared out of us and were just glad to see the back of it—sealing it inside the ship proved to be the right decision. Until now."

"Linda managed to write down the number plate of the car." Vic paused as he fixed Jerry with a glare, "the plate belongs to a Commonwealth Car in Canberra."

Jerry screwed his eyes shut and scowled. "And I'll bet London to a brick on, that I know which Department is currently using it. I know just the person who can confirm my suspicions." Leaving Linda and Vic to finish their late breakfasts, Jerry headed for the pay phone outside the restaurant.

"Commissioner Duncombe."

"Andy, its Commander O'Rourke. Congratulations on the promotion by the way!"

"Jerry O'Rourke, now there's a name from the past! I hear you received your third stripe, so same to you. What can I do for you, Commander?"

"'Jerry' please, I hope we're still on a first-name basis?"

"Yes, of course—unless the reason for this call puts that at risk?"

"It may just do that Andy but I believe a young man's life is at stake so I'm compelled to ask it anyway. Andy, I'm going to give you the registration details of a Com Car and I'm hoping you can tell me the make, model and who is currently operating it?"

"By the sound of it, I'm guessing you need this information as soon as possible?"

"If you can, please Andy. I'm having coffee in a restaurant; can you ring the information through to me there?"

"Can't see why not, what's the number?" Jerry gave the Commissioner the telephone number of the restaurant that was conveniently and prominently blazoned across the front of the awning stretching over the tables and chairs on the footpath and then re-joined Vic and Linda to wait for the call.

158

Vic leaned in conspiratorially—despite the restaurant being almost empty—took hold of Linda's hand and said confidently, "I can almost guarantee that Bobby is still alive. The recovery of the box and its contents has been on the kidnappers' agenda for over twelve years. They/he will use every trick in the book and go to extremes to pry that information out of him—but they need him alive at all costs." Linda nodded. Assured.

"Having said that, the kidnappers will also go to the extreme not to get caught—if you get my drift?"

Again, Linda nodded.

"That's why I'm sitting here with you two fine upstanding, law-abiding people about to break every rule in the Police Handbook when it comes to investigating kidnappings. Why? Because if we were to follow normal police procedures and inform Uncle Tom Cobley and all, I suspect that the kidnappers would learn of that fact through their Cumberland Asylum informant and cut their losses—which would certainly lead to Bobby's demise. Now you may ask where all this jabber is leading to?"

"Where is all—" Jerry started to say.

"OK, smart arse! It's leading to 'The Plan'. Well, come on then Mr Wise Guy," this directed at Jerry.

"Alright, I'll bite—What would that plan be, Senior Sergeant Know-it-all?" Jerry replied.

Linda chuckled, "Can we please hear the plan without the banter?"

"Sorry, miss," they replied in unison.

Jerry leaned across the table and looked Linda directly in the eyes and said firmly, "We're going to get him back."

"Thanks, Jerry. Thank you both. Now, what about this bloody plan!"

"A few years ago, I was involved in a sting organised to apprehend a well-organised group of jewellery thieves. The robberies all had one thing in common; the getaway car was a very expensive but unmodified, maroon W111 Mercedes with bogus number plates. While we couldn't track the vehicle from its registration, an eye witness reported this particular model Merc had a very distinguishing feature—it had chrome strips around the front wheel arches. Of the 520 registered in Australia at the time, 180 were in New South Wales, 74 were maroon but only 15 had the chrome strips.

"Long story short—we had Mercedes, Australia put out a bogus urgent recall notice for owners of the W111 to return their vehicles to an approved inspection station where the 'free maintenance' would be carried out.

"Sure enough, fifteen suspect vehicles turn up, we followed each of them home, obtained search warrants for fifteen properties and the rest is now residing at Her Majesty's pleasure in Long Bay Goal."

"That sounds great, Vic," Linda commented, "but I couldn't tell you what make or model the car was?"

"With a bit of luck, I'll be getting a phone call that will solve that problem, Linda," Jerry responded. "Our next hurdle will be overcoming the fact that most cars in the Com Car fleet are regular Holdens or Ford Falcons—and there are thousands of them!"

The group was into its third round of coffees when the call from Commissioner Duncombe came through.

"*The vehicle in question has been used by the office of the Chief of Naval Intelligence here in Canberra, however, fuel receipts received by Com Car show the car has been used exclusively in Sydney since October. The car is a 1964 MkIV Humber Super Snipe of which Com Cars operate three.*"

"Wow, you've really belt and braces my request, Andy. I'm not sure how and if I can repay the favour anytime soon?"

"*I do have another piece of information that may or may not be relevant, but the majority of the fuel receipts show the driver using the Pearl Service station in Woolloomooloo almost exclusively.*"

"Andy, as they say in the classics, your blood's worth bottling! Many thanks my friend."

He couldn't keep the smile from his face as he returned to the table. "The good news is, the vehicle we're looking for is a black MkIV Humber Super Snipe. The even better news is that there are only three operated by Com Cars and the excellent news is that one has been located in Sydney since October and it is most likely based somewhere near the Pearl Service Station in Woolloomooloo."

"It arrived in Sydney when Bobby was in Cumberland!" Linda added. "Would your plan work now we're armed with all that information Vic?" she asked.

"Well from here, it's working out what the fastest method is of locating where Bobby's being held. As I see it we now have two options. One, we stake out the Pearl servo or two, we find out who the Humber agent is in Sydney and try to convince him to issue a bogus recall notice."

"I think we probably need to find a more suitable meeting place," Jerry suggested. "This place will be filling up with lunch time crowds shortly and what we're planning isn't for public disclosure."

Vic thought for a while and then his eyes lit up. "I know just the place!"

Fifteen minutes later they entered the doors of the most impressive police station Linda and Jerry had ever seen.

"'Roy' Rogers as I live and breathe!" The desk Sergeant lifted the counter flap and the two policemen hugged and back-slapped. "What brings you back to Darlinghurst Police Station—or more rightly; what disaster made you leave Barclay's Creek?"

"Sergeant Noel Hockey, please meet Miss Linda West and Mr Jerry O'Rourke."

Handshakes were exchanged and then Vic took Sergeant Hockey by the arm and led him out of earshot of the other two.

"Noel, I need a huge favour."

Several minutes later, Sergeant Hockey returned to his stool behind the counter and in his best menacing voice addressed Linda and Jerry.

"You two are lucky it was an off-duty Sergeant Rogers that arrested you on suspicion of car theft," he said with a wink. "You are not being arrested at this stage but charges may be laid following Sergeant Rogers' interview. Sergeant Rogers, please escort the suspects to Interview Room 2," then he leaned over the counter and whispered, "Lunch will be served shortly."

"There's more to you than meets the eye Senior Sergeant *Roy* Rogers!" Linda told the smiling Vic Rogers.

Chapter 34

1:40 p.m., Monday 7 December 1969, Darlinghurst Police Station, Sydney

Their lunch would have had anyone else unfortunate enough to be seated in this room, green with envy.

It had been Noel himself that had walked across Taylor Square to the well-frequented *Leong's Chinese Restaurant* and had returned with three steaming hot bowls of curried prawns and rice.

With the evidence of their meal deposited in a waste bin outside the Station—just in case the Station Commander just happened to poke his head in the door—Vic addressed the group.

"Noel and I have known each other since we were cadets at the Police Training Centre. This was our first posting; talk about being thrown in the deep end! I was disappointed when they assigned me to a small, country Station but since visiting Noel in the hospital twice, recovering from knife wounds, I've grown to love and appreciate the peaceful and mostly boring, Barclay's Creek.

"Noel has kindly given us the use of this 'Interview Suite' for the rest of the day so we'd better put our thinking caps on."

They began by mulling over the best course of action how to uncover the kidnapper's hiding place.

"Now that they have Bobby stowed away and drew a blank trying to find Linda," Vic began "it's highly unlikely that they'll be needing to refuel the car anytime soon, so staking out the Pearl Service Station is probably a waste of time. Our best bet is to try the 'Urgent Vehicle Recall' sting—if we can persuade the Humber Australian agent to issue it."

"Is it worth trying both?" Linda asked. "It won't take three of us to speak with Humber; why don't I stake out the servo while you and Jerry lean on the Humber bloke?"

Jerry agreed that it was worth a shot and Vic nodded his assent.

"Before we all go rushing off, is there any other way we can trace this car?" Vic asked.

"No, I have no idea. If it hadn't been for you and Jerry, I'd still be floundering in the dark!" Linda replied a short time later.

"Me neither. Having never been involved in a kidnapping case, I'm clueless!" Jerry added.

"Right then, we go with Linda's suggestion. First off though we need to find out who and where the Humber agent is. I'll go and grab a phone book."

Vic returned with a Sydney Telephone Directory and turned to the Yellow Pages. "Here we go *Car Dealerships*; Holden, Honda—ah ha!, Humber—180 William Street! Jerry, you have a much more refined vocabulary; why don't I let you go and ring the Sales Manager to find out who the head honcho is in Australia?"

"I think I can manage that but it's probably advisable that we all leave together seeing we're still in your custody?"

"Yeah, you're right there!"

"Umm, it's now 3:30," Jerry pointed out. "Are you and Linda staying in the city tonight?"

Linda intercepted Jerry's question, "Well, I was going to offer Vic the use of the spare bedroom at my place tonight seeing Mortlake is only thirty minutes away. But if my place is being watched, that's out of the question!"

"That's very kind of you Linda, but, do you still have a key to Bobby's apartment?"

"Yes?"

"I suggest you sleep there tonight—just in case your apartment is being watched. I seriously doubt that the people who have Bobby have the numbers to afford a twenty-four-hour watch on your place but better safe than sorry.

"I have some serious catching up to do with Sergeant Hockey—and I owe him dinner for his help today. I'll crash on his lounge tonight—if his wife has forgiven me for my indiscretion last time I stayed there that is!"

"Well that's tonight sorted," Jerry said, "but can we just summarise our roles for the rest of today?"

After Jerry and Linda had quietly thanked Noel for the use of his Station and the excellent lunch, they waited outside while Vic arranged his evening.

"See you at the restaurant we were in this morning Linda at 8:30 and don't spend all night staking out that servo. We need you bright-eyed and bushy-tailed tomorrow."

Vic and Jerry headed over to William Street while Linda quickly walked back to Bobby's car.

Chapter 35

6:45 p.m., Monday 7 December 1969, Location Unknown, Sydney

Terry and 'Doris' had returned from the Concord Repatriation Hospital empty-handed. A thorough search of Miss West's apartment had revealed absolutely zilch and Terry's mood was even blacker after they found out she was taking some time off work. They would have to come up with something soon or else they could kiss their substantial monetary reward good bye!

Bobby was tucking into a plate of baked beans with a fried egg and two slices of toast. Every joint in his body felt as if someone had replaced the cartilage with sand, including his finger joints. Even though it hurt like hell just holding the plastic knife and fork, he was determined not to grimace every time he cut through the toast.

'Hey, I managed to push the pain from my bullet wound to the back of my mind for a pretty girl, so putting up with this shit from a couple of trained monkeys is going to be a piece of cake!' he had said to himself when 'Daphne'—or it could have been 'Doris'—had handed him his freshly cleaned clothes to put on.

"You see Mr Massey, we can be reasonable men, can't we boys?"

"Very reasonable, Boss."

"Over-the-top reasonable, Boss."

"So, as reasonable men, we thought you might respond in kind and be reasonable with us? Isn't that right, boys?"

"Absolutely, Boss!"

"Too right, Boss!"

"I'm sorry we had to put you through so much pain Mr Massey. We hope that the soft bed, the warm shower, the clean clothes and 'Doris' wonderful breakfast, have shown that we are willing to negotiate a win-win outcome for both of us. What do you say Mr Massey?"

"Doris—which ever one you are," Bobby said waving his fork in their direction, "this is the best breakfast I've had since I arrived. Thank you! I must say it's a vast improvement on the 'pee' soup you served me earlier—way too much salt! Is there a chance I could get a black tea with one sugar to wash the beans down?"

'Doris' rumbled something and started towards Bobby.

"'Doris', please make Mr Massey his cup of tea." Bobby was sure that the 'Boss' had managed to say that through clenched teeth! He gave 'Doris' a huge smile as the monkey trudged to the kitchen.

Once 'Doris' had returned, Bobby wiped the remains of his breakfast on the paper napkin, picked up his cup of tea and leaned back in his chair.

"'Boss'—is it OK if I call you that?" an almost imperceptible nod from the chief monkey. "'Boss', at a rough guess, I'd say you're the most senior monkey of the three of you, oh! did I say 'monkey'? How impolite of me; I should have said 'henchman'. Is henchman the correct terminology 'Doris'?" No answer. "'Daphne'?" No answer.

"I'll take that as a 'Yes' then. 'Reasonable'? Interesting proposition I must say, but, let's check the facts shall we? Was it reasonable when you broke into my apartment and destroyed all my belongings—no, it was not. Was it reasonable to break into my apartment a second time, drug and kidnap me—no, it definitely wasn't. Was it reasonable to torture me with electric shocks and deprive me of food and sleep to the point where I couldn't tell up from down let alone what *fucking time of the day it was*—no it wasn't.

"Now you 'allow' me a bed to sleep in and feed me a plate of beans and expect me to shake your hand and tell you what you want to know, well I have something 'reasonable' to say—you and your two henchmen *can go fuck yourselves!*"

Bobby saw the punch coming but, in his current state, didn't have time to duck and it caught him square on the temple. He saw the concrete floor racing to meet him and then everything went black.

"Throw him back in the light and sound box. I'm going back upstairs for a kip, being reasonable has tired me out. Let him stew in the box without food or any contact for a few hours. 'Daphne', set up the drugs chair and spotlight, please. 'Doris', take a walk around the block to settle your temper and bring us all back a pizza."

"It's pissing down outside, Boss, alright if I take the car?"

"Yeah, OK. Wake me when you get back.

"Wait! Forget the pizza. I want you to drive over to Mortlake and stake out Miss West's apartment for a couple of hours. I'm going to give 'Debra' a call—see if he wants to earn some cash. If I'm successful, he'll relieve you and then you can pick up some pizzas! If our luck changes and Miss West is either at home or arrives while you're there, please ask her to join us. I'm sure the sight of his girlfriend being threatened with all sorts of nasty things will loosen Mr Massey's tongue! Take a 'Nighty Night' syringe with you just in case she declines your invitation."

"On it Boss!"

****

"'Debra' it's Terry."

"*Yes, Boss?*"

"You interested in making some spending money?"

"*Does it have anything to do with the Massey job, 'cos you know where I stand on that one?*"

"Well, yes and no. Let me explain; Massey is in our 'care' so no, it doesn't in a direct sense. What I'm asking is that you carry out surveillance of his girlfriend. We tried to contact her earlier today without luck so I'm staking out her apartment and that's where I need an extra body. Let's say $5,000 for 24 hours of your time?"

"*That sounds fair; when do I start?*"

"'Doris' is on his way there now; can you get to Mortlake by 2200 hundred hours?"

"*I'm on my way.*"

"Thanks, mate. If she happens to show, ring me and we'll come and take her into custody—so to speak. 'Doris' will give you the details during your handover."

Chapter 36

9:00 p.m., Monday 7 December 1969, Woolloomooloo, Sydney

"This is ridiculous, Linda," she told herself. "It's raining cats and dogs, the windows keep fogging up and you haven't had dinner!"

She started the Cortina, turned the heater controls to 'defogger' and stared at the Service Station pumps, willing a black Humber to pull up at the bowser while she waited for the windscreen to clear. With a resigned sigh, she pushed the gear lever into first and drove to Bobby's apartment in Strathfield.

Jerry lay on his bunk staring at the ceiling and went over the events of the day in his mind. He'd had a feeling Peter Fleming's fingers were deeply in this pie—the information from Andy Duncombe just confirmed his suspicions. The Commodore had always been a stickler for compliance with the Naval Disciplinary Code so why steer way off course with this particular case? Jerry believed it had more to do with a 12-year-old bruised ego than any sense of duty. Peter Fleming would stop at nothing to extract the bug from his backside that was the unsolved unauthorised entry into a facility that was under his ultimate control.

He still had serious doubts about Bobby being found alive and being brutally honest, whether their plan had a snowball's chance in hell of coming to fruition.

He had spoken to the Manager of the Humber Dealership in William Street and to his and Vic's disappointment, had been informed that the General Manager was based in Melbourne. Vic had commented that it was going to be much harder to intimidate someone over the phone; harder but not impossible.

Meanwhile, not far from where Jerry lay, Vic and Noel had just finished their counter-dinner in their favoured watering hole, the *Courthouse Hotel* and were about to get stuck into another schooner of beer when Vic worked up the courage and asked Noel for a favour.

"You fucking what?" Noel had asked incredulously.

"Look, it's not as if I'm going to use it, but if we find these pricks, odds on they'll be armed—with loaded guns! They're not going to lay them down if I turn up with only my dick in my hand!"

"Especially with the size of your wanger! Look mate, you know I'd go the whole nine yards to help you out but this, this is just hanging my arse out waiting for the Commissioner to fuck me over!"

"Noel, I'm going to set this boy free. I never had kids of my own but when that beautiful young lady sat on my lounge and told me hers and Bobby's story, it nearly broke my heart. The lad's a Vietnam Veteran for fuck sake and ever since he's been home he's the one that's been fucked over. No more, Noel, no more."

"Are you tearing up?"

"Fuck off, Noel, it's just the bloody smoke in this place!" he said as he wiped the back of his hands across his eyes.

"It's against my better judgement," Noel sighed, resigned to the fact that he was going to help the big bastard despite his protestations, "but I tell you what I'll do, I'll see if there's a sawn-off in the evidence room that's not likely to be called up as evidence in the near future. If, and I'm not saying there is, if there is one, I'll let you have it for a couple of days but please, please don't get caught with it?"

Chapter 37

8:00 a.m., Tuesday 8 December 1969, Sydney City

Vic, Linda and Jerry we're back in the same booth, in the same Greek restaurant as they were yesterday, but rather than a big breakfast, they all opted for teas and toast.

"Has anyone had a revelation overnight?" Vic asked, showing absolutely no ill-effects of his night out with Noel, although the blood-shot eyes belied his physical appearance.

"I did come up with a variation on the 'vehicle recall' sting but it will depend on how convincing either myself or Vic can be?" Jerry offered.

"Well, don't leave us in suspenders!" Vic said.

"What I'm suggesting is that we cut out the middleman, so to speak and deal directly with the Com Car Maintenance Manager.

"The time spent talking to Humber, getting the recall notice printed, sending it out to all owners, is time we can't afford. I propose that one of us—namely *moi*—go back to the dealership in William Street and sweet-talk the Service Manager there, into revealing what would be likely to fail on the Super Snipe that would result in an urgent recall being issued.

"Armed with that information and a great deal of bravado, either Vic or myself contact the Com Car Maintenance Manager, posing as someone from Humber Head Office and ask them to urgently inspect the three Super Snipes that they have in their fleet."

"Sorry to pour cold water on your suggestion with the obvious question," Vic posed, "if you speak to the Com Car bloke, what's stopping him from ringing Humber Head Office to confirm the information?"

"Yeah, good point!" Crestfallen, Jerry slumped back in the seat. "Thought it sounded too easy!"

"What if we try combining both ideas?" Linda suggested. "Rather than making up some bullshit story, we explain our situation to the Humber General

170

Manager and appeal to his better nature? He could then ring Com Car rather than us?"

Vic and Jerry mulled this over and then Vic said, "I agree with everything that's been proposed and Jerry's right when he says that Bobby probably doesn't have time on his side so my suggestion really isn't an option.

"Jerry's proposal has the problem of the Com Car Manager contacting Humber. So, Lindy-Loo, we'll try your plan."

"Thanks, Vic, but if you ever call me 'Lindy Loo' again, you're off my Christmas card list—for ever!" she said angrily, fire burning in her damp eyes.

Taken aback by Linda's sudden mood change, Vic held up his hands and said apologetically, "Sorry Linda, won't happen again."

"Right then," Jerry cut into the tense pause, "guess we need a number for the Humber Head Office? I'll go and call 'Directory Assistance' while you two can mend some fences." Jerry poked Vic in the ribs as he headed for the pay phone, leaving the red-faced lug to face Linda.

"I'm truly sorry, Linda, if I'd have known you hated the nickname that much, I never would have said it."

"Apology accepted, Vic. I'm sorry that I over-reacted, but, it's what my Nana—my mum's mum—used to call me. She practically lived next door to us in England and was my surrogate mother for a long time, looking after me when Mum was working long hours at the hospital. I loved her very much and it broke my heart when we immigrated and left her behind.

"We were all living in Council flats in Bethnal Green; Nana was only three doors away. Dad was working at the Ford factory in Dagenham and Mum was a nurse at St Bart's Hospital in the city. Both would have to leave early to catch the train to work, leaving Nana to dress me, make my breakfast and get me ready for school. She was there for me in the mornings and I would go to her flat after school. If Mum had to work late, Nana would cook me dinner and I would sleep in her bed—she was more of a mother to me than my real mum.

"It was only ever Dad that had wanted to come here and Mum would bitch day and night about why everything in England was better than Australia. The first three weeks here were hell for me. I didn't want to go to school but, with the tension between my parents, I didn't want to go home either.

"All I wanted to do was go and cry in the arms of the only person who would understand how I felt; my Nana.

"Don't know if they had it in your school days, but the Barclay's Creek Dairy Co-Op would drop off a churn of milk and 'milk monitors' would ladle out a cupful for each kid. One day, when I was almost at rock bottom, sitting all alone in a shady corner of the playground, this boy came up to me at morning recess and offered me a cup of milk.

"Without waiting for me to answer, he plonked himself down beside me—and I mean, that close that he's sitting on my tunic close!—and said, '*Did you forget your cup this morning?*' He's got this stupid grin on his face and he's still holding out the cup—and I promptly burst into tears! Do you know what he did? He put an arm around my shoulders and said, '*Come on, drink this, it will make you feel better!*' and with that my tears turned to fits of laughter. With that kind gesture and a stupid comment, he dragged me out of the hole I was in.

"That boy's name was Bobby Massey and from that day on, we became best mates. I actually looked forward to going to school and my parents bickering faded into the background.

"Looking back at that moment, I believe Bobby saved my life. It's my turn to return the favour."

Vic leaned forward on his elbows, "I never found the time to get married and have kids, but if I was your father, I would be proud of you and what you're doing. Very proud indeed!"

Just then Jerry returned with a piece of note paper in his hand. "Ah, good," noticing Vic holding Linda's hand. "Fences mended then I see. Right, who's the best person to ring the GM?"

The waitress appeared at their table, a look of concern creased her face, "Are you OK, miss?"

"Yes, thank you. Reminiscing that's all," Linda replied with a smile.

"Can I get you folks anything else?"

"I think three coffees and Baklava would go down a treat," Jerry replied.

"Coffees and Baklava it is then."

"You want *me* to try and convince the General Manager of a prestige car company to lie to one of his customers?" Linda asked dismayed.

"Linda, out of the three of us, you're the one with the emotional attachment to the victim." Vic pointed out, "Without even realising it, that close attachment to Bobby came through very clearly when you told me your story on Sunday night. With a bit of luck, the General Manager will be a married man with a daughter your age and if so, he can't help but understand what you're doing and why. However, rather than chuck you in the deep end, I'll have a word with him first—in my capacity as a Senior Sergeant with the NSW Police Force—and then put you on the line. OK?"

"Yes, OK."

"This phone call is going to take longer than five minutes and I don't think the two of you will squeeze into that phone box outside! I suggest we find somewhere more comfortable to do this," Jerry said. "The Chevron Hilton is just up the road; why don't we head there and use one of the phones in the lobby?"

Chapter 38

11:40 a.m., Tuesday 8 December 1969, Chevron Hilton Hotel, Potts Point, Sydney

"Good morning, Humber Australasia, how may I help you?"

"Good morning, my name is Senior Sergeant Rogers. I'm with the NSW Police. Would you put me through to the General Manager please?"

"Certainly, Sergeant. Please hold while I transfer your call."

"Good morning Sergeant Rogers, my name is Pamela Chambers and I'm Mr Blakely's secretary. Can I enquire as to the nature of your call?"

"Good morning, Pamela, the reason for my call is personal and confidential and very urgent so if Mr Blakely is in, please put me through."

"Very well, I'll see if he can take your call," she said sounding miffed.

The phone stayed quiet for a couple of minutes and then an equally miffed-sounding Mr Blakely came on the line.

"Good morning, Sergeant."

"Excuse me sir, but that's *Senior* Sergeant."

"My apologies, Senior Sergeant. How can I be of assistance to the NSW Police Force?"

"Mr Blakely, I'm going to hand the phone over to a very distressed young lady. I appreciate that you are a very busy man but I'm asking that you put all thoughts aside about Humber's profit margins and listen very carefully for the next ten to fifteen minutes as she tells you the story behind what is causing her distress. Can you do that for me Mr Blakely? You can? Thank you sir. The lady's name is Linda West."

"Hello?"

"Miss West, you have something you wish to tell me?"

"Yes sir, but please call me Linda."

"Linda, I'm Archie."

"Archie, I'm very nervous speaking to a man in your position so please excuse me if I stumble over my words."

"*No need to be nervous, Linda—imagine I'm sitting in my office in my underwear,*" Archie Blakely said lightly. Linda laughed.

"Are you wearing sock suspenders?"

Vic and Jerry exchanged puzzled looks.

"*Absolutely! And my wife's pink fluffy slippers!*"

Linda laughed even louder and after a few deep breaths said, "Thanks Archie, that settled the nerves somewhat at least."

Linda then proceeded to tell the same sorry tale she had told Vic just two nights ago, but this time, she managed to keep the tears at bay.

Almost twenty minutes later she said her goodbyes and handed the phone back to Vic.

"Mr Blakely, it's Vic Rogers back again."

"*Vic, Archie. I'm guessing that the reason you had Linda tell me her story, is because it's the precursor to something you're going to ask me to do. Something that probably lays outside of the law. Would that be a fair assumption?*"

"Your assumption is correct, Archie. We need to find out where the kidnappers are holding Mr Massey; our greatest chance of achieving that is by following their car back to where he's being held.

"What I'm asking you to do is ring the Commonwealth Car Fleet Maintenance Manager and strongly advise him to have their three MkIV Super Snipes visit an approved Humber workshop at the first available opportunity for an urgent inspection of—and I'll let you add the part—following a serious accident in the UK.

"The Com Car Manager, if he's on the ball, is going to ask you the location of an 'approved workshop' in Sydney. I'm going to give you the location of a Pearl Service Station in Woolloomooloo that's going to instantly become 'approved'. Do you have a pen handy?"

"Well, that was easier than I thought!" Vic remarked as he hung up the phone. "Now, all we have to do is convince the Pearl servo owner to loan us his workshop."

"Linda, do you mind?" Jerry opened his arms and Linda walked into them, "You were brilliant, young lady. Bobby would be so proud." He then let her go and opened his arms to Vic. "Get out of it you silly bugger," Vic said, "you'll have everyone in the lobby talking about us!"

Chapter 39

3:20 p.m., Tuesday 8 December 1969, Pearl Service Station, Woolloomooloo, Sydney

The Pearl Service Station was in a prime location in Woolloomooloo and would most likely have enjoyed a roaring trade a few years ago. Now, it was probably only utilised when drivers didn't have enough fuel to make it to the next one. The driveway was cracked and pot-holed, the pumps were that faded it was hard to discern whether you were filling up with 'Super' or 'Standard' and the roller-door to the workshop looked like it hadn't been opened in decades!

Jerry and Vic walked into an office crammed with boxes of engine, transmission and differential oil, a desk with a till on one end and a pair of greasy boots at the end of overall-clad legs propped up in the centre.

A face with a remarkable resemblance to Albert Steptoe appeared from behind a newspaper.

"Help you, gentlemen?"

Jerry couldn't help himself, "G'day Albert, where's your son, Harold?"

"Ha fuckin ha, I'd like a fuckin quid for every fuckin time I've heard that fuckin one!"

Vic swept 'Albert's' feet off the table and sat. "We're here to make you an offer you can't refuse." He flashed his NSW Police Service badge in 'Albert's' face. "My partner and I need to 'borrow' your workshop for a couple of days."

"Why the fuck would I help the fuckin pigs! Hardly a fuckin week goes by without my fuckin till getting fucking robbed or some arse 'ole nicks somefin out of me fuckin shop and wadda the fuckin pigs do—fuckin nuthin! That's what, fuckin nuthin!"

"Well, look on the bright side, you'll have a policeman onsite for as long as we're using your workshop! Couldn't get better protection than that if you paid for it eh?"

"S'pose you're right. Will I get compo for not be'in able to use me fuckin workshop?"

Jerry and Vic looked around he deserted workshop.

"Tell you what, we won't charge you a cent for security if you don't charge us for the use of your workshop. Deal?"

Vic held out his hand, secretly wishing that this greasy little weasel despised coppers that much, he would refuse to shake his hand—sadly, he didn't. "Deal."

Jerry and Vic walked back to the Cortina that was parked in almost the same spot where Linda had parked the night before.

As she pulled into the traffic, Jerry asked if they could all go back to Bobby's apartment. "We need to put our heads together and seriously think about what to do if and when the Humber turns up at the garage," he said.

"No problem at all," Linda replied. "I can knock us up some of Linda West's excellent Spaghetti Bolognese. Bobby may even have a bottle of 1968 Seppelts Moyston Claret that I gave him gathering dust somewhere. Not a big fan of wine is our Bobby."

"It will also enable us to all arrive back here at opening time," Vic added.

All their scheming and planning had been carried out seriously and with a sense of purpose, but also with a nervous sense of fun. That had now ended; having cast the hook into the sea, all they could do was hope and pray that the fish would take the bait.

"On second thoughts, drive us back to Mortlake. There's only one way to find out how serious the kidnappers are. Is there a back way into your apartment Linda?"

"No, the only way in is via the driveway off Livingstone Street."

"Is there a cross-street you can drive down rather than your street?"

"The closest one is about 200 metres away."

"Perfect! If they're watching your apartment, they're not going to park that far away. Drive down the cross-street and park near the intersection with your street. I'll take a walk 'round the block and check for anyone lurking close by."

Linda parked the Cortina in the shadow of an overhanging tree—just in case the kidnappers decided to turn into this street on their way home—then Vic got out and disappeared around the corner.

Vic had been involved in enough stake-outs to know that the best vantage point would be on the opposite side of the road but with a clear line-of-sight to the main access point. He spotted the Humber as soon as he crossed to Linda's side of the street.

There were two issues with conducting covert surveillance in the quiet, tree-lined streets of Sydney's more affluent suburbs. One was the fact that the thick, lower branches of the mature Brush Box trees obscured most of the buildings until you were almost directly in front of their driveways. The second issue was that, unlike a city stake-out, a car parked in the street was a rarity. The poor bloke stood out like a sore thumb.

If he was on the ball, the driver would have spotted Vic in his rear-view mirror as soon as he had crossed the road. The trick now was to act as nonchalantly as possible. He was about twenty feet from being level with the car when he had an idea.

Vic passed the car and then purposely looked directly at the driver. He hesitated then stopped and crossed to the car. Leaning down to peer in the window, he said, "G'day mate, are you lost?"

"Uh, g'day. No, not lost. Why do you ask?"

"Sorry for sounding nosey, but I've lived just down the road for nearly twenty years and I can count on one hand the number of local cars that park under these trees at night. They're a trap for young players—it's the honeydew, you see."

"Honeydew?"

"Yeah, bloody Maple trees! They look fantastic and provide wonderful shade but the leaves attract bugs like aphids that 'crap' a substance called 'honeydew' that sticks to every surface of your car. You stay here much longer and next time you turn your wipers on, the wiper arms will move but the rubbers will stay right where they are!"

"Oh, well, I, uh—I'll park round the corner and come back for my wife. She's visiting her sister but I can't stand the cranky cow, that's why I'm in the car."

"Righto then, you have a good evening."

"Thanks for the advice." With that 'Doris' started the car and headed in search of another surveillance spot. "But not till that nosey bastard pisses off."

Ten minutes later Vic returned to the Cortina.

"Well, we now know that the kidnappers are very serious. I just gave one of them a Botany lesson."

Linda and Jerry exchanged puzzled looks.

"I scared him off—for probably five minutes. There is one other minor problem with our plans for tomorrow.

"It's amazing how a walk in the cool air concentrates the mind; half way back to the car I suddenly realised that we're going to have a problem following the Humber once it leaves the workshop. We have to assume that the kidnappers know this Cortina belongs to Bobby, so at the moment, we don't have a chase vehicle."

That revelation made the mood even more sombre. Their whole plan had been predicated on following the kidnappers back to their lair. Without verbalising their thoughts, each of them knew what they were all now focusing their minds on; 'where in God's name were they going to find another vehicle at such short notice?'

"Umm, I've suddenly lost the enthusiasm for cooking; do you two mind if we pick up takeaway instead? There's a great curry house in Strathfield that has the best Tikka Masala in Sydney. We can also grab some 1969 vintage Resch's Pilsner at the *Railway Hotel* to wash it down with."

"Sounds good to me; Jerry?"

"If it's as good as the Curry Cafe in Sembawang in Singapore, it's got my vote."

The curry was indeed, very tasty and while the Moysten Claret was off the menu, they found the icy cold beer paired very nicely with the Tikka. Vic and Jerry had washed up and dried up the dishes, much to Linda's annoyance and then the trio topped up their glasses and moved into Bobby's lounge room.

"We need to brainstorm the problem with the chase car," Jerry said. "One thing I can rule out completely is hailing a cab and asking the driver to 'follow that car'!"

"What about renting a car?" Linda suggested.

"Time is against us with renting," Vic replied, "we have to be at the servo and in the workshop by 9.00 a.m. tomorrow. It would be close to lunch time by the time we get to the rental company and fill out the paperwork."

"I could sign out a car from the Motor Transport section in *Kuttabul* but a light blue car with Royal Australian Navy 'Z' number plates, will easily be spotted, even by the dumbest kidnapper!" Jerry offered half-heartedly.

"Rather than worrying about another car, why don't we use the kidnapper's?" Linda suddenly and excitedly exclaimed, "The kidnapper presents his car for the inspection—hopefully—we grab him and make him drive us back to their hideout?"

"Brilliant Linda! Why didn't I think of that!" Jerry said and they both turned to Vic.

"Sounds like a great idea and while it works in the movies, these people aren't actors in a movie following a script. These are intelligent, professionally trained men.

"Trying to physically force this bloke to 'take us to your leader' would only have him rolling around the floor laughing. So no, attempting that would only result in Bobby being 'disposed of' sooner than they planned."

The flame of excitement that had run through Linda and Jerry was suddenly extinguished and they returned to forlornly sipping the remains of their beer.

Some minutes later Vic sighed, drained his glass then stood, "Linda, can I use your phone please?"

"'Course you can, it's on the bench in the kitchen."

"Thanks. Back in a minute."

Jerry and Linda could hear the tone of Vic's phone call but not what the conversation was about. They knew that whatever it had been about, it didn't end happily. Linda thought Bobby may need a new handset following the loud bang as Vic hung up.

Vic ended his call to Sergeant Noel Hockey and hung up the phone forcibly, angry with himself over what he had asked his mate to do.

Noel had been in the same Police Recruit intake as Vic in 1936. Physically, they were like two peas in a pod. However, where Vic was calm and careful in simulated stressful situations, his instructors found he was too slow to react. Noel, on the other hand, wanted to kick down doors and charge in, all guns blazing, without giving enough thought to the consequences.

Their training officer saw the potential in both of them and paired them up. At first, they nearly came to blows on several occasions over the best way to achieve the desired result. Then the penny dropped and they discovered that if they listened to what the other had to say, they could quickly determine what approach to take in any particular situation.

Then they had become friends and on graduating, work colleagues, in the same Police Station. Not that they stopped having a go at each other, it was now more friendly banter than venom-filled invective.

They did have one falling out though—and it all started the night of Vic's promotion to Senior Constable.

There was a tradition in the Darlinghurst Police Station that called for everyone to buy the newly promoted officer a beer in the Courthouse Hotel. Noel dragged the—moderately—reluctant Senior Constable across Oxford Street and into the Lounge Bar that the constabulary had the use of until 6.00 p.m. when the pub closed.

Vic was on his eighth or twelfth free beer when the most gorgeous woman he had ever laid his bloodshot eyes on walked into the Lounge.

Instantly sober (or so he thought at the time) he stood up and approached the vision of loveliness only to fall over a chair and land at her feet. While this brought a round of applause and hoots of laughter from his so-called mates, the woman bent down and helped him to his feet.

"Are you alright?" she asked, genuinely concerned.

"Yes ma'am, just a bit pi—drunk ma'am." He lent down and managed to pick up the chair that he had tripped over. "Would you like a seat, ma'am?"

"No thank you—?"

"Vic, Vic Rogers."

"No thank you Vic. Margaret Cooper," she offered Vic a gloved hand which he took hold of like it was a delicate piece of glass. "Pleased to make your acquaintance, Margaret."

"Umm, can I have my hand back?" Vic dropped Margaret's hand like it was a hot potato.

"Sorry, forgot where I was for a moment!"

Margaret glanced around at the grinning and guffawing police officers then smiled up at him, "I guess you've just been promoted?"

"Guilty as charged ma—Margaret. Are you sure I can't buy you a drink?"

"That's very kind of you but my father's expecting me upstairs. He's the Publican of this hotel. I am free tomorrow afternoon after five though?"

"Oh, wow, umm, gosh!"

Margaret laughed, rested her hand on his arm and said, "I guess I'll see you tomorrow then?"

She then turned and climbed the stairs with Vic watching her every move. It was only when she had disappeared that he became aware of Noel standing beside him.

"Sorry mate, what was that?"

"I said 'Put your eyeballs and tongue back in and drink those three schooners before the bar closes' you dopey bugger!"

Vic did meet Margaret in her father's pub the following afternoon and then irregularly after that. It became a matter of finding the time between her studying for a Law Degree and his shift work.

The struggle continued for nearly six months. In the end, they both agreed that their relationship had no future as long as they continued trying to juggle work/study commitments and a social life. They parted on good terms and on the odd occasion had a drink together in her father's pub whenever their paths crossed.

Nearly twelve months later Vic received an invitation in his pigeon hole at the Station.

'Messrs Stanley and Elizabeth Cooper

Cordially invite

Mr Vic Rogers

to the wedding of their daughter

Margaret

To

Mr Noel Hockey

son of—'

Vic couldn't continue reading. He screwed up the invitation so tight in his fist, the veins were bulging in his forearms.

Noel had been waiting for Vic to pick up and read the invitation that he had placed in the pigeonhole ten minutes earlier. He watched and saw the rage build in his friend's body and walked up behind him, ready with the apology he had been agonising with for a couple of days.

"Not now, Noel!" was all Vic said without turning around. He dropped the screwed-up card into the nearest waste basket and, without looking back, walked out of the Station.

"Vic?"

"Hey Maggie! Hi there! Come and have a shelabratory drink! Drink to my old mate, Noel Hockey! Eesh getting married you know! Fanshy that, me old, two-faced, back-stabbing, duplish—dushlip—deeesheetful mate's getting married?"

"Vic!"

"What! What Maggie? You want my bleshing, is that it? You want me to be happy for you? Well, guess what Maggie—you can both go to hell!"

And then he passed out and slumped onto the table.

"Oww!" Vic's arm flopped over his eyes as the curtains were opened. Slowly opening one eye, but still shielding it from the light, he tried to see where he was.

"Ah, the piss-pot awakens!"

"Noel? Where the fuck am I?" Vic tried to sit up, but a bomb went off in his head and he collapsed back on the pillow. "What the fuck did I drink?"

"Language, big fella, ladies present."

"Morning, Victor," Margaret said sweetly.

Vic pulled the pillow over his head, "Nff hyffry, Myhhgy."

"I'm sorry, what was that?"

He lifted the pillow slightly, "I'm so sorry Maggie!"

"And so you bloody well should be! Carrying on like a jilted teenager! But," her voice softened, "we're sorry too. We didn't know how to tell you and kept finding excuses not to!" Then harder, "Not that we bloody well had to tell you! You and I agreed our relationship wasn't going anywhere, so why should I feel bad about marrying your best mate!" Then Maggie lay down across his chest and sobbed, "because I do feel really, really bad!"

An hour and three Aspirins later, Vic joined Noel and Maggie at Noel's kitchen table. He poured himself a black coffee and looked each of them in the eye.

"Maggie, Noel—I was out of order yesterday and was so wrapped up in self-pity that I failed both of you as friends. You didn't deserve my tantrum and I'm extremely sorry for any hurt I've caused you both. If I've lost your friendship then that's down to me, but, if you can forgive me, I would be very grateful."

"Hey, nice speech! What do you reckon Maggie, we give this big ox a second chance?"

"No way—unless—"

The proviso was that he was Noel's Best Man at their wedding. Rubbing salt into an open wound? Maybe, but he got over it.

But this? This, was maybe a bridge too far.

"We'll have another car delivered to the service station tomorrow morning," he told them sadly.

"Umm, can I ask, if you managed to find us another car, why the long face?" Linda asked.

"No, you cannot—ask that is. But *can I ask*, what the sleeping arrangements are tonight?"

Puzzled with Vic's demeanour, Linda got up and led him through the apartment, pointing out the bathroom and the second bedroom.

"If you need an extra pillow or blankets they're in this cupboard."

"Thanks, Linda."

She gently grasped his elbow, "Are you OK?"

"Not really but I'm a big boy, I'll handle it." With that he stepped into the spare bedroom and quietly closed the door.

Chapter 40

8:45 p.m., Tuesday 8 December 1969, Location Unknown, Sydney

"Welcome back to the land of the living Mr Massey. I hope your manner has improved since we last spoke?"

"Ghnn gherrd!"

"Oh, having trouble speaking, are we? Don't worry the effects of the sedative we gave you will wear off in a few minutes and then you and I are going to be the best of mates. Being great mates, we tell each other everything, don't we Daphne?"

"No secrets between mates Boss, that's for sure."

Bobby was having trouble holding his head up for a couple of reasons; one, because his head felt like it was perched on top of a mound of jelly and two, because a very bright light was burning holes in the back of his eyes that for some reason he couldn't shut?

Ah, so we have moved onto the drugs! Bobby knew all about truth drugs, shit, he had even experimented with them as a teenager! Well, not LSD! Hell, even 'Doctor Tooheys' loosened lips! But he had been told the secret behind fooling the interrogators—make up some bullshit story close enough to the truth to make it believable but, at all costs, keep your thoughts away from the key points.

"Oww!" Bobby was yanked out of his reverie by a sharp pain in the back of his hand.

"Very good, Mr Massey, you've regained your ability to speak! That pain you just felt was the very amateurish attempt by 'Daphne' to administer a drug that's going to take all your aches, your pains, your anger away—in fact, Mr Massey, in short, you will be conscious but your body will be unconscious? Won't that be wonderful?"

"Yesh, Bosh."

"Excellent! Now, Bobby—it's OK if I call you that isn't it, now that we're mates?"

"Yeth, Bosh," Bobby managed to say after wrestling with a tongue that was flopping around his mouth like a fish out of water.

"Terrific. As I was saying, you and I are going to have a nice little chat. You'd like to chat, wouldn't you Bobby?"

"Yes, Boss," Bobby had finally brought his tongue under control, "a chat over a nice cup of tea Boss."

"Great idea! 'Daphne' go and make us a pot of tea please," he said while shaking his head in the negative.

"Bobby, while we wait for the tea, you're going to tell me all about yourself, where you went to school, what sport you like, what your girlfriend's name is—you do have a girlfriend, don't you, Bobby?"

"No Boss, no girlfriend, Boss."

"Right!" Annoyed. "We'll come back to that later. So where did you go to school—"

The questions kept coming and the drugs were compelling him to answer but his mind was still alert enough to respond negatively to the two salient questions—who is his girlfriend and where is the small green box? His answers to all the other questions were true but he definitely did not have a girlfriend and he didn't know anything about a green box.

Did he live in Barclay's Creek—Yes, Boss.

Did he enter a secret tunnel—Yes, Boss.

What's the name of your girlfriend—No girlfriend, Boss.

Did you enter a secret tunnel—Yes, Boss.

And so it went on until the effects of the Scopolamine began to wear off.

"Time for a cup of tea now, Boss."

"Yes Bobby, time for a cup of tea," the Boss said wearily, "but not for you, arsehole!"

"Mates don't call each other 'arsehole'!" Bobby replied angrily.

The Boss rested his hands on Bobby's forearms that had been taped to a chair and leaned down inches from Bobby's taped-open eyes temporarily blocking the bright light.

"Now, you listen to me you fucker, the only reason you're still alive is because I answer to a higher power and because I have been telling him there is still a chance Mr Massey will give me the information he needs. Well, guess what sunshine, I've just changed my mind!"

Bobby, still tied to the chair, was thrown back into the dark damp cell, fortunately, he landed on his side and not his head; unfortunately, while the chair cracked, it didn't break.

"Well that went well, don't you think? Stuck it right up that bastard's nose though eh? You do know that talking to yourself is the first sign of madness, don't you Bobby Massey?"

"Sir, it's now been over sixty hours since we grabbed Mr Massey. I've tried every standard torture technique I know and either the bastard is mentally stronger than all the men I've tortured in the past or he genuinely doesn't know anything about the box."

"I understand. There is one thing we haven't tried and I'd like you to try it out when Mr Massey recovers."

Terry listened intently to what his boss was suggesting and then said, "You do realise that this multiplies the risk of being caught?"

The Commodore suggested dumping a bound, sedated and blind-folded Bobby outside the Cumberland Asylum and then waiting for his girlfriend to come running to the hospital. They grab her as she gets out of her car and then contact Bobby with the ultimatum—the girl for the box.

"Yes I do, but, do I think a possible positive outcome is worth that risk, again, yes I do. You have until midnight Friday to achieve an outcome—regardless of whether Mr Massey gives us the information or not. Do I make myself clear?"

"Yes sir, crystal."

"Oh, a small housekeeping matter has come up. The Humber has a possible defect in the steering tie rod—whatever that is—that needs to be inspected urgently. As luck would have it, the authorised Humber workshop in Sydney is the Pearl Service Station in Woolloomooloo. Have 'Doris' drop the car in there tomorrow."

"Yes, sir."

Chapter 41

7:00 a.m., Wednesday 9 December 1969, Mortlake, Sydney

"Morning Vic," Jerry said as Vic came into Bobby's small kitchen/dining area, "cup of tea?"

"Yeah, black, one sugar please."

"Linda's having a shower but has left us out Cornflakes or toast and jam or Vegemite?"

"No thanks, mate, I'll just have the cuppa."

Jerry bought his and Vic's tea to the table and sat down opposite the brooding policeman.

"You OK, mate?"

"No, not really."

"Vic, how many years have we known each other, twelve going on thirteen? In all those years, I've never known you to sulk like a nine-year-old, now, how about swallowing the bile that's obviously rising in your gizzard and tell me what's going on in that big head of yours!"

Vic slumped over his tea. "I've never been one for making friends. Always told myself that in my line of work, it was too risky. The only real friend I ever had in my nearly fifty years on God's earth, was Noel Hockey—last night I put that friendship at risk for a total stranger and a young lady I would be proud to have as a daughter. Am I sorry I did what I had to do, no, but do I like it—not one fucking bit!"

The next thing he knew, long wet hair fell over his face and Linda was clinging to his neck like a limpet.

"Hey, what's all this then?" he asked as he untangled himself from Linda's embrace.

"I'm sorry, but I overheard everything you just said." Linda managed between sobs, "You have absolutely no idea how grateful I am to have you and

188

Jerry helping me find Bobby. The last thing I expect you to do, however, is to sacrifice any relationships you have for my or Bobby's sake."

"Linda—"

"Please let me finish. You said you would be proud to have me as a daughter, well, Vic Rogers, you have gone above and beyond what any loving father would have done in similar circumstances and I will never, ever be able to thank you enough." And with that she once more wrapped herself around his neck with a fresh round of tears.

"I guess it's truth or dare time?"

Jerry had gone to have a shower leaving Vic and Linda to talk in private.

"Only if you want to and only if it will help us concentrate on what we have to do today."

"Right. The other night when Noel and I went out, I asked him to get me a gun?"

"You what!?"

"Easy! Let me finish."

"Sorry. Go on."

"As I said last night, the men who are holding Bobby are professionals. We have no idea whether there are three or thirteen of them. Regardless of their number, one thing is certain; they will be armed to the teeth and the first person to die if they're discovered will be Bobby. You are not going anywhere near their hideout that leaves Jerry and I.

"Do you think for one moment that we can simply knock on the door and ask them to release Bobby? Not a snowball's chance in hell of that happening.

"Even with one gun, there's every possibility that we'll fail—and that's where I put my friendship with Noel on the line."

"You asked him for two guns?"

"And a car."

"This is probably a stupid question but what was his answer?"

"A car with two fully loaded 12-gauge, pump action, sawn-off shotguns will be parked in the Pearl Service Station by 8:30 tomorrow morning—with the promise that if it all goes tits up, Noel will arrest me and throw me in jail himself. From the tone of his voice; with a well-deserved boot to the backside for good measure!"

"Better get your arses into gear you two," Jerry said as he zipped up his navy-blue overalls.

"My, aren't we looking all brutish in our tradesman's outfit!"

"I'll have you know young lady that under my normal suave, svelte exterior lies a motor mechanic waiting to be released."

"'Re-leashed' more like," then Vic added, "Come on then 'Captain Spark Plug', I believe a young man in distress needs rescuing."

They arrived at the service station at 8.30 a.m. just as the Weasel was pushing up the roller door to the workshop. Linda dropped the two men off and went to park the Cortina somewhere out of sight and then try to find a cafe that was open to buy them all coffee.

"Hoo-fuckin-ray! The fuckin cavalry have arrived!"

Vic got out of the car and menaced the scrawny man, "Now Weasel—"

"Me fuckin name is—"

Vic loomed closer, "'Weasel', yes I know, now close your mouth and listen carefully. A lovely young lady will be arriving shortly and she does not want to hear another 'fuckin' escape your weaselly lips, if she does and I'm within earshot, I'm going to stuff that greasy rag that's hanging out of your pocket into your mouth! Is that clear Mr Weasel?"

The Weasel swallowed audibly and managed a stuttered, "Yes, sir."

"Excellent! Two things; firstly the keys to the black EH Holden parked over by the workshop?" Vic held out his hand into which the Weasel placed the keys. "See how easy that was and not a 'fuckin' in sight! Now, be a good chap and show me and my colleague here around the workshop."

****

Not that far away, three men, balaclavas discarded, were finishing off 'Doris' favourite dish—baked beans on toast with a fried egg and lashings of Heinz 57 Tomato Ketchup—and discussing how to put 'the Man's' new plan into action.

'Daphne' was sceptical, "Boss, you know I'll go along with anything that gives us a result, but, I reckon Mr Massey's got our measure on this one. What 'the Man' suggests is really just clutching at straws!"

"I agree, however, if we want to get paid, it's best to acquiesce to his wishes—regardless of our personal views. Talking about his wishes; 'Doris', when you finish clearing up, I want you to take the Humber to the servo in Woolloomooloo—there's a problem with the front end that needs an inspection. The mechanic there will be expecting you."

"No problems Boss. Be nice to get out in the fresh air!"

"Wait a minute, wait a fucking minute! I'm so clever sometimes it scares me! Doris, drop the clearing up and come here."

Once the three men had regathered around the table, the Boss laid out *his* plan. After he had finished, he spread his arms, "What did I say, am I brilliant or am I brilliant?"

"The brightest, I reckon," said 'Daphne'.

"More brilliant than the brightest star!" said 'Doris'.

"Well then, off you go, 'Doris'! And don't stop for a quickie!"

"No, Boss."

"'Daphne', please go and make sure Mr Massey is comfortable. Better yet, give him something to eat and then clean him up. We want him to look presentable for his reunion, don't you think?"

"Absolutely, Boss!"

Chapter 42

9:30 a.m., Wednesday 9 December 1969, Woolloomooloo, Sydney

"Oh shit! Jerry!" Linda called urgently. Jerry looked up sharply from the magazine he was reading. "It's here, the Humber, it's here!"

"OK, relax. Stay out of sight, Vic and I will take it from here."

As calmly as he could on legs that had turned to jelly, he walked out to the workshop.

"It's alright, Jerry, I see him. You know what to do." A statement, not a question.

The Weasel, unaware that this was the target, walked out and greeted the man as he got out of the car. "Help you?"

"It's OK Wea—Warren, I'll take care of the gentleman." Jerry wiped his hands on a greasy rag and offered his right one to 'Doris'.

"Good morning sir, the first cab of the rank. Good for you, less waiting time. We'll have this beauty inspected and, fingers crossed, she'll be back on the road in." Jerry studied his watch, "say, thirty minutes?"

"Uh, couldn't do it any faster?"

"Busy day eh, places to go, people to meet and all that?"

"Uh, yes!"

"Ooo, tricky that. You see, if I get the mechanic to give it the quick one, two and then the part fails, well, Humber blames me and I lose what is a very good job. Now I can see that you're a diligent, hardworking man yourself and I can bet you wouldn't enjoy being hurried up by a customer, would you? Of course you wouldn't, so why don't you walk up the road and grab a coffee and drop back in thirty minutes?"

'Doris', resigned to the fact that the inspection wouldn't be finished one second sooner than thirty minutes, grabbed his hat from the car and walked up Dowling Street in search of a cafe.

Jerry sat in the plush leather driver's seat and stroked the Walnut burl dashboard. The Super Snipe was a luxury car manufactured for those who couldn't afford a Mercedes or a BMW, shame it didn't have the following of the motoring public that Humber would have liked. He moved the column shift into first and drove it into the workshop.

"While we've got it here, may as well give it the once over, see if the bastards have left us any clues," Vic said as Jerry slid out of the car.

"Bugger!" Jerry exclaimed. "I have no idea what we're supposed to be inspecting!"

"Have you still got Blakely's number?" Vic asked.

Jerry rummaged through his pockets, "Yes!" and he hurried through to the Weasel's office.

"Sorry mate, need you to lend me your office for five!"

While Jerry was calling Archie Blakeley, Vic was going through the interior of the Humber.

"Hello, hello, hello, what have we here then?"

The Humber had beautifully crafted pleated leather door pockets and in the front passenger side, he found a slim black folio case. Inside we're various signed authorisations but the document that caught his eye had the letterhead 'Office of Naval Intelligence'. Taking a gamble that the driver wouldn't check the contents of the folio when he returned, he folded the document and tucked it into his top pocket.

"'Steering arm tie rods' wherever they are?" Jerry shouted as he emerged from the office.

"Here, I'll show you," the Weasel pulled over a large trolley jack and proceeded to raise the front of the car. "See here, this rod with the ball joint on the end is the tie rod."

"Thanks—what is your name by the way?"

"Albert, Albert Glendinning."

"Thank you, Albert! I did get your first name right then?"

"Don't rub it in!"

"There you go sir. Right as rain. Your car has the beefed-up tie rods so no problems at all. Here are your keys and have a great day." Vic sat in the idling chase car as Jerry handed possession of the Humber back to the driver. No sooner had it turned onto the road, when Vic pulled up and Jerry piled in. "Follow that car!"

"Smart arse! One piece of useless information; the driver is the same bloke that was assigned to stake out Linda's apartment last night. Now, that could tell us something or nothing—my gut instinct tells me that the kidnap team are short-staffed. Firstly, you wouldn't send the Humber on a stake-out; it stands out like dog's dusters! Secondly, a serious stake-out would have at least a team of two— Sid the Chauffeur here, was all on his Pat Malone. Definitely, short-staffed!"

Linda watched from the office as Vic and Jerry left the service station. The new, revised plan was that she would wait at the servo until either of them rang with news—good or bad. If she hadn't heard anything by 4:00 p.m., she could assume the worse and call Sergeant Hockey and tell him everything.

She knew it was going to be the longest, most stressful day of her life.

Vic had expected the Humber to head in any direction but the one it was taking.

"Where in the blazes is this bloke going?" he thought aloud as the Humber turned towards Kings Cross and then into a narrow side-street.

"I don't fucking believe it, they're holding him in a brothel!"

"Are you sure, it looks like a standard Sydney terrace house—ah, I see!"

"Don't look at me like that! And no, it's not that I'm a customer! I know it's a brothel from the number of times we raided it when I was a wet-behind-the-ears constable. OK?"

"Vic, you're a single man—an old single man mind—and if visiting brothels is the only way you can get a girl, then you do what you got to do!"

"Piss off, Jerry!"

"Wouldn't a brothel be a bit too busy to be a hideout?" Jerry asked.

"You'd be surprised what goes on in that lovely old terrace house Jerry, besides the usual fornication that is! But I do take your point, besides, your average gangster wouldn't be seen dead in a Humber! We'll just sit here for a few minutes before we go inside."

"Hey, maybe Mr Kidnapper has urges and has just dropped in to relieve his carnal desire?" Jerry suggested.

Vic reached into his pocket and pulled out the folded document he had taken from the folio in the Humber and held it out for Jerry. "You might like to read this while we're waiting."

Jerry unfolded the 'Authorisation'. His eyes went straight to the signature at the bottom. "I'm not at all surprised to see Fleming's moniker on this. You do realise this is just protecting his arse in the event his team get caught?"

"Yeah, I got that. He'll still have a lot of explaining to do at the end of all this. I can't understand why they just didn't go completely off the books?"

"Ah, that's because he's smarter than your average Police Sergeant or Navy Commander! You can bet London to a brick on, that he has a similar document signed by the Minister squirrelled away in his safe. Investigators turn up; 'I was only doing what the Minister directed me to do!' No doubt he believes he's bullet proof. Can I hang onto this?"

"Fill your boots, I've got no use for it. Stuff this, I'm going in to renew acquaintances and see what Sid the Chauffer is up to."

"You sure they'll let you in dressed in overalls?"

"You've never been in a brothel have you? Mate, they don't care what you're wearing when you walk in as long as you're wearing a 'raincoat' when you're inside—if you get my drift?"

Vic climbed out of the car and walked up the steps into a fug of incense, cheap perfume and the unmistakable aroma of cannabis. Georgia, the Madam of the house, artificially enhanced breasts all but spilling out over the large ornate mahogany desk she was sitting behind, welcomed him with a voice rough with age and cigarettes.

"Well hello, tall, blonde and well-hung. Welcome to the *Princess Palace*. How can we service you today big boy?"

"That line never worked on me twenty years ago Georgia and it certainly won't now we're both twenty years older!"

"Victor? My god, is that really you? You look so, so—old!"

"Careful, 'pot and kettle', Georgia!"

"Ooo, meow! Now I know you're not here to donate to my pension fund, so why are you here?"

"Guy about my size in a suit and Fedora hat came in here about five minutes ago; what did he want?"

"Come on Victor, you know I can't divulge any of my client's details."

"Georgia, you be a good girl and tell Uncle Victor all he wants to know or I'll get Uncle Noel Hockey to send some of his Constables to carry out a 'training exercise' in illegal casino raiding techniques of your establishment."

"The passing of the years hasn't made you any less of a prick you know! The weirdo you're inquiring about is on a shopping trip. He paid very well just to look at every girl I have working today. If he finds 'the one', he'll pay twice as much again. Hey, don't give me that quizzical expression! You know we get all types in here—we even get coppers with nothing better to do than harass a legitimate business woman!"

"Thanks, Georgia."

Vic climbed back behind the wheel of the EH Holden.

"He's window shopping."

"What?"

"Yep, paid a great deal of money just to look with the promise of more if he finds the right girl!"

"That's the problem with kidnappers these days; get paid way too much, if they can afford to be fussy!"

"Hang on, here he comes. Wait, he must have found what he was looking for—he's got a hooker with him?"

"Maybe he's picking up takeaway for the rest of the crew?"

They both chuckled as the kidnapper bundled the girl into the passenger seat.

"Did you notice anything about the girl?" Vic asked as he eased the car into the traffic two cars back from the Humber.

"Well, her tits were too small and her legs were too skinny for my tastes—Why are you looking at me like that?"

"I meant, did she look like someone we know?"

"My God, the long black hair in a pony tail—Linda!"

"Exactly, now why would they want a hooker that looks like Linda?"

"Interrogation basics—get the captive to believe you're going to do some nasty things to a loved one, nine times out of ten, they'll reveal all."

"Got it in one, my boy! As far as we know, the kidnappers only saw Linda from the back as she walked to the telephone box the night they searched Bobby's apartment. They were denied capturing the real Linda, hence they needed a girl about Linda's height and with long black hair."

The Humber had driven back down William Street and was now waiting to turn right into College Street which ran along the eastern boundary of Hyde Park.

"This bloke has me confused. First, he picks up a hooker, now he's heading for the business end of town, rather than the suburbs?"

Then to Vic's total amazement, the Humber turned into the Hyde Park Barracks.

Hyde Park Barracks had been built by convict labour in the 19th century. An imposing yet architectural plain red-brick building, it had served a number of purposes over its 150-year history, from a convict barracks at the start of its life, a hospital, mint, and courthouse, to its present-day use by the Department of Attorney General and Justice.

Vic pulled over to the kerb opposite the Barracks building and shook his head.

"Well, I certainly have to take my hat off to these villains, a building being used by the Justice Department, is the last place I'd have looked!"

Jerry was watching the Humber, just in case it was a decoy move. But there was no movement of the car nor its occupants.

"What are they doing—or don't I want to know?" Jerry asked.

"If our assumptions are correct, I'd guess Mr Kidnapper is briefing faux-Linda on her role. But where are they headed is the 64,000 dollar question? I've been in that building many times and for the life of me, I can't think of a more unsuitable place for a hideout?"

Jerry opened his door, then closed it again when he realised he was still wearing overalls.

"Where are you off to, sunshine?"

"It's smoko time so some of the staff will be stretching their legs in the forecourt; I'm going to join them and hopefully see where our pair are headed."

"Just remember, he's seen your face at the servo!"

"Got it."

Jerry had managed, with great difficulty, to remove his overalls while still in the car.

Straightening his tie and smoothing his hair, he crossed the road and into the Hyde Park Barracks paved forecourt. After strolling up and down for five or so minutes, a bench became vacant close to where the Humber was parked. Close enough that he could smell the prostitute's cheap perfume as it wafted out of the car window in overpowering waves.

Chapter 43

10:30 a.m., Wednesday 9 December 1969, Hyde Park Barracks, Sydney

"Are you absolutely clear on what you have to do?"

"Listen sweetheart, for $500 you wouldn't get a better performance out of Natalie fucking Wood!"

"Right then, Act One is about to commence. This is a busy place during the day. Cars in and out of the car park and people backwards and forwards to the various offices—and the toilets at the rear of the building. As soon as we get out of the car, we're a married couple. Our destination is that side entrance over there. We're about to enter the building when you excuse yourself and walk around the back of the building to where the toilets are.

"When you get there, you'll notice a narrow alleyway between the toilets and the main building. Check that no-one's around and quickly walk down the alley. When you're almost at the end, you'll find a door on your left with a 'No Entry' sign. Quietly open the door, step inside and close the door. It's pitch black once the door is closed so just wait there until I join you. Got that."

"Too fucking easy, sweetheart."

Jerry raised both hands straight up in a stretch motion signalling Vic that the driver was on the move. He got to his feet and turned away from the Humber as the driver got out and came around to the passenger side to open the door for the girl. Once out of the car, she pulled down the hem of her mini-skirt, took the man's offered hand and the pair headed to a side entrance.

They were nearly at the door when the woman leaned in, whispered something in the man's ear and then headed for the rear of the building.

Jerry had just resumed his casual walking when Vic, still dressed in his overalls, flat cap pulled low on his head and carrying a large duffle bag, walked up to him.

"*Don't acknowledge me*," Vic whispered, then in a louder voice. "Hey mate, where's the tradesman's entrance?"

"Uh—"

"*Point to where the woman went.*"

"Sorry, million miles away! The workman's entrance is just down there," loud enough for people 50 metres away to hear.

"*I'll be just inside the door, knock when the man joins the woman.* Very kind of you, thank you." Vic tipped his cap and, with the possibility that the driver may recognise him from the previous night, walked directly in front of him and opened the door.

"You coming in guv'nor?"

"Umm, no, no thank you. Waiting for the missus. Can't go ten minutes without needing the loo!"

No, didn't recognise me; you pathetic excuse for a stakeout man!

"OK mate, have a good day."

"You too."

Oh, I intend to, you fucking scum bag, I intend to!

Three minutes later, Jerry knocked sharply on the door.

"They've both gone round the back of the building to the toilet block," Jerry said as Vic emerged from the main building.

Vic peered cautiously around the corner.

"No sign of either of them. Check the 'Gents', I'll check the 'Ladies'. Not expecting them to be in there but better safe than sorry."

The toilets were empty as anticipated. Vic looked around the rest of the lot. "Nothing, so where are you?"

"Down here!" Jerry called out softly.

"Just as well I'm not a few pounds heavier, I'd never squeeze down there!"

"We need to have a plan of attack before we open this door because I have absolutely no idea what's behind it! The first thing we have to do is get out of sight of anybody coming to use the toilets."

"How are we going for time? I'd hate to think that we're going to be too late?"

"No chance of that. The dummy Linda has only just arrived. The kidnappers will still be prepping Bobby for her performance so I'd say we've got at least thirty minutes or more before the curtain goes up."

After a short deliberation, Vic and Jerry agreed that they were best hiding in plain sight, so they went back to the bench Jerry had occupied when he first arrived on site.

"I'm going to leave the overalls and cap on—if they happen to catch us entering, I can act as if I have every right to be there and question why they're here. It also gives me a reason for carrying this bag with my 'tools' in it. As soon as we're safely inside, I'll give you one of the shotguns; have you used a pump action before?"

"A few times on the rifle range."

"You OK with shooting someone?"

"Honestly, I don't know. However, if the kidnappers are armed and start pointing their guns at me or anyone I care about—I'll shoot first, and attend therapy later!"

"Good man."

"These are loaded with fifteen shells each. For safety, there isn't one in the chamber. Once inside, I'll manually load a shell into each chamber—quieter than pumping the gun to load. If you can, remember to count your shots; you don't want to be standing in the open with an empty gun."

The door opened silently on well-oiled hinges. Closing it gently behind them, they were plunged into total darkness.

"Stay still until your eyes adjust to the darkness."

Ever so slowly, a weak light coming from somewhere below, picked out sandstone steps winding their way down and around a central column some two metres in diameter. As planned, Vic loaded one of the guns and handed it to Jerry with the warning, "*No safety, keep it pointed skywards.*" After loading his own gun and discarding the bag, Vic led the way slowly down the steps.

The steps seemed to go on forever but eventually emerged into a large, dark, wet, brick-lined tunnel with a smooth concrete floor.

"*I know where we are,*" Jerry whispered. "*We're in the disused railway tunnel near St James Station.*"

"Which way?" Vic asked.

"A calculated guess would be left towards the station. That's where any office spaces would have been built."

They had gone about sixty metres when Vic held up his hand and dropped to a crouch against the tunnel wall. Jerry crouched behind him.

"Can you hear that?"

Jerry listened and despite the background rumble of trains nearby, he could just make out voices.

****

"Mr Massey, come in! Please, have a seat. Are you feeling better now the drugs have worn off—to some extent anyway?"

It felt to Bobby that the drugs hadn't worn off one tiny little bit, but he would continue to play their game.

"I'd feel almost human again if you let me have a quick shower."

"That's an excellent idea! I tell you what, you go and have a long hot shower and I'll put the kettle on shall I?"

"Is that what they call 'facetiousness' Boss?" Bobby asked.

"Well, yes and no. You see, my original offer is still on the table—you tell me where the green box is and I'll let you go. I'll even make you a cup of tea to seal the deal. So, one final time; where's the box?"

"And for the final time; I have no idea what you're talking about!"

"Are you absolutely positive that you don't know anything about an olive drab box about the size of a rectangular 'Erinmore Flake' tobacco tin?"

"Absolutely positive!"

"'Daphne'," the Boss shouted.

The scream when it came shook Bobby to the core.

"Ahh, recognise that scream do we?" The 'Boss' walked over to a doorway and opened the door. A bright light framed the silhouette of a naked young woman with long dark hair tied to a chair. 'Daphne' was holding what looked suspiciously like an electric cattle prod.

"Again, please, 'Daphne'."

The woman shook violently and screamed even louder. Bobby jumped out of his chair but 'Doris' two beefy hands slammed him back down.

The screaming eventually stopped and the woman's head slumped forward.

"You look depressed, Mr Massey. What, no smart-arse remarks, no witty rejoinders, no clueless insults? You disappoint me, Mr Massey! All that sass knocked out of you just because your girlfriend's getting her nipples fried? Now, can you please end all this fucking around *and tell me what I want to know!?*"

****

Jerry flinched visibly when the piercing scream echoed down the tunnel.

"Fuck me!"

"Steady Jerry, she is only acting."

"Sadly, Bobby doesn't know that and if that scream scared the bejesus out of me, I can't imagine what's going on in his head at the moment!"

"I think it's time the cavalry saved the day don't you?"

"Let's go!"

"Easy, even the cavalry used scouts before they charged over the hill!"

"Right!"

"Go on then—scout!"

"Me?"

"Am I built for skulking around quietly?"

"Fair point. Back in a tick."

While he was prepared the second time, the scream still set Jerry's teeth on edge. "Much closer this time though," he whispered to himself.

Rounding a curve in the tunnel, Jerry came across the space that would have been the platform for a station on a rail line that was never finished. He stuck his head around the corner of the platform and saw a pair of black-painted wooden double doors with glass panels in the top half. A light was shining through the panels.

He eased himself up onto the platform and looked with one eye into an empty short linoleum-covered passageway. There were two wooden doors off to the left and a solid-looking steel door at the end of the passage.

Disappointed that he couldn't see any kidnappers or Bobby and knowing that it would be suicide to go in by himself, he eased himself back into the tunnel and hurried back to where Vic was waiting.

Jerry wasted no time in detailing the scene and a short time later the two of them crouched below the level of the platform. Listening.

"I can only make out two voices," Jerry whispered.

"Yeah, me too. We know that there are a minimum of four people inside there; Bobby, dummy Linda, Humber driver and whoever was babysitting while Humber driver was out. Linda said there were three men in the car the night they abducted Bobby. We have to assume there are more than three. In fact, I can't see how they could have managed an operation of this scale with only three people. My guess is there's at least one or possibly two others—whether they're all in here now is an unknown.

"The steel door most likely is where they keep Bobby between interrogation sessions. Right now, judging from the screams, we can almost guarantee that the head honcho is either trying to get or has succeeded in getting, the information he's after, most likely with one of his muscle men watching over Bobby.

"Another trained ape is looking after the hooker. That leaves the most dangerous person unaccounted for. He's the most dangerous because he could be fucking anywhere!

"Because we don't have a clue about the office layout, we're going to have to risk entering the corridor.

"You OK with that?"

"No, but let's do it anyway!"

Thankfully, the passageway door opened easily with a minimum of noise. The doors leading off the passageway to the two rooms, unfortunately, didn't have the same glass panels as the double entry doors but now they were seated directly out side, they could just make out what was being said.

They had just placed their back against the wall when Jerry noticed a white plastic-covered sign with red lettering fixed to the wall just inside the entry doors.

"*Bingo!*" He nudged Vic and pointed to the sign. "*Our luck's just changed. That's the mandatory fire escape plan and it should show a layout of the whole office complex.*"

The two of them stood and quickly studied the plan. The two wooden doors opened into mirror-image large office spaces with three smaller rooms off to the sides. A set of double doors interconnected the large offices. Vic gave Jerry a thumbs up and they returned to crouching in the passageway.

No sooner had they done so when they heard Bobby's voice.

"Let her go first."

"Now why would I do that? The first piece of real leverage I have to loosen your tongue and you want me to let her go? I don't think so."

Bobby was racking his brain trying to remember if he'd slipped up at any time and unintentionally revealed Linda's name.

No, there was no way he could have revealed enough information for them to have kidnapped Linda. Yes, he might have let her first name slip but he would have realised his mistake as soon as they probed for her surname and address. No, this was just another part of the game—he would play along until they grew frustrated as they had with all the other attempts.

Vic held up two fingers and mouthed 'Bobby' and pointed to the right-hand door.

"Look, I'm sorry I've been stuffing you around, OK? But I'm smart enough to know that once I give you what you want, I'm a dead man! Please let Linda go and I swear to you I'll drive you to where I hid the box and place it in your hand. Please, please, just let Linda go." Then Bobby buried his face in his hands and sobbed convincingly.

"Bobby, come on be reasonable! What would you do in my shoes? I was given a relatively simple job to do and you, you fuck, have made it more difficult than it should have been. Hey, it's a small box that probably means nothing to anyone except the person you stole it from. It certainly can't mean anything to you or you wouldn't have squirrelled it away somewhere. So, I'm going to ask you one more time and if you don't tell me where the box is, I'm going to have 'Daphne' and 'Doris' fuck your little Linda in every hole in her body! Is that fucking clear!"

'Thanks arsehole, you've just told me how many of you there are,' Vic said to himself and then whispered, "*three baddies*" to Jerry then held up one finger and pointed to the door on the left. He steeled himself to enter the room where Bobby was being interrogated. He lifted the shotgun across his chest and then hand-signalled that he was going to enter the room with Bobby in it and for Jerry to enter the other room. He then held up a closed fist, the universal signal to wait. "*Come on Bobby, hit him with it,*" he said quietly.

Bobby slowly lifted his head and looked at the 'Boss' with a puzzled expression.

"'Boss', I'm pretty naïve when it comes to matters of a sexual nature, but, when you say your monkeys are going to fuck Linda in every hole—they must have very small dicks to be able to fuck her ears?"

Vic almost burst into laughter but instead released his fist and kicked open the door. To make sure everyone knew he was armed he fired a round into the ceiling.

"*Everyone on the floor, NOW!*"

As that was happening, Jerry went to kick down the other door, but unfortunately failed at his first attempt. While the second attempt saw the door slam back on its hinges, the delay was enough to enable 'Daphne' to draw a pistol from the back of his waistband and get off a hurried shot. The bullet unluckily caught Jerry squarely in the right kneecap but before the pain could overcome the adrenaline racing through his system, he did manage to turn 'Daphne's' head into a nice red and grey abstract mural on the wall behind him.

Meanwhile, although 'Doris' and Bobby were lying prone side by side, the 'Boss' concluded that being blasted with a shotgun was the preferable option to being incarcerated so, he also drew his pistol—unfortunately, he didn't manage to get a shot away.

Bobby Massey, looking like death warmed up, rolled onto his back and smiled up at Vic Rogers who returned the grin with a broad smile. "You've got balls, son, I'll give you that." He then placed the still-hot and smoking barrel of the shotgun on the back of 'Doris' neck.

"Hands behind your back arsehole! Bobby, have a hunt around and find something to truss this turkey up with."

He reached out and grabbed Bobby's hand and hauled him to his feet. Bobby found a coil of rope lying nearby then he and Vic made sure that 'Doris' wouldn't be able to bat an eyelid without it causing him pain.

"Hey Jerry, you ready to go?" Vic had heard Jerry's shotgun fire and assumed he was fine.

"*I think I need an ambulance,*" came the weak reply.

"Shit, shit, shit," Vic muttered as he raced into the adjoining room with Bobby close behind. There was no sign of the hooker who had grabbed her clothes and scarpered the moment that 'Daphne's' head had departed his body.

Vic knelt down next to Jerry who was gripping his leg and gasping in pain, "Bobby Massey, Jerry O'Rourke. Bobby, I need something to strap Jerry's knee to stop the bleeding. Have a look around and see if you can find anything". Then to Jerry, "Hang in there, sailor!"

While Bobby went looking for makeshift bandages, Vic searched 'Daphne's' body and was rewarded when he found a knife attached to the belt he was wearing. Taking both the belt and the knife, he sliced Jerry's right trouser leg to above the knee and used the belt as a tourniquet to stem the flow of blood.

Bobby returned with a towel. "Will this do?"

Vic folded the towel several times then bound Jerry's knee as tightly as he could. He then turned to Bobby.

"I need to get Jerry some help. I was hoping to get you back to Linda but she's going to have to wait a bit longer. Stay here with him, I'll be back as soon as I can."

Jerry grabbed Vic's arm, "We can't alert the authorities to what's just transpired down here. We—the three of us—need to get out of here, get the Holden and the Humber back to the service station and think of a way to sort this," he waved an arm around, "this shit fight, out."

"I hate to point this out Jerry, but you're not going anywhere on that knee!"

Bobby cut in, "I did a Field First Aid Course during army training, I reckon there's enough material laying around here to fashion a makeshift splint for the knee. As long as the knee remains static, Jerry should be able to hobble on one leg."

Vic and Jerry both looked at Bobby quizzically then Vic clapped him on the shoulder, "Well, you've proven you're not just a pretty face, so show us what you've got soldier!"

Bobby searched around the rooms that his captors had been using, obviously for some time too, judging from the amount of clothing and provisions he found.

Twenty minutes later, Bobby returned ladened down with an assortment of items—including an ice-cold bottle of Grey Goose vodka, "We can use this as an antiseptic."

Jerry reached out for the bottle. "Not before I use it as a pain killer you won't!"

"By the way, who was the girl?" Bobby asked as he tended to Jerry's knee. "The bastards had me believing it was Linda for about 5 seconds!"

"What made you so sure it wasn't?" Vic asked.

"Well, I was ninety percent sure I hadn't given them enough information for them to identify her but as soon as they opened the door and I saw her silhouette, I knew it wasn't Linda—her tits were too small!"

That was it for Vic and Jerry who both burst into fits of laughter.

"What did I say?"

Vic recovered enough to clap Bobby on the shoulder, "Long story Bobby, worth saving until we've got you and Jerry out of here!"

Jerry's knee had been bathed with ice-cold Grey Goose vodka (which Jerry insisted on helping himself to on several occasions—'purely to numb the pain' of course) and wrapped in more strips of absorbent towelling. The knee was braced on either side by two wooden clothes hangers—that had been made with the almost perfect angle that caused Jerry the least amount of pain—secured in place by lengths of ripped sheeting.

Once Bobby and Vic had helped him stand, Jerry was able to support his weight on his left leg. With the aid of an upturned broom and mop bound with more towelling, as crutches, he was able to move, albeit painfully, down the short corridor and out onto the platform.

"Ahh, small problem! How, in God's name am I going to get down from here?"

Again, Bobby proved his worth. He went back inside the office and retuned moments later with an office chair with castors.

Once Jerry had gently eased himself into the chair, Vic and Bobby pushed the chair carefully over the edge of the platform and slowly lowered him to the concrete floor.

"There's no way I'll be able to negotiate the steps back to the Hyde Park Barracks car park!"

"I imagine there's an exit onto St James Station down that way," Vic pointed in the opposite direction from the stone stairway.

"We'll roll you down there in the chair then lift you onto the unused platform that would have had access from St James Station. Once onto the platform, you and Bobby enter the station and take the elevator to the Elizabeth Street exit and then drive the Holden back to the servo. Bobby, here are the keys. I'll clean up any traces of us being down here and meet you back in Woolloomooloo with the Humber. OK?" Jerry and Bobby nodded their agreement and the trio set off.

Vic was right about the unused platform having access to St James Station. Jerry tried to get out of the chair but the Grey Goose had worked its magic and he slumped back down.

"Fuck it! Bobby, wheel me to my chariot!" which Bobby took great delight in doing!

Vic returned to the kidnapper's lair and carefully and methodically cleaned what needed cleaning and packed anything that could link any of them to the place into two large plastic bags he found in the small kitchenette.

He then checked the two bodies and 'Doris' for ID and found none—'Doris' did have the keys to the Humber though. He deposited the two shotguns and the kidnapper's three 9mm pistols in the bags along with three unopened bottles of Grey Goose vodka.

"To the victor, go the spoils—no pun intended!" he said to the empty room.

On his way out, he delivered a hefty kick to 'Doris' ribs and was rewarded with a pained 'Oooof'.

"Hang in there pal, the police will have you in a nice dry cell by midnight."

Turning off all the lights as he left, he hefted the plastic bags over his shoulder and made his way back up the sandstone steps to the Hyde Park Barracks exit door.

He deposited everything into the duffle bag he'd left by the door and making sure no-one was in the narrow alley, stepped out into a dazzlingly bright, sunlit park.

Chapter 44

2:45 p.m., Wednesday 9 December 1969, Pearl Service Station, Woolloomooloo, Sydney

Vic parked the Humber next to the black EH Holden and had just stepped out of the car when a tearful Linda raced across the driveway and leapt onto him like a spider monkey clinging to a tree. Gasping for air, he finally managed to untangle himself from her embrace. "What's got into you, young lady? Anybody would think you've just been reunited with your boyfriend!"

"Vic Rogers, you and that one-legged drunken sailor in there," she pointed in the direction of Albert Glendinning's office, "are either two of the most stupidest men in Australia or—and this is the one I'm leaning toward—two of the bravest, most selfless men I've had the greatest pleasure knowing and loving!"

"Eh! Enough of the 'loving' bit!" Bobby jokingly scolded, then much to Vic's surprise, he also wrapped Vic in a bear hug.

"Linda and I owe you and Jerry so very much that I can't begin to think how we're ever going to show our profound gratitude! Thank you, Sergeant Vic Rogers, from the bottom of my heart, thank you!"

"Well, that's very kind of you both, but, you haven't received my bill yet!" he managed to say with a straight face. He maintained the icy policeman's stare until he saw the excitement start to drain from their faces and then with a full-on belly laugh, wrapped his arms around each of them. "Come on let's go check on sailor boy. Had you going for a while there though didn't I? Come on, admit it, you were wondering how much my fee would be, eh?"

"I was just hoping that I wasn't going to have to sell the Cortina to pay for it!" Bobby replied. "Or put Linda on the streets! Oww, that hurt!"

"You're still a wimp, Bobby Massey!"

Their laughter was more relief than from any joking remarks.

Bobby's makeshift splint and bandaging had worked a treat. So much so, that despite the rough handling and jarring it received getting from the tunnel to the car, there was no sign of blood seeping through the bandages. Jerry was fast asleep on the lounge in Albert's Office, his injured knee propped up on two cushions. The couple of swigs of vodka he had consumed in the tunnel had done wonders.

"First thing, we need to do is work out where we take Jerry to get his knee looked at. Does anyone have any ideas?" Vic asked.

"I know a fuc—doctor that's very discreet!" Albert offered.

"Albert, you're a dark horse, how would you know a shonky Doctor?" Vic said.

"I didn't say he was fuc—shonky, I said he was 'discreet'!"

"Same horse, different jockey—so how do you know him?"

"Well, sometimes me greyhounds—"

"A bloody vet! We're not taking Jerry to a shonky vet for crying out loud!"

"Maybe a cup of tea will help us think," Vic suggested and then, "Thanks Albert, don't mind if I do—black and two please."

While a mumbling Albert went into his back room to make the tea, Linda went behind his desk and picked up the phone. Before she dialled, she said, "Don't get your hopes up. This is a long-shot but I have to try. I do need to do this confidentially so if you don't mind—?"

Bobby and Vic rose as one and went to help a surprised Albert make the tea.

She dialled the number and when connected she said, "Hello my name is Linda West, would you put me through to Doctor David Ramsay please?"

Twenty minutes later, Linda joined the men in the back room. Bobby made her a cup of tea.

"Well, come on then, the suspense is killing me!"

"Vic, you told me this morning that last night you had put your friendship with Noel Hockey at risk when you put him on the spot asking for 'equipment' to assist in Bobby's rescue. I've just asked a highly respected Orthopaedic surgeon to carry out illegal surgery on a gunshot victim. Much to my surprise, he agreed so why do I feel like crap!"

Vic grasped her arm gently. "Now, you know how I felt. The question you need to ask yourself is 'could I *not* have asked for his help'—knowing you as I do, I suspect the answer is 'no, I couldn't'."

Bobby, the pragmatist, "So Linda, what's the plan?"

Linda relayed the instructions Doctor Ramsay had given her and at 8.00 p.m. sharp, Jerry was placed on a stretcher and wheeled into the Operating Theatre of the Durham Hills Private Hospital.

"Jerry, my name is Doctor David Ramsay. I understand you've had a nasty accident on your motor bike?" Jerry, having been briefed on the scenario replied, "Yes, Doctor. Rode too close to my brick gate post that collided with my knee."

"Right then, we'd better get you prepped."

"How are you feeling?"

Jerry was still woozy from the anaesthetic but slowly managed to focus on Doctor Ramsay.

"Yeah, good—I think?"

"Excellent! I'll leave you in the hands of Nurse West who will monitor you for twenty-four hours. I've left a souvenir for you with the nurse."

David Ramsay turned to face Linda as Jerry nodded off again. "Linda, this probably is the last thing you expected from me, but, thank you. Thank you for not only trusting me with your secret but having the faith in me not to simply turn you all over to the police.

The surgery I carried out on Jerry's knee was purely to remove the bullet and stem any blood loss. He will need a full knee reconstruction, however, it is doubtful that even with that surgery, he will ever walk unaided again. Have him come and see me in Concord Repat when he recovers."

Linda reached out to him and kissed his cheek, "Thank you!"

After Doctor Ramsay had gone, Linda pulled up a chair next to Jerry's bed and took the crushed lead slug from her pocket, "Bloody bullets! Two men I love shot—what are the odds of that?"

While Jerry was undergoing surgery to remove the lead slug from his knee, Vic was reporting a suspected shooting in the abandoned tunnels near St James Station to the Surry Hills Police Station.

Chapter 45

3:30 a.m., Thursday 10 December 1969, Darlinghurst Police Station, Sydney

At 3:30 a.m. on the morning following the rescue of Bobby Massey, the gates to the Darlinghurst Police motor vehicle compound swung open and a sparkling clean black 1964 EH Holden swung in and parked as far towards the back of the lot as it could.

In the boot of the Holden was a nondescript grey/green duffle bag containing two freshly cleaned 12-gauge shotguns—the NSW Police Evidence tags reattached to the trigger guards. Not that these guns would ever be called before the court as evidence because the charge sheets and all other documents relating to their crime will eventually be destroyed on the orders of the Attorney General himself.

With the car safely parked, the rather large, well-built driver stepped from the vehicle, carefully wiped the steering wheel, and locked and gently closed the door. On his way out of the compound, he stopped to pet the large German Shepherd that sat obediently inside the compound and then handed the car keys to the person standing ready to close the gate. They shook hands, exchanged an understanding nod and then the gates were closed and locked.

Several seconds later, a black—or possibly metallic green—medium-sized sports sedan, its lights extinguished, pulled up to allow the Holden driver to climb into the passenger seat. Then, with its lights still off, the sedan drove slowly down the quiet back street.

At 7:30 a.m. that same morning, a call was received by a young female Probationary Constable in the Darlinghurst Police Station from a Mr Albert Glendinning, proprietor of the Pearl Service Station in Woolloomooloo, reporting a Humber Super Snipe that was illegally parked in his service area.

Apparently, the owner of the said vehicle had failed to collect it after a mandatory inspection of the tie rods had been carried out. Mr Glendinning was quite adamant that the, quote, *fuckin pigs get off their fuckin' arse's and get the fuckin' piece of fuckin' shit out of my fuckin' car space!*

Chapter 46

8:00 a.m., Thursday 10 December 1969, Canberra, ACT

"Breaking news from Sydney this morning where New South Wales police have sealed off St James Station and parts of Elizabeth Street. Details are still sketchy, but the ABC understands that two bodies were removed from the station around 4.30 a.m. this morning. A third man in handcuffs was seen being led away from the scene by detectives. More on this story as it comes to hand."

Commodore Fleming listened to the news passively. It wasn't entirely unexpected given the nature of the mission. His biggest concern wasn't that it would take the average detective only five minutes to link him to the affair, it was that he still hadn't recovered the box. He slammed his hand on the desk top and uttered a frustrated, "Damn it!"

Recovering quickly, he changed into his golf clothes and walked out of his office. Stopping at his adjutant's desk, he addressed the young Lieutenant, "I'll be out of the office all morning, David. Anything urgent comes up, contact the Club Captain." He made a show of checking his watch, "Depending on my partner's game, I should be back in the office around 1400."

Commodore Peter Fleming then took the fire stairs down to the basement car park—and disappeared.

Peter Fordham, recently retired from the travelling sales business, donned his $25 sunglasses, pulled his floppy white hat low on his brow, placed a booted foot on the back wheel of his Victa lawn mower and pulled hard on the starter cord. No luck.

"'bout time you mowed that flamin' jungle," his neighbour shouted good-naturedly over the fence. "Spark plugs probably oiled up, it's been that long since you used it. Hang on, I'll come over and give you a hand. Have a cold one ready!"

Chapter 47

9:00 a.m., Thursday 10 December 1969, Office of the Minister for Defence, Canberra, ACT

George Peterson walked confidently into his outer office trying hard not to reveal the extreme stress that was churning in his gut.

"Good morning, Henry."

"Good Morning, Minister." His Private Secretary stood and was in the process of gathering papers and documents in preparation for his usual morning briefing with the Minister.

"Not just yet, Henry. I need to make some urgent private calls before our meeting. Would you be so kind to bring me in a pot of tea please?"

"Certainly, Minister."

George Peterson's stomach had been doing cartwheels from the moment he heard the morning news. He had tried to ring Commodore Fleming but his Adjutant had said he wasn't available—which only meant one thing; Commodore Fleming had fled the coop!

George's first call was to 'a man who knew a man' regarding his escape plan.

"*Yes sir, all ready and waiting. Please deposit the quoted fee in our Post Office box. Once received, the documents will be couriered to the address provided.*"

"Thank you. The fee will be in your box by 5:00 p.m. today."

His next call could wait until he'd had his cup of tea.

"*John Forrester?*"

"Morning John, are you available for a meeting in our usual place."

"*Not today, George. I'll ring you with a time and place.*"

Not today—that meant only one thing; his three comrades in arms needed some time to exorcise any link between them and what went down in St James Station. With Peter Fleming now 'on the lam', as the Americans would say, George Peterson was the remaining link.

"Thinking cap on, George," he lay back in his arm chair and tried to think of ways to turn current events in his favour.

He was stirred from his reverie by Henry buzzing him from the outer office. Reluctantly, he walked over and pressed the intercom, "Yes, Henry?"

"Sorry to disturb you, Minister, but I wonder if now is a good time for our daily briefing?"

"Sorry, Henry! With a million things on my mind at the moment, I'd forgotten all about it! Please, come on in."

Thankfully, most of what Henry needed his attention for was routine and was quickly dispensed with. What it did achieve, however, was that it cleared his mind of thinking reactively. He needed to be proactive and deliver the first blow.

But first, he needed to organise some insurance.

****

"Army Provosts, Sergeant Thomas."

"Sergeant, is the Military Police aware that one of their Special Air Service soldiers is at this very moment, being interrogated by the NSW Police Force regarding the deaths of two of his colleagues in St James Station this morning?"

"Who is this? Hello. Hello?

"Corporal, get onto Sydney Area Police Command and ask them if they have any Army personnel in custody!"

****

Friday came and still no call from John Forrester.

"Not as easy to get rid of me as you thought eh Forrester?" the Minister asked his empty office.

"OK George, let's go shopping!" He replaced his recently purchased new identity documents back in their envelope and then asked Henry to order a Com Car to take him to the city.

Armed with his new identity documents, George Peterson pulled his Fedora low over his eyes and walked into the first used car dealership he came upon. A glossy black sedan caught his eye and he was sitting in the driver's seat when a salesman approached him.

"Very low kilometres on this one Mr—?"

"Fredrickson, George Fredrickson."

"Well, Mr Fredrickson, I can tell you know a great deal when you see one. Just three years young, this XY Ford 500 is a beauty; only one owner, serviced regularly by us and not a scratch on her. Would you like to take it for a test drive?"

"Thank you, I'd love to. Do you mind if I take it home to show the wife?"

"Not at all Mr Fredrickson—take as long as you like, but we close at 5:00 p.m.! Ha, ha, ha!"

Putting on a pair of dark sunglasses, George took the opportunity of being anonymous for an hour or so to open a new bank account at a small bank branch in the suburbs; apply for an American Express Gold card and visit his usual bank in the city to transfer most of his savings to the account of George Fredrickson.

"She drives beautifully! Tell you what; if you can transfer the registration to NSW for me by Monday, I'll pay cash for what you're asking?"

"Mr Fredrickson, I do believe you have a deal! Come to my office and we'll fill out all the necessary paperwork."

****

"*Hello?*"

"Is that Mrs Williams, Mrs Moira Williams?"

"*Yes?*"

"My name is Sam Tyson, Detective Sergeant Sam Tyson, Wollongbar Police Station." George Peterson was banking on Moira Williams taking 'Detective Tyson' at his word and not later ringing Wollongbar Police Station to check to see if he actually existed. "Mrs Williams, do you recall the events that resulted in the increased security measures being constructed around the old Barclay's Creek Quarry nearly twelve years ago?"

"*Well, no, not really. Yes, Bill and I witnessed the construction of the new security fencing, but we weren't aware of anything that might have caused that to happen!*"

"Are you and your husband able to drop in to the Wollongbar Police Station next week and sign a statement to that effect?"

"*Of course, Detective, we go into town every second Tuesday for supplies, so we could drop in next week if that's OK?*"

216

"Tell you what, it's not urgent so how about I call in next time I'm out your way?"

"We're here most days Detective and you're welcome anytime."

"Thank you, Mrs Williams."

George Peterson ticked off the plan on his fingers. "OK, drive the car to the farm next Tuesday—the Williams' will be out so no witnesses, taxi into Wollongbar, train back to Canberra, wait for the Bill to pass through both Houses organise the transfer of the goods to General Mpoto, pass 'GO' and collect 1,000,000 US dollars thank you very much and disappear overseas! On the other hand; Forrester comes looking for blood—high-tail it back to the farm, pick up the car, assume the new identity, kiss goodbye to $1,000,000 and disappear overseas. Hmm, with one million dollars at stake, I definitely need to turn things around with John Forrester!"

"Henry!"

"Yes, Minister?"

"I need to go to Sydney next Tuesday on a personal matter. Will you make sure my diary stays empty for then?"

"Certainly, Minister."

George Peterson leaned back in his chair and folded his hands behind his head, "That's you sorted George—now, how to get Forrester off my back?"

By the next morning, George Peterson had come up with a scheme to remove John Forrester's hands from around his neck.

"Good morning, it's George Peterson—I'm ringing about a barking dog that needs silencing and was wondering if you know of anyone that can help?"

"Good morning, Minister. As a matter of fact, I have just the person. His prices are scaled to the size and breed of the dog so if you can give me the relevant details, I'll ring you later today with a quote."

George knew going down this path was expensive but if he was to share in the four million dollar prize, it would be worth every penny.

****

John Forrester was the first to admit that he was a fifty-four-year-old lecher. He figured that all the hard yards he put in at the gym to keep his body toned, would be wasted on one particular woman—especially when the Canberra nightclubs were full of twenty to thirty-year-olds in need of a man with his 'experience'. OK, maybe the fact that he splashed money around like confetti helped.

George Peterson's 'dog controller' couldn't believe his luck! "This will be the easiest thousand bucks I've earned in a long time!"

"The photos are very—what's the word?"

"'*Revealing*'?"

"Yes, 'revealing' in more ways than one! And he participated voluntarily?"

"*Took to it like a duck to water; even paid for the privilege!*"

"You're kidding?"

"*I kid you not, Minister. Mind you, if he knew his activities were being filmed in widescreen technicolour he may not have been so forthcoming, so to speak!*"

"True. Thank you for another great service; your fee plus a bonus will be in your post office box Monday afternoon."

"*Thank you Minister, as always—it's been a pleasure doing business with you.*"

****

John Forrester entered his office on Monday morning at precisely 9:00 a.m.—a spring in his step and a smile on his face. His day had started at 5:00 a.m. with a run around the lake then forty minutes in the gym followed by forty laps of the pool. The start of another working week and life was good.

First order of business; check the diary—nothing until the Heads of Section meeting at 10:30 a.m. Next; check the 'In' tray—usual crap, hello, what's this then?

He turned the A4 buff-coloured enveloped over—nothing? Someone must have personally dropped it off. He sliced open the top and pulled out six large full-colour photos of himself naked, *flagrante* with a woman and a man in all combinations possible. A small 'With Compliments' note was attached to one of the photos; it read *Rose Garden 9:30 a.m.*

"Good morning, John, you're looking flushed! You need to watch your blood pressure!"

"You fucking bastard!"

"Now, there you go again! Getting all worked up, you really do need to calm down old boy! Here, come and sit down and let's discuss our respective dilemmas."

John Forrester seethed with anger as he paced up and down in front of the bench where George Peterson was sitting. In the end, common sense won out over the desire to stab George Peterson in the heart and damn the consequences. He slumped onto the bench in defeat.

"There you go! Now, John, this is how we're going to move ahead of our respective fuck-ups and continue with our original plan. I know that the three of you were planning my demise and quite frankly, if the shoe was on the other foot, I'd be doing exactly the same thing. However—and you're going to have to take my word for this—there is absolutely no way that I can be linked to what happened in Sydney.

"As far as our client is concerned, everything is as it was when handshakes were exchanged. I've taken care of the one remaining witness to what went down in St James Station and the news will reveal that it was an SAS training exercise that went tragically wrong. End of story.

"In the meantime, I will continue to actively search for the missing container. If it's still out there, by hook or by crook, I'll retrieve the bloody thing!

"As far as the photos of your exploits go—as long as I stay alive, they stay safely locked away."

George Peterson extended his right hand, "Deal?"

John Forrester took several seconds before shaking the offered hand, "Deal."

****

'Doris' wasn't saying anything. Despite almost thirty-six hours of being interrogated by detectives, the only word to pass his lips had been 'toilet?'

The NSW Police were no closer to determining what had taken place in the abandoned St James tunnel complex after four days of investigations. Behind the steel doors at the end of the corridor, they found two cells both set up with equipment synonymous with torture. They had two unidentified bodies, killed by shotgun blasts but no shotguns or spent shells.

They had evidence of injury to another person from bloodstains some distance from the shotgun victims and hundreds of fingerprints, some of which belonged to the victims. There was no evidence of any drugs nor any large sums of cash. There were no documents of any kind, not even shopping receipts, nor were there any identifying labels on any of the victim's clothing. Their only clue to the events was currently lying in a cell and even that was about to disappear.

"Detective, there's an Army Provost Corporal here to see you."

"Why the hell is an MP asking for me? Better bring him through then, Sergeant."

"Morning, Detective, I'm Corporal Harrison. I have here a Warrant for the release into my custody of a soldier you have in your cells."

"Sorry to disappoint you, Corporal, but we're not holding any soldier in our cells?"

"Detective, I understand that you are holding a person in relation to the deaths of two men found in tunnels near St James Station—we have reason to believe that this man is a member of the Australian Army."

"And just how the fuck do you know that Corporal?"

"May I speak to the prisoner?"

'Doris' stood as the MP Corporal entered the cell.

"Name, rank and serial number soldier!"

'Doris' immediately snapped to attention.

"Brauer, Raymond, Sergeant, X694534, Sir."

"***Do I look like a 'sir' Sergeant?***" the Corporal barked.

"No Corporal, sorry Corporal!"

"About face Sergeant, hands behind your back!"

Despite the protestations of the detective, Sergeant Raymond Brauer was handcuffed and frogmarched out of the Police Station and into the back of an Army Land Rover parked outside.

****

The NSW Police Commissioner has revealed that the events leading to the closure of St James Station and a section of Elizabeth Street early last Friday morning, were the result of an Army Training exercise going tragically wrong.

The exercise was being conducted in one of the abandoned railway tunnels near St James Station and was initiating members of the Australian Army's elite Special Air Service into interrogation techniques. Sadly, two soldiers were killed while a third is now awaiting Court Martial. Jodie Marshall, ABC News, Sydney.

Chapter 48

Wednesday 4 March 1970 Office of Mr Jerry O'Rourke, CEO, Nova Aurora Security

"Come on in, Mr Edwards. You'll have to forgive me if I don't stand."

"Of course, Commander," replied Henry Edwards, Private Secretary to the Minister for Defence, "and please, it's Henry."

Jerry manoeuvred his wheelchair back behind his desk.

"Just 'Mr Jerry O'Rourke' these days Henry. Please have a seat," Jerry indicated the chair in front of the desk. "Would you like tea or a coffee?"

"No, thank you." Henry Edwards lifted his briefcase and sat it on his lap. "While not being privy to the contents of the document that I have in here, the Minister did admit that giving you this goes against everything the Australian Intelligence Agency has fought to keep secret since 1943. That being the case, I strongly advised the Minister against giving you such information. As my presence here indicates; my advice was ignored."

Henry opened the briefcase and extracted an A4 buff envelope. Laying it on the desk in front of Jerry he said solemnly, "You do realise that once you break the seal, you can't put the genie back in the bottle?"

"Yes Henry, but too many lives were changed for the worse by someone working on orders from the Minister via the Office of Naval Intelligence.

An apology to those affected by those traumatic events has never been offered by the Navy or successive Governments and to this day, no explanation as to why those people put their careers and sometimes their personal safety, on the line. At least after reading whatever's in that envelope, I can contact those still living and give them closure."

"You do realise that the first page will be a Non-Disclosure Agreement?"

"I do and I won't. I haven't wandered that far from the mast Henry."

"Understood and I apologise for the inference."

The Minister's Private Secretary snapped his briefcase shut, stood and extended a hand, "I wish you well Jerry."

Jerry accepted the offered hand, "Thank you, Henry."

After Henry had left, Jerry buzzed his assistant. "Make me a double espresso please David then hold all calls for an hour."

"*Yes, sir.*"

Jerry waited for his coffee before sliding himself from the wheelchair onto his studded leather Chesterfield, lifted his damaged leg onto a matching Ottoman, broke the seal and opened the envelope.

Thirty minutes later, Jerry lay his head on the back of the sofa, closed his eyes and uttered a single word; "Fuck." Not an angry 'fuck!' or a surprise 'fuck!' just a resigned sort of 'fuck'. The sort of 'fuck' one would utter when one comes to realise the reason for the feeling of weightlessness is mainly because they've jumped from 5,000ft and their parachute is still in the aeroplane or when you fill up your brand new petrol-engine Ferrari and on returning the fuel hose to the bowser, you read the word 'Diesel' for the first time.

He lifted the letter and re-read it.

Dear Commander O'Rourke (this crossed through and replaced with a handwritten 'Jerry')

The facts I'm about to reveal to you in this letter are known to four people— five now—myself included.

Having read your exemplary service record, I need not stress the weight of responsibility that now rests on your shoulders and the utter frustration you will feel in having to carry the burden of this knowledge to your grave.

In 1942, the forerunner to the British Intelligence Service was the Special Operations Group. This group carried out many telling raids behind enemy lines. One such daring raid resulted in the abduction of one of Hitler's chief scientists, a Doctor Stefan Jensen.

After months of interrogation and God knows what else, Doctor Jensen agreed to help the allies in their fight against the Nazis. Before he was taken from Auschwitz, Doctor Jensen had been working on a biological weapon that was so deadly, he estimated that it could cause the collapse of the Allied forces in under a hundred days. The beauty of this weapon was that it cost almost nothing to develop and was easy to mass produce.

The allied leaders positively salivated over the thought of ending the war within three months. The weapon went into full production at a secret location just outside of Reading in Berkshire and in just four weeks they had 500,000 all packed and ready to be shipped to the front.

What was the weapon—it was a strain of the Spanish Flu. Doctor Jensen had discovered a way to put the virus into a state of suspended animation but he also created a solution that not only brought it back to life but also acted as a growth stimulant. All that was required was to load the two totally harmless glass vials into a special hollow shell and fire or drop it into enemy territory. The shell lands, the vials break, the contents atomise and anyone down breeze is infected with an extremely virulent dose of the flu.

Within days, the infected soldiers are not only contagious and spreading the virus further, they become weak and disoriented. Within a week they become completely incapacitated. Only the fittest would survive and even then be so weakened from the illness, be absolutely useless to any fighting force. The mortality rate was estimated at 85%.

The problem with Doctor Jensen's weapon was that it was indiscriminate so before the virus could go anywhere, the scientists had to develop a vaccine that would inoculate our troops against it. Unfortunately, a vaccine couldn't be developed in time and the whole project was disbanded.

The allies now had the problem of how to dispose of 500,000 vials of an extremely contagious and deadly virus. Suggestions included incinerating them at Maralinga and/or Bikini Atoll during the testing of the atom bomb but it was unknown whether the virus would be entirely destroyed by an atomic blast or revived and blown to all corners of the earth.

In the end, after intense lobbying from the Brits and the Yanks, Australia 'volunteered' to store them indefinitely or until a vaccine was developed. All parties agreed and the general population was none the wiser until a rockfall unearthed a hastily hidden tunnel.

And unfortunately, you know the rest.

I'm hoping that, while you and many others have suffered immensely from successive Government procrastination and inaction, you now understand why we had to conceal the contents of the cave in Barclay's Creek from the Australian public and do everything in our power to find that missing canister.

To you and all those that suffered at the hands of unnamed Government agents, I extend a personal and heartfelt apology.

Yours sincerely,
George Peterson
Minister for Defence
Canberra

Chapter 49

Friday 6 March 1970, Office of Mr Jerry O'Rourke, CEO, Nova Aurora Security, Pyrmont, Sydney

"Concord Repat, how can I help you?"

"Would you put me through to Miss Linda West Please?"

"Can I ask who's calling?"

"Yes, sorry, it's Jerry O'Rourke."

"Thank you, Mr O'Rourke. One moment please."

Jerry had read the Minister's letter a third time and then a fourth time; something about it wasn't quite right, but, he couldn't put his finger on what was the cause of his consternation. In the end, he decided to get in contact with Linda and quiz her once more about the box.

"Hello, Jerry! To what do I owe the pleasure?"

"Hello, Linda. Look, I know you're busy, so I won't go into the reason for my call, but, can we meet for coffee somewhere at a time that's convenient for you?"

"Ooo, very mysterious! Jerry, I owe you more than I can ever repay so if it's urgent, I'll be there as soon as my little legs can get me there!"

"No, not urgent, but, could you and Bobby come into my office tomorrow morning, say, 1030?"

"Umm, don't know, Bobby usually cooks pancakes for us on Saturday mornings? Of course, we'll be there—we'll bring the pancakes with us!"

Jerry chuckled, "I'll look forward to it. See you then. Bye."

"Bye."

"Bobby and Linda are here to see you, sir."

"Thanks, David; please take their beverage order and then send them in."

"Espresso for you, sir?"

"Yes, please."

"Come in! Please sit anywhere that's comfortable."

Bobby came over and grasped Jerry's offered hand in both of his, "Great to see you again, Jerry!"

"Likewise, Bobby."

Linda bent down and hugged him then held him at arm's length. "Good to see your business is doing so well, but, how are you facing up physically?"

"Oh, you know, up there one day, down here the next. All things considered, I really can't complain."

They were still shooting the breeze and marvelling at the view when David knocked on the door and entered wheeling a trolley laden with tea and coffee pots and all amounts of milk, cream, sugar, artificial sweeteners—if you could add it to tea and coffee, it was on the trolley. Taking pride of place was a steaming hot stack of freshly reheated blueberry pancakes.

Once David had cleared away the 'debris' of morning tea—and helped himself to a leftover pancake—Jerry retrieved the Minister's letter and wheeled himself over to where Bobby and Linda were seated.

"This is the reason I've asked both of you here today. This is a letter from the Minister for Defence outlining the reasons the Government, wittingly or unwittingly, sanctioned Bobby's abduction and torture. By law, I'm unable to allow you to read the letter or divulge its contents.

"I've read the letter four times, and there is something either in the letter or missing from it that is gnawing at the back of my mind.

"So, if I can't reveal the contents of the letter, my only other option to scratch this itch, is to ask both of you to tell me the whole story of the little green box you took from the Barclay's Creek Quarry Storage Facility. But only if you feel comfortable doing so."

Bobby and Linda exchanged looks, and then Linda took Bobby's hand.

Looking into his eyes she told him about finding the box when he had demolished his apartment in a psychotic rage and how she had then kept it in her office at the hospital.

"You probably had already guessed that I had the box when you couldn't find your model ship."

She turned to Jerry, "Now, I'm guessing that part of the Minister's letter details what the contents were and how lethal they are, etcetera, etcetera."

Jerry smiled, "There I was desperately trying to find a way of telling you what is in this letter when I should have realised you would have put the pieces together! You're exactly right! So what is it that's still troubling me?"

"Probably the same thing that has me puzzled from the moment Bobby and I entered the storage facility; why the fuck—excuse my French—are there still half a million of these supposedly lethal boxes still in that cavern?"

"Right, that is worrying, but that's not what's bugging me. It does answer one question though; when you asked for my and Vic's help in finding Bobby, one of the questions I asked you was 'wasn't either of you tempted to open the box?' and your reply was something like 'well, we knew it wasn't a box of lollies'.

"Now, the normal response to that question would be either 'yes' or 'no'. But you said you 'knew' that it wasn't lollies which infers you also 'knew' what the box did contain. Correct?"

"Correct."

"Would I be correct in assuming you've had the contents tested?"

"Correct, but, the tests were carried out in a commercial and industrial laboratory and not in a medical facility. The findings were inconclusive."

"Do you still have the remaining contents?"

"No, apparently, standard laboratory operating procedures require any unidentifiable matter to be destroyed in their very high-temperature incinerator along with anything else that was used during the testing."

"So, we come back to the question as to why is the Government still holding onto a stockpile of supposedly lethal weapons? And, more importantly, why have they given up looking for the missing box—or have they?"

"Jerry, now all this has come to light, Bobby and I need to have a long, private discussion. Do you mind if we cut this meeting short?"

"Of course not!"

Linda and Bobby stood, said their goodbyes and sombrely left Jerry's office.

Bobby held the car door open for Linda then sat behind the wheel of his Cortina. He sat there silently staring through the windscreen for half a minute before turning in his seat to face Linda.

"Linda—"

She gently placed a hand on his knee.

"Not here, Bobby. Let's go home and I'll explain everything."

Chapter 50

Saturday 7 March 1970, Mortlake, Sydney

"So the original lab report and the empty box are stashed in your office at work?"

Bobby was seated on the lounge while Linda paced up and down the small lounge room.

"Yes."

Bobby sat silently mulling over everything that Linda had told him, occasionally asking a question to clarify the details he didn't fully understand. Finally, he posed the question Linda knew was coming.

"So why haven't you told me any of this before today?"

She sat down beside him.

"You know I love you deeply right?"

"Nearly as much as I love and adore you!"

"What I did or didn't do—I believed at the time—was always, *always*, with your best interests in mind. If looking back on what transpired between the time of us fleeing the quarry and sitting here today, happened as a result of something I did, then I'm profoundly sorry. Would I have acted in any other way knowing what we know now? Absolutely! But would I change what we did if we had our time over, absolutely not! Now, Bobby Massey, do we move forward together or do you want to wallow in the drama of the past?"

Bobby took hold of her hand and manoeuvred her until she was sitting crossways on his lap.

"Nice speech, now it's my turn. I have loved you all my life. The moment you drank milk from my cup in Primary School—"

"You remember that?"

"Sshh, don't interrupt my train of thought!—from that moment, I knew without a doubt that in thirteen years, five months, two weeks, three days, eighteen hours," he glanced at his watch, "and precisely fourteen minutes, I would have you sitting in my lap purring like a kitten. Ow, that hurt!"

"I don't purr!"

"Now, I've forgotten what I was going to say! No, hang on, yes that was it! What I was going to say was that it was only the thought of you and the thought of what those pricks would have done to you if they'd succeeded in breaking me, that kept me alive long enough for Vic and Jerry to rescue me. Do I 'blame' you for me being here; yes I do, because if you hadn't done what you did, I wouldn't be. Wadda you reckon, good speech?"

"Nah, I'm still ahead on points!"

"Want to try double or nothing in the bedroom?"

"Hey! the Groucho Marx eyebrow wiggle is my trick!"

With that, she jumped off his lap and ran towards the bedroom. Kicking off her shoes and pulling her jumper over her head she yelled over her shoulder.

"Last one naked makes dinner!"

Chapter 51

Saturday 7 March 1970, Office of Mr Jerry O'Rourke, CEO, Nova Aurora Security, Pyrmont, Sydney

The gunshot wound Jerry had sustained in the rescue of Bobby Massey had been deemed by the Naval Medical Board—under the direction of the Minister for Defence himself—as a 'severe and permanent injury received in the line of duty'. He was discharged from the Navy 'medically unfit for service' with a full disability pension and a substantial monetary compensation package.

The money he received as compensation went towards paying Doctor David Ramsay for reconstructing his knee.

During his convalescence in the care of his parents or more correctly, the people employed by his parents, Jerry had time to think about what he was going to do for the rest of his working life. It was only when he received a 'Get Well' card from Lieutenant Bill English that he realised where his talents lay. He finally admitted to himself that the most exciting time of his Naval career wasn't commanding a ship during exercises with Australia's allies in the South China Sea, but when a chain of unforeseen events was triggered by an alarm sounding in Hangar 43 at HMAS *Dolphin*.

"A security firm? Are you sure Jeremiah?" Only his mother was allowed to call him 'Jeremiah' "I'm sure Father and I could find you something—what's the word I'm looking for?"

"Upper class?"

"Jeremiah, that's certainly not the word! We're not that kind of people, are we Father?"

"No dear."

"Mum, I'm 45 and quite able to decide what career path to take. I'm letting you know what that career is, not asking your permission. I am hoping that both of you will support my decision—and help me find suitable office space?"

In the end, his father used his vast contacts to not only find him office space on the 24th floor of a complex in Pyrmont with spectacular views of Sydney Harbour but to fit it out ready for him to occupy within six weeks of informing them of his decision. His mother chipped in and insisted she hired and paid the wages of his own Personal Assistant. David had become his right-hand man but Jerry suspected he was also his mother's spy.

Sitting behind his desk, admiring the magnificent view, he couldn't get the nagging thought of why the Department of Defence had permanently sealed the half a million boxes in the cavern rather than destroy the contents?

Linda's revelation regarding the testing and ultimate destruction of the box's contents had rekindled his desire to finally put a full stop to the whole sad and sorry mess. He just needed to work that nagging thought into something tangible and logical.

Chapter 52

Monday 9 March 1970, Office of the Honourable George Peterson MP, Minister for Defence, Canberra, ACT

Henry Edwards knocked on the Minister's door and then entered without waiting for a response.

"Ah, Henry, how did your meeting with Commander O'Rourke go?"

"As expected Minister. Mr O'Rourke is—or was when I left him—still aggrieved over the Government's involvement in the kidnapping of Mr Massey and himself being wounded. Although, to be honest Minister, if I was in his shoes, I think I'd be more than just aggrieved!"

"Quite right Henry. Sadly, with the benefit of knowing the whole story as I do, the Government had little choice but to act the way it did. Did Mr O'Rourke hand you anything to give to me?"

"No, nothing. Was he supposed to?"

"Not really. I was hoping he would return something. Pity. Oh well, can't be helped."

The Minister then walked over to his safe and removed two plain envelopes, one white and the other blue.

"While you're here I have a job for you. Before I tell you what the job is, I need to know that I can rely on your absolute discretion?"

"Minister, I thought that would have been obvious by now, but, if you need affirmation, yes, you can trust me to keep everything that goes on in and on behalf of this office, strictly between the two of us."

"Even if called to give evidence before a Senate inquiry?"

"Yes Minister, my word is my bond."

"Thank you Henry. Do you know where the 1st Military Correctional Establishment Holsworthy is?"

"Yes sir, it's in southwestern Sydney."

"Correct. I have a confidential letter for a prisoner there. I want you to meet with him and have him read this letter in front of you."

The Minister handed his Private Secretary the white envelope, "If, after reading it, he asks you to burn the letter, you are to carry out his wishes and then give the blue envelope to the Establishment's Commanding Officer. You will then drive the shackled and hooded prisoner to this address near Canberra airport."

The blue envelope and a slip of paper followed the white envelope. "If the prisoner places the letter back in its envelope, you will thank him for his time and return to the office. Do you understand what I'm asking of you?"

"Yes, Minister. When do you want me to leave?"

"I'll arrange for you to meet with the prisoner at 1030 Wednesday. Ring me from the Establishment CO's office after your meeting and let me know what the prisoner's decision was."

"Yes, Sir."

"Thank you, Henry."

Chapter 53

Tuesday 10 March 1970, Mortlake, Sydney

"Good Morning, Jerry."

"*Good Morning, Bobby, what can I do for you.*"

"Can you come here for dinner tonight? I mean, would you like to come to dinner tonight?"

Jerry chuckled. "*It's OK, Bobby; yes, I'm capable of catching a cab to your apartment and I would love to come to dinner. Is Linda cooking her amazing Spaghetti Bolognese?*"

"How did you guess?"

"*She threatened to cook it for Vic and I while you were otherwise engaged.*"

"What saved you?"

"I can hear your conversation you know!"

Bobby lowered his voice, "*Takes after her mother; can hear a fly fart 100 feet away. Ow, that hurt!*"

"I take back the rude comments about your Spaghetti Bolognese; it was absolutely divine! And you were spot on with the wine pairing in the 68 Seppelts Moyston Claret too. Thank you." Jerry raised his glass to an obviously pleased Linda.

"Thank you for coming over. It can't be easy?"

"Thankfully, it's getting easier every day. So, what are we celebrating?"

"Help yourself to some more wine while Bobby and I clear away the dishes then we'd like to share a theory with you."

Bobby and Linda joined Jerry in the lounge room about fifteen minutes later. Linda sipped her wine and then addressed Jerry.

"I'm going to hazard a guess and paraphrase the Minister's letter; 'the Government regrets the pain and anguish blah, blah. Please accept our heartfelt apologies blah, blah.

We had no option blah. Contents of box highly dangerous, needed to recover no matter the cost blah, blah and sincerely, blah! That sound about right?"

"I'm pretty sure there were no 'blahs' but other than that, spot on!"

"Right, so what was he hoping to gain? Ministers don't put anything on paper unless he was expecting something beneficial was going to come from it. What is it that he's been after since Day One?"

Jerry's eyes grew wide when the realisation of the obvious answer to Linda's question finally dawned on him.

"The box! He thought I had the box! The letter was basically saying, 'the Government stuffed up, we're sorry, can we have our box back?"

"Exactly!"

"So, what do you suggest we do?"

"Bobby and I have been tossing that question back and forth all weekend. The one thing we can't understand is why they permanently sealed the only access to the stockpile?"

Jerry leaned back in his chair with a huge sigh and slapped his forehead, "The sealing of the tunnel—that's what's been niggling away at the back of my mind! Smoke and mirrors! Yes, the tunnel entrance was permanently sealed giving the illusion that the contents were no longer accessible. But they are!"

"What!?" Linda uttered incredulously.

"When I was investigating your 'break in', I came across a blue steel door at the back of the cavern with 'Emergency Exit' stencilled on it. The door opened into a long tunnel that I'm assuming opens out somewhere on the opposite side of the quarry. The rudimentary plan Commodore Fleming sent for me to navigate my way around the facility had no mention of the 'Emergency Exit'. The four people who know the full story of the cavern didn't want the Commodore or anyone else to know it existed. Why? Because they still want access to what's in those boxes!"

"My God!"

"Well, come on you two." Bobby piped up, "how are we going to make sure that never happens?"

"Bobby, how would you and Linda like a drive in the country?"

Chapter 54

Wednesday 11 March 1970, 1st Military Correctional Establishment, Holsworthy, NSW

"Good morning, Mr Brauer, my name is Henry Edwards and I'm the Personal Assistant to the Minister for Defence, the Honourable George Peterson MP. Please sit."

Henry had been expecting the 'Visitors Lounge' to contain bolted-down stainless steel tables and chairs and armed guards standing close by. He was therefore surprised to find vinyl-topped tables and padded wooden chairs and not a guard in sight!

"To what do I owe the pleasure?"

"Mr—is it Mister or Sergeant?"

"'Mister' is fine."

"Mr Brauer, the Minister has asked me to hand-deliver this letter to you." Henry slid the sealed envelope over the table.

"Is this my 'Get out of Jail Free' card?"

"I have no idea of the contents of the letter, but putting two and two together, I'd say it may well be."

The ex-Special Air Services Sergeant opened the envelope and read the letter. After reading it, he leaned back in his chair and closed his eyes, obviously seriously considering the contents of the letter. After several minutes, he sat forward, pinched the bridge of his nose, sighed and then folded and slid the letter back across the desk.

"Fuck it! How much further can I fall—Burn it!"

Three hours later, Henry removed Mr Brauer's shackles—he hadn't seen the need for the hood remaining on once they were on the highway—and let him out of the car.

"I guess you know the layout of this place?"

"Yep and where the front door key is hidden. I just hope the code for the alarm system hasn't been changed."

"Sorry, can't help you there. Good luck, Mr Brauer."

They shook hands before Henry returned to his car and drove back to Parliament House.

"Do you have everything you need, Sergeant?"

"Well, a bottle of 18-year-old Glenmorangie would have been a nice welcome-home present! But apart from that, yes, I do have everything I need.

"When do I get the information on the target?"

"The package will be in a briefcase identical to the one that's sitting on your dining room table.

"You will wear the charcoal suit and hat that's in your bedroom wardrobe and visit the Australian National Library at 0930 tomorrow. Go to the information desk and ask to see the Canberra Times archives then leave your briefcase in the Cloak Room. Go to the reading room and take the microfilm spool to the reader on the far left near the 'Exit'.

"Place your Cloak Room check ticket on the left-hand side of the machine. Someone will brush past and knock it to the floor. That person will bend down, pick it up and place another ticket in its place. Continue scanning the microfilm for another thirty minutes before retrieving the replacement briefcase.

"Ring me on my private line if you have any questions, otherwise, I expect to hear or read of your success within three days from midnight tonight. If the mission is a success, a car will be delivered to the house. In the boot, you will find your new identity documents, fifty thousand US dollars and a one-way ticket to Argentina."

"Thank you, sir."

Chapter 55

Wednesday 11 March 1970, Barclay's Creek Police Station

"Can I help you?" the young Constable asked from behind the counter of the Police Station.

"Yes Constable, can you tell Senior Sergeant Rogers that Jerry O'Rourke would like to see him and that Madam Georgia sends her regards."

A minute later a booming laugh came rolling out of Vic's office followed by a bellowed, "***O'Rourke get your malingering arse in here!***"

A smiling Constable returned to the counter and opened the door for the trio to enter.

Vic was holding his office door open so Bobby could push Jerry's wheelchair inside.

"Well, the band's back together! Where's our next gig?"

"Funny you should ask, but you'd better close the door before I lay it out."

Vic thumped his desk. "The duplicitous bastards! So from what you're saying, the 'Faceless Four' were using the Office of Naval Intelligence and an unwitting Commodore Fleming to do their dirty work—recover the box and its lethal contents at all costs! Unfortunately, they didn't anticipate the tenacity of a brave young soldier and the cunning of his girlfriend.

"You do realise they will still be determined to recover their property? The one thing in your favour is that they are shit-scared of being even remotely linked to any overt action against you. Their next attempt will be better planned and—I hate to say it—have a more dire outcome than the last."

"That's why we have to strike first! How far does your area of jurisdiction extend?" Jerry asked.

"In which direction?"

"Let me put it another way; does it include the far side of the quarry entrance?"

"Yes, the highway is our border so we cover an extensive area on the other side of the hill. It's all open grazing land though?"

"Do you mind if we take a drive over there and have a look?"

"Not at all."

Vic pulled off the side of the road in a position where they looked out over the whole hillside.

"As you can see, there's certainly no tunnel! The house down there on the right belongs to the Williams and the house over there half way up the hill is owned by Peter Ferris."

"Have you met the owners?" Jerry asked.

"Yep, the first job in taking up the position—visit the locals. Bill and Moira Williams took over the farm from their father who inherited it from his father, one of the pioneers in the district. They subdivided the farm in the early fifties; a Mr Peter Ferris has owned the carved-off farm since 1958 but I've never actually met him. I'm assuming he's a Macquarie Street farmer and just purchased the property as a tax dodge."

"There must be an exit from that tunnel somewhere on that hillside. It would be completely illogical to only half construct an emergency exit! Can we drive up to the Ferris place?"

"No problem."

Bill Williams was slashing one of his paddocks and waved as the Police car drove past. Vic stopped at the entry to Peter Ferris's property, "Can you get the gate for me, Bobby?"

Bobby hopped out and went to open the gate; five seconds later he was back, "No can do, Vic, the gate's chained and locked. Been that way for a while I'd say judging from the spider webs clinging to it. Do you want me to jump the fence and knock on the door?"

"No, if Mr Ferris was in, the gate wouldn't be locked. What you can do though, is go and walk through the paddock behind the house and see if you can find anything resembling a door to a tunnel. In the meantime, I'm going to have a chat with Bill."

"On it. Linda, fancy a tromp through the hay?"

"Didn't they teach you anything in school; it only becomes hay when it's cut and dried, but yes, I'll 'tromp' through the grass with you."

Bobby easily lifted Linda over the fence and the pair skipped through the knee-high grass like two teenagers.

"Ah, to be young again," Jerry sighed.

"I can't remember being that young!" Vic reversed the car back down the gravel road to the Williams entry and then drove over the cattle grid up to the house. Moira must have seen the car coming and was waiting for them on the front veranda.

"G'day Vic, haven't seen you out this way for a while?"

"Morning, Moira. Hope we're not disturbing you?"

"I was just taking some scones out of the oven but apart from that, nothing till Bill takes a break for lunch. Come in, I'll put the kettle on."

Vic retrieved a pair of crutches from the boot and then helped Jerry out of the car.

"You right with the steps?"

"As long as take my time."

Vic and Jerry were just finishing their tea and scones when a breathless Bobby and Linda knocked on Moira's kitchen door.

"It's open!"

"You are not going to believe this!" Bobby managed to say.

"You two look like you need a nice cup of tea." Moira greeted the pair, "Sit yourselves down and help yourself to a scone while I make a fresh pot."

"Did you notice how the Ferris house is built on a cut into the side of the hill?" Bobby continued.

Both Vic and Jerry nodded.

"Well, when we walked up the hill on the far side of the house we noticed something unusual; the back of the garage butts up against the rock wall. Now why, with all that acreage to play with, would you do that?"

"To conceal the exit from the tunnel!" Jerry exclaimed.

Having spoken with Bill and Moira about Peter Ferris they discovered that the last time he was on the property was about this time three years ago.

"I remember it was around this time of the year because he borrowed our slasher to cut his grass. Look at it now! A grass fire would go through there like pork fat through a duck!"

Once the group had polished off another helping of Moira's tea and scones, they returned to Vic's office to discuss their findings.

Vic produced an A4 pad from his desk and started writing.

'I, as the Officer in Charge of the Barclay's Creek Police Station and with the assistance of,

"I'll add your names and contact details later,"

'have established that a cache of biological weapons is stored inside the supposedly sealed cavern behind the abandoned Barclay's Creek quarry. We know that a cabal in Canberra orchestrated the abduction of Bobby Massey in a failed attempt at retrieving one of half a million small boxes from that cache that allegedly contain an unknown and currently inert bacterial strain.

'The same group tried in vain to keep a so-called 'Emergency Exit' tunnel a secret. Following an inspection of a homestead leased by a Mr Peter Ferris but now apparently abandoned, situated on the opposite side of the quarry, I have reason to believe that the garage to the homestead conceals the exit from that tunnel.

'I also have reason to believe that the Canberra group comprise four high ranking Government officials; the Minister for Defence, Mr George Peterson is one of those officials. The other three remain unknown. Evidence to support many of the above assertions is available.'

"Have I covered everything?"

"I believe you've encapsulated what's taken thirteen years to determine, yes," Jerry replied. "The question now is; what are you going to do with it?"

"Can I make a suggestion?" Linda asked.

"By all means, because, at the moment, all I can see happening is that we're about to hit a hornet's nest with a cricket bat!"

"Thanks, Vic. Before I do though, I'd just like to say that deep down in my heart, I believe that no matter what righteous path you and Jerry choose, the 'Faceless Four' will walk away unblemished and unpunished. After what those—and I can't use the word that immediately comes to mind—those fucking arseholes put Bobby through, I'm not going to let that happen! Now my suggestion is that you and Jerry seek a confidential and off-the-record meeting with Australian Federal Police Commissioner Duncombe and present him with your report. Hopefully, his boss isn't one of the Four!"

"I agree with everything Linda has said and what she has implied," Bobby added. "We are not going to let those pricks get off Scot-free!"

Linda touched his arm. "Thanks, Bobby. Vic, Jerry—if you'll excuse us, Bobby and I need to have a private chat." With that, they walked out of Vic's office.

"That young lady is too smart for her own good! What do you think Jerry; is a meeting with Commissioner Duncombe a viable option?"

"Andy Duncombe is his own man and wouldn't let anyone dissuade him from conducting an investigation—if he believes there is something to investigate."

"OK, do you have his number?"

Chapter 56

Wednesday 11 March 1970, Barclay's Creek

"Linda," she stopped and faced him. "You have a look in your eyes that I've never seen before and, quite frankly, it's scaring the hell out of me!"

She carried on staring at him with a steely determination until her pulse rate had slowed and the seething anger slowly abated enough to reply.

"How long are we going to let those bastards control our lives Bobby?" the venom in her quavering voice revealing the depth of her feelings, "How many times are we going to wake at night at the slightest creak or banging of a door? When are we going to be able to go anywhere without checking to see if anyone is following us? They're out there, Bobby." She swung both arms around.

"Right this minute they're out there, if not actively looking for us, they'll be planning and plotting to ensure that two insignificant 'Neddy Nobodies' never, ever reveal the secret that lies behind that fucking quarry! If I'm scaring you, that's good, because I'm shit scared myself." With that, all her emotions crashed and she collapsed crying hysterically in Bobby's arms.

On leaving the Police Station, Bobby had suggested they walk down to the *Lakeside Inn* and grab a counter-lunch. After that, they could talk about whatever Linda had in mind when she excused herself and Bobby from Vic's meeting. They were only halfway there when Linda had her meltdown. Bobby steered her to a nearby bus stop and sat her down. He knew there was nothing he could say that would make her feel better so he just sat beside her and held her until she had cried herself out.

Three minutes later she lifted her head and smiled lamely up at Bobby. "I suppose I look like the wreck of the Hesperus?"

Bobby handed her a handkerchief. "Well, I have seen redder eyes in photos but only just!"

Linda dabbed her eyes and blew her nose then held out the handkerchief to return to Bobby.

"Eeuw, I'll let you keep that one thank you very much."

Linda hugged him and snuggled into his side. "What would I do without you?" Standing, she held out her hand, "Come on, let's get to the pub before lunchtime finishes."

"We have to strike the first blow. We can't just cringe in a corner and wait for the bogeyman to turn up." Linda had regained her composure completely and together they were nutting out a first-strike plan. "But how do we hurt someone when we don't even know who they are or where they are?"

"First order of battle; 'know thine enemy'—don't know who I pinched that from, but it sounds good, secondly, don't start a war unless you're sure you have a bloody good chance of winning and lastly, make sure you have enough ammunition!" Bobby offered. "So we don't know who the 'Faceless Four' are—apart from the Minister for Defence—but we do know their methods so, we fight fire with fire!"

"Any suggestion as to how we do that?"

"Yes—but you won't like it!"

"That's not as crazy as you think!" Linda remarked after Bobby has sketched out his plan, "Do we get Jerry and Vic involved?"

"No, unfortunately, Jerry's injury rules him out and both have got too much to lose if the plan turns to custard."

"You do realise that the whole plan rests on our supposition that the 'Faceless Four' have no local agents?"

"They have survived at least twenty years by playing their cards close to their collective chest. They're certainly not going to employ anyone to watch an abandoned farmhouse."

Chapter 57

Wednesday 11 March 1970, Barclay's Creek Police Station

"*Commissioner Duncombe.*"

"Commissioner, it's Senior Sergeant Vic Rogers from Barclay's Creek."

"*Yes Sergeant, how can I help you.*"

"Commissioner, I have you on speaker for the benefit of Jerry O'Rourke."

"*Jerry, how are you? Understand you had a bad accident on your motorbike? Funny that, seeing you've never owned a motorbike or possessed a motorcycle Licence.*"

"Now, that's one of the reasons I suggested to Vic that we call you—nothing gets past you!"

The Commissioner chuckled, "*Good to speak to you again, Jerry. What are you after this time?*"

Vic chimed in, "Sir, we have uncovered a very serious crime perpetrated by high-ranking Australian Government officials and would like an off-the-record meeting with you as soon as possible."

"*Vic, I should have warned you earlier, but all my calls are recorded. I can delete this conversation but I recommend that we terminate this call and I'll ring you back on a secure, unmonitored line. Give me five minutes.*"

Commissioner Duncombe rang them back in under five minutes and agreed to meet with them in *The Winding Road Pantry* in Jugiong about two hours from Barclay's Creek at 11:00 in the morning.

Bobby and Linda booked a room in the *Lakeside Inn* then returned to the Police Station to let Jerry know that they had decided to stay overnight. Jerry was delighted because he too was staying overnight as he and Vic had a meeting with Commissioner Duncombe in the morning.

At 2:30 a.m. Thursday morning, Bobby and Linda, dressed in newly acquired navy blue overalls, gloves and black beanies, slipped out of the hotel and keeping to the shadows wherever possible, made their way up the road to the quarry. Without stopping at the quarry, they continued along the dirt road until they were adjacent to the Ferris property.

"Does this feel a bit déjà vu?" Bobby asked.

"Yes it does. I'm just hoping the Williams don't have any dogs!"

"There weren't any when we were there yesterday."

"Here, let me lift you over the fence."

"The front door is securely locked and bolted."

"So is the back door!"

"The windows are sliding sash type and I bet they're nailed shut.

"Have a hunt around and see if you can find something to deaden the sound of a breaking window."

Two minutes later, Linda returned with a front door mat.

"Will this do?"

"One way to find out! Hold it over the lower pane and turn your head away."

Bobby took the Cortina's jack handle from inside his overalls and gave the middle of the mat a healthy blow. The breaking glass made the most noise as it fell onto the bare floor boards inside the room. It was doubtful that it would have been heard at the front of the house let alone the Williams place over half a kilometre away.

Bobby carefully removed the remaining shards from the window frame then reached inside and opened the lock. Surprisingly, the window wasn't nailed shut and opened easily. Using the front door mat to cover the broken glass, he climbed into the house and then felt his way carefully to the back door and unlocked and opened it for Linda. There was enough ambient light to allow them to see the scant pieces of furniture scattered here and there and they made their way through the house without tripping over anything.

They had just turned a corner in the hall when Linda pointed to the glow emanating from under a door at the end of a short passageway.

Linda twisted the door handle and pushed on the door.

"It won't open. I think it's locked on the inside."

"Try pulling instead of pushing."

The door swung into the passage and revealed a spacious garage softly bathed in a red glow from a large control panel on the back wall. Taking up most of the space though was a dusty black 1966 XR Ford Falcon 500 sedan with a pristine red vinyl interior—with the keys in the ignition.

"Wow!"

"I bet you say that to all the Fords! Do you think it could crash through that locked gate if the need arises?"

"What and scratch the duco? Not bloody likely!"

"OK, enough drooling, let's do what we came here to do!"

The pair of them walked to the rear of the garage, where, as expected, was a plain white door. Bobby went to try the handle but Linda stopped him.

"Before we go charging in, let's just have a look at what we have in here. How much light do you reckon would leak through that roller door?"

"Too much. There's a six-inch gap at the top and about half an inch down both sides. On a moonless night like tonight, it would stand out like a lighthouse."

"Let's have a look in those lockers on the side there. We might find a torch."

As luck would have it, the lockers held work clothes, hard hats, goggles and head lamps.

Out of the four available, only one had power remaining in the battery. Holding her hand over the beam, Linda allowed just enough light to seep out for them to inspect the various switches, dials and signs.

The one switch they were most interested in had the label *Alarm Isolating Switch*. Unfortunately, it required a key to unlock it and turn it off.

"Bugger!"

"How are we going for time?"

"3.15—we have roughly another forty-five minutes before we have to leave."

"Right. Ten minutes to search for the key. I'll check the lockers, you take the torch and check obvious places; hooks near the front and back doors, drawers in the kitchen, and drawers in anything that looks like an office desk. Go!"

Eight minutes later Bobby returned, "Nothing."

"Nothing here either. Shit, shit, shit!"

"I did find these though; spare batteries for the head lamps. Wearing these we could be in and out in under twenty minutes. We'd be having breakfast before anyone arrived to investigate the alarm."

"No. That defeats the purpose of us being here. Come on let's cut our losses and head back."

With heads hung in disappointment, they headed for the back door. Linda had just opened the door when Bobby exclaimed, "The Ford!"

"Bobby, be realistic, there's no way you could possibly take the Ford!"

"But I could, couldn't I?"

"No! What are you going on about?"

"Think about it—I *could* take it."

"Oh, for crying out loud Bobby, sometimes you—" her eyes widened. "No, they wouldn't be that silly would they?"

"One way to find out!"

They hurried back to the garage where Bobby took the Ford's keys out of the ignition and approached the control panel. Sorting through them he found a small key that most certainly wouldn't have fitted anything in the car. Nervously, he slipped the key easily into the switch and turned it off.

"You fucking beauty! Oh, sorry Linda!"

"Don't worry—you took the words right out of my mouth!"

Dawn was breaking when two tired and dirty people deposited overalls, gloves and beanies in the Hotel's rubbish skip and quietly made their way back to their room. A small, sealed, *Erinmore Flake* tobacco tin1-size, army olive drab box was placed on their bedside table.

Chapter 58

Thursday 12 March 1970, *The Winding Road Pantry,* Jugiong, NSW

Vic parked the unmarked police car in the carpark beside *The Winding Road Pantry*. He was helping Jerry up the six wooden steps to the entrance when a man almost the mirror image of Vic, but with more hair, came out of the cafe.

"Here, let me help you up these steps." then lowering his voice, "*Grab a coffee to go and meet me in the park opposite.*"

"You mean I'm struggling up these steps for nothing!" Jerry grumbled.

"There you go champ! Try the Banoffee cake; it's fabulous!"

Ten minutes later, after Jerry had struggled back down the steps, they found Andy Duncombe sitting at a picnic table concealed from the Cafe and the road by a large weeping willow tree.

"Andy, good to see you again." Jerry shook his hand, "Andy Duncombe, Vic Rogers."

Andy extended his hand, "Very pleased to me you after all this time Senior Sergeant Rogers."

Vic took Andy's offered hand, "Likewise Commissioner, but please, it's 'Vic'."

They shook hands, each testing the grip of the other, "Andy."

"These are extremely serious and worrying allegations—and Miss West has the evidence to support them?" Andy asked after reading Vic's report.

"She does."

"I guess both of you have considered the possibility that my boss, the Minister for the Interior, could be one of the four members of the group?"

Jerry fielded the question. "We have, but, as I pointed out to Vic, I think I know you well enough to believe that it won't stop you from investigating these allegations."

"You're right, but it makes my job very difficult—not impossible, but almost!

"I'll need some time to assemble a team of special investigators, in the meantime, I would like to deputise you both temporarily. The idea behind it is the fact that you're already up to speed plus each of you is close to the scenes of both crimes.

"Before I head back to Canberra; how committed are you and Vic to seeing this through? Because I have to warn you that if you thought the kidnapping was the group's end game, you will be sadly disappointed. No matter how hard I try to keep the investigation under the radar, sooner or later, they'll find out and it's not me with the target on his back!"

"Andy, my job is to uphold the law regardless of any personal danger. I think I'm also correct in saying that Jerry hobbling around on one leg is testimony enough of his commitment. Would I be right there, Jerry?"

"One hundred percent, my friend!"

"Right then, I'll set the wheels in motion. I'll contact Vic when and if there are any developments. Please give my regards to Miss West; without that young lady's courage and tenacity, we wouldn't be having this conversation."

The Commissioner got up from the table and returned to his car leaving Vic and Jerry to finish their coffees and Banoffee cake—that was indeed, delicious.

Chapter 59

Thursday 12 March 1970, Government Precinct, Canberra, ACT

"I still think Vic should be involved in this part!"

Bobby and Linda were huddled in a phone box a short distance from the Lakeside Inn. 'Just in case calls to Parliament House can be traced!' Linda had reasoned.

"Listen to me, while Vic the man would agree to help us in a heartbeat, we can't ask Vic the policeman to knowingly break the law. No Bobby, we, that's you and me, have to do this on our own."

She picked up the handset and made the call.

"Minister, I have a Miss Linda West on the phone asking to speak to you. She refuses to tell me what it's about but she does sound quite upset."

"Thanks, Henry, I'll take the call on my private line in the ante room."

George Peterson smiled. "Finally, she's come to her senses!" He settled back into his armchair with a supercilious smile on his face and lifted the receiver from the unmonitored line.

"Good morning, Miss West, how lovely to hear from you. How's Bobby coping after his terrible ordeal?"

Linda broke down into a fit of sobbing.

"There, there my poor child! What's got you so upset?"

The sobbing eased and a quivering little voice said, *"I'm sorry!"*

"What was that?"

"I said I'm sorry!"

"And well you should be, young lady! Stealing that box has not only caused you and your boyfriend great distress but the Australian taxpayer has spent thousands of their hard-earned dollars trying to retrieve it! The galling part of all this is the fact that you still haven't returned the Government's property! So if you're expecting forgiveness, you will be sadly disappointed!"

Linda drew a deep breath. *"No Minister, I don't expect or seek forgiveness, but I am looking for redemption. I still have the sealed box in my possession and I will gladly return it to you just to assuage this guilt that is dragging me down."*

"Well thank you, at last, Miss West, I'll send my Personal Assistant to retrieve it. What's your address?"

Linda's tone changed abruptly, *"Minister, don't take me for a fool! You know what my address is seeing your goons raided it in a bungled attempt at recovering your precious box. Do I for an instant believe you will accept the box and leave Bobby and I to live the rest of our lives in peace; no! So before I hand over the box to you personally, you will give me written guarantees that you will call off your dogs. Once you hand me those documents, then and only then, will I hand you the box."*

If the sudden change in Linda's voice surprised him, the Minister didn't outwardly react.

"How can I be so sure you actually have the box and that you'll stick to the deal?"

"You can't, but they're my terms. I'll give you twenty-four hours to confer with the other three members of the 'Faceless Four'. I'll ring you this time tomorrow. Oh, I nearly forgot—you really, really don't want to refuse my offer!"

*"**Are you threatening me!**"* he screamed into a disconnected line.

What he didn't hear was Henry Edwards carefully hanging up the party line.

****

When Vic and Jerry returned to Barclay's Creek, they found Bobby and Linda in the waiting room of the Police Station.

"How did your meeting with the Commissioner go?" Bobby asked.

"Come on through to my office and we'll fill you in."

"Does that make you feel more at ease Linda?" Jerry asked once they had passed on the details of their meeting with the Commissioner.

"Let's put it this way; it's a step in the right direction. Do I believe the Federal Police will ultimately charge all those involved; no, I don't. But, to tell you the truth, I'm tired of the whole business and would like nothing better than retiring to my chalet in the Swiss Alps—if I had one!

"Jerry, Vic thank you again for all you have done for us both, but now it's in the hands of the Federal Police, Bobby and I are going underground for a few days to just relax and try to forget that damn box! We've decided to stay another night in the pub before heading off to places unknown. Are you OK getting back to Sydney, Jerry?"

"Don't worry about me, I'll manage. Might even stay the night myself and catch the morning train home."

Chapter 60

Friday 13 March 1970, Government Precinct, Canberra, ACT

"We need some bolt cutters to open the gate to the Ferris place."

"Good idea Bobby, but if my intuition is correct, Peter Ferris AKA George Peterson, will have a key to the padlock."

"If Peterson refuses to cooperate, won't the Mr and Mrs Williams be suspicious if two cars leave the property?"

"When Peterson arrives, we turn the houselights on, the Williams then realise it must be Peter Ferris returning after all this time and go back to watching *Division Four*."

Linda nervously checked her watch for the umpteenth time. "You clear on what you have to do and more importantly, are you sure you can go through with it?"

"Hey, I'm nervous as hell but I can't wait to get the bastard here so I can return a long overdue favour!"

"You'll be fine! Before I ring Peterson, let's just run through the plan one more time."

"*Minister, Miss West.*"

"Thanks Henry, put her through to the ante room.

"Miss West."

"*Minister. Sounds like some of the wind has gone out of your sails. Your three chums not happy with you?*"

"Stop with the games, Miss West, just tell me how I get my property back."

"'*Your property'—surely you mean 'the Government's property', Minister? Never mind; you have exactly three minutes and forty seconds to reach the payphone in the street fifty yards to your left as you exit the building. Starting— now!*"

George Peterson had been caught off guard. He was hoping to have sufficient time to organise a support team. Two seconds was all it took to make up his mind as to go or try to delay the process—he paused long enough to grab his hat and coat and then raced from the building. He heard he phone ringing and then suddenly stop when he was ten feet away.

"Shit!" He turned around, trying to see if anyone was watching him, but the whole area was empty. Ten seconds later, the phone started to ring again. Flinging open the door, he snatched the handset off its hook.

"What the fu—" the line went dead. "Ahhh!" The phone rang again. Calmly, he put the phone to his ear.

"Are you calm now, George? The last thing Parliament needs is one of their Ministers dying from a heart attack on its front steps."

"Yes, I'm calm!"

"You don't sound calm? What you need is a holiday in the country! Now I hope you remembered the signed guarantees in your haste to answer the phone?"

The silence lasted all of two seconds.

"Oh dear, the one and only bargaining chip you had and you left it sitting on your desk! Tell you what, I'm going to forgive you George—only because I have some typed up and ready for your signature when you arrive. Now, have you regained your breath, you have, excellent, because now you have two minutes and thirty-six seconds to run over to the Albert Hall and climb into the passenger seat of a green Cortina parked in the driveway. Starting—now!"

He made it in just over two minutes and collapsed into the seat next to Bobby. As he turned to see who the driver was an elbow smashed into the bridge of his nose and he slumped forward, unconscious.

A minute later, Linda climbed into the back seat behind the Minister.

"Just as well I put that towel in the wheel-well, he's bleeding like a stuck pig!" Bobby complained.

Linda pulled the lever that allowed the front seat to recline and pulled it back against her knees. Grabbing the back of Peterson's coat, she yanked him back in the seat.

"The stupid prick forgot our signed guarantees! I don't think he planned on us attacking him on his home turf. No one is tailing him so he obviously hasn't had time to organise a back-up crew. Pass me the towel Bobby then let's head back to the house."

She cleaned George Peterson up with the already bloody towel and pinched his nose to stem the flow of blood. She was pleased to hear Peterson breathing through his mouth. The last thing they needed was a dead bargaining chip!

Once the blood flow had slowed, she pulled his arms behind the seat and tied them together, then roughly patted him down to see if he was wearing any recording devices. His wallet was in his jacket but nothing looked suspicious so she put it back. All the other coat pockets were empty but his right trouser pocket contained a bunch of keys.

She knew she had hit the jackpot when she identified a small key that fitted the *Alarm Disable Switch*. The Law of Probabilities meant that one of the others would fit the padlock on the Ferris property gate. The one thing she couldn't reach was his shoes but she hoped that the gadgets 'Q' provided James Bond were only movie fiction.

The only remaining thing she had to do was mix four of Bobby's Valium capsules in some water and pour it down George Peterson's throat. With his nose blocked with congealing blood, Peterson's gag reflex coughed up the first mouthful. After that, she would wait until he woke up and then let him drink it himself.

One of Peterson's keys did open the locked gate and as she was closing it behind the car, she saw a light coming from Moira's kitchen window as she moved the curtain aside.

"We'll have to wait and see if our arriving has her ringing the police," she said to the star-filled sky. George Peterson had come around an hour earlier and had started twisting violently in the seat and cursing and swearing loudly.

Linda had grabbed his ear and twisted it viciously, "You have two options George—one, I put the seat upright and let Bobby give you another taste of his elbow or, two, you can lay back and think of England!"

A few seconds later, Peterson sighed and sank back in the seat. "Excellent choice, George!

Now, if you're going to behave, I'll give you a drink. Are you going to behave George?" He nodded his assent. Linda held the water bottle to Peterson's lips and he drank greedily, blissfully unaware of its contents.

One of Peterson's keys also fitted the front door and now the pair of them were half assisting half dragging a very relaxed and smiling Minister for Defence into the house.

Against her better judgement but bending to the ethics of her profession, she had straightened Peterson's nose and stuffed it with a gauze bandage she had found in a first aid kit.

As Linda had suggested, they turned the lights on in the house to allay any concerns the Williams had when Moira had seen the car drive through the gate. Bobby reversed the Falcon out of the garage, drove the Cortina in and then closed the roller door just to add weight to the charade.

Peterson awoke feeling very relaxed—right up until the moment he realised he was bound to a chair and that; "*I can't see a fugging thing! Oww, whad happened to my node?*"

"Ah, sleeping beauty awakens! Good morning, Minister, I trust you slept well?"

"Fugg you!"

"Bobby, lights please."

The storage cavern lit up and when George Peterson realised where he was, he knew he was a dead man walking. His head sagged to his chest and his whole body seemed to deflate.

"Bravo, Miss West! If my hands were free, I'd even applaud. We underestimated you, young lady. In just over six months you've single-handedly undone over twenty-eight years of secrecy."

"For what, George? Twenty-eight years of secrecy for what? So that four power brokers in Canberra could get rich selling these," she waved an arm in the direction of the dull green crates, "these 'weapons' to the highest bidder?"

"You don't understand! Yes, we stood to make some money from any future transaction, but, how else are we going to stop the yellow hordes from robbing us of the democratic society we have come to treasure?

"Do you think for one moment that the Communist Chinese will stop with the fall of Democracy in South Vietnam? South Vietnam is only the springboard to Malaysia, Singapore, Indonesia and finally Australia and New Zealand. When—not if—when they reach our shores, for how long do you think we could put up at least a decent fight? Our own Defence analysts predict seventy-two hours, three fucking days Miss West! The Prime Minister may as well stand on the wharf in Darwin and give Chairman Mao the key to the country and save countless Australian lives."

"So these so-called weapons are going to prevent that from happening? I'm guessing you still haven't developed a vaccine against this virus?"

"No, but we are actively working on it!"

"And how long do you think it would take the scientists in China to develop a vaccine?"

Silence.

"Exactly! So stop feeding me bullshit George and tell me which third-world nation these are being sold to!"

Silence. Then as a last attempt at escaping with his life, George Peterson said, "Regardless of whether I tell you what you want to know, you realise I'll be dead within twenty-four hours of leaving here?"

"Remember, my first phone call to your office? I said I was seeking redemption—it was all bullshit, of course—but," Linda bent down and looked the Australian Government Minister for Defence straight in the eye. "What you have to decide right here, right now, George, is do you want to die as the scum-bag Minister that used the powers of his Office to keep secret a cache of biological weapons for his own personal gain or seek redemption by turning whistle-blower and ending up in a Witness Protection program whiling away the rest of your pathetic life in Surfers Paradise?

Before you decide, I'm going to provide an incentive for you to vote in favour of the latter; if you choose the former," Linda paused and removed the sealed box that she and Bobby had retrieved the previous night from her pocket. George Peterson's eyes grew wide in horror as he watched Linda slowly remove the tape sealing the box, "then Bobby and I will simply leave you tied to that chair with a mixture of these two vials in your lap and reseal the complex!"

"You don't have the guts!"

"Try me! Here's a sample of what to expect—I'll be back in two hours. Bobby, lights!"

Linda switched on her headlamp and then she and Bobby returned to the house.

****

"Good morning, Vic, have you listened to the news this morning?"

"*Good morning, Commissioner and yes I have. I guess you'll be run off your feet until you find him?*"

"Unfortunately no, I'll be stuck behind a microphone most of the day trying to explain how the Minister for Defence has walked out of Parliament House and disappeared.

"What hasn't been disclosed is that the Federal Police wish to speak with one Miss Linda West who's private phone conversation was illegally listened to by the Minister's Personal Assistant, Mr Henry Edwards. In the overheard conversation the Minister refers to a box that Miss West allegedly stole from him. She then advises the Minister that she will call back with instructions on how the box can be recovered.

"At the same time the following day, Miss West rang the Minister again. Approximately two minutes later, the Minister grabbed his hat and coat and raced from the building. A security guard standing on the steps of Parliament House reports seeing him go into a telephone box and then race off in the direction of the Albert Hall. I'm sorry but I have to ask; have you seen or heard from Miss West in the last twenty-four hours?"

"No Andy, the last Jerry and I saw of Linda and Bobby was when they left my office around 1630 yesterday afternoon and headed back to the Lakeside Inn."

"Thanks, Vic. I must advise you that two Federal Police Officers are on their way to interview you and anyone who may have spoken to or seen them since Tuesday. One other thing concerning the matter we discussed recently; suffice to say Mr Edwards has been singing like a canary about the Minister's, shall I say 'out of portfolio activities'! Please contact me directly if either Bobby and/or Linda resurface."

"Roger that."

****

George Peterson had never been so scared as he was right now. His entire body was shaking with fear. He had never experienced the 'feel' of darkness or more correctly, the absolute absence of light. The blackness was clinging to him like a shroud, he could feel it in his mouth, working its way down his throat. He had tried coughing it up but then he had to inhale it into his lungs. It coated his eyes and no matter how much he blinked, it stuck firmly in place. He knew without a shadow of doubt that if he stayed in this void of imagined viscous black nothing for much longer he would go completely insane.

And then the lights came on.

"Thank you, thank you, thank you!"

"Well George, what'll be, more bullshit and what's left of your pitiful life—once this biological 'weapon' has its wicked way with you—spent in total darkness or a chance of redemption."

"Anything, anything you want but please, please don't turn off the lights!" he whimpered pathetically.

"Good boy."

Linda snapped the lid back on the box and Bobby removed the ropes that bound the Minister's arms to the chair.

"Lean forward and put your hands behind your back." Bobby roughly tied Peterson's hands and then removed the remainder of his bonds.

Linda locked and sealed the exit door from the tunnel and rearmed the alarm system.

Bobby marched Peterson through the house to the kitchen breakfast bar where he tied Peterson's legs to a stool and then untied his hands. Sitting on the breakfast bar was an A4 notepad and two pens.

"There you go sunshine, confession time. Take your time, leave nothing out and I mean nothing. Even if you went for a piss during a meeting with your three mates, I want to know. When you've reached the end of the first page, I run my 'bullshit meter' over it, if it passes, I'll give you a cup of tea; the second page—breakfast and so on. However, if the 'bullshit meter' dings, we put you back in the pit of doom forever. Understood?"

"Understood."

Four and a half hours later, a smiling Bobby drove the Falcon 500 to the Barclay's Creek Police Station and presented Vic with five neatly handwritten A4 pages signed by 'G. Peterson, Honourable Minister for Defence' – although someone had crossed out 'Honourable'. He also handed Vic the resealed box they took from the cavern the previous night.

"Here's what all the fuss has been about. Linda and I don't believe we'll need to hold onto this 'insurance' from being hunted by George Peterson and his cronies any longer!" He just hoped there wouldn't be another stocktake of the cavern anytime soon.

Two hours after that at 3:15 a.m. Saturday morning, the Minister for Defence, the Honourable George Peterson MP was arrested by Senior Sergeant Rogers and charged with multiple offences including the kidnapping and torture of Sapper Robert Massey.

Miss Linda West and Mr Robert Massey were also arrested—albeit, reluctantly—by Senior Sergeant Rogers and charged with the abduction, assault and unlawful detention of Mr George Peterson. Charges that were subsequently dropped when the victim chose not to press charges following a private one-on-one meeting with Senior Sergeant Rogers.

After Bobby and Linda had been released from the hastily cleared cell in the Barclay's Creek Police Station, Bobby asked Vic if he could keep the black Ford Falcon 500 that had been impounded. Vic laughed at Bobby's audacity but suggested he contact the Department of Motor Transport to find out who the rightful owner was.

Three weeks later, the DMT wrote to Bobby advising him that the Mr George Fredrickson, who had initially registered the Ford didn't exist. Vic then determined that as it had been obtained illegally, most likely by George Peterson, he immediately impounded it. After six weeks, the Barclay's Creek Police Station put the Falcon up for disposal at a no-reserve auction. Sadly for the police coffers, the only bidder paid five dollars for it.

The first thing that Bobby did when he got the Falcon back to Mortlake was to detail it inside and out. It was when he went to vacuum the boot that he discovered a black vinyl sports bag with the Balmain 'Tigers' rugby league team logo on the side. Inside the bag was a folder of official documents, including a new passport, a NSW Drivers Licence and a gold American Express card all in the name of Mr George Fredrickson. The picture in the passport was of Mr George Peterson.

The thing that made Bobby smile though were the banded bundles of fresh United States one hundred dollar bills.

Linda simply said, "To the victor goes the spoils."

Chapter 61

Friday 13 March 1970, Bankstown, Sydney

Peter Fordham's body clock had always woken him at precisely 5:30 a.m. for as long as he could remember. He was surprised then when he woke, glanced at his bedside clock and discovered it was only 3:00 a.m.

"Good Morning Commodore, hope I didn't wake you?"

"What the fu—!" the former Commodore started to say but pulled up short when the soldier he knew only as 'Doris', turned on the lamp he was seated under. Although it wasn't the sight of 'Doris' that had changed his anger into fear, it was the silenced 9mm pistol that 'Doris' was pointing at his chest.

It took Peter Fordham AKA Peter Fleming, almost thirty seconds to realise that he would never see another sunrise. He sat up and slowly moved a spare pillow behind his back.

"I guess George Peterson sent you?"

"Correct."

"Am I supposed to confess to something before you shoot me?"

"Do you *want* to confess to something, Commodore?"

"Apart from being stupid enough to be used as George fucking Peterson's puppet, no, nothing. So, as they say in the movies—'fire away'!"

"Well, here's the thing; there's been a development." 'Doris' reached behind him and retrieved the Commodores dressing gown that had been hanging over the back of the chair. Tossing it on the bed, he said, "Put that on. We're going to watch the news."

—this stage, we are still gathering physical evidence and talking to persons of interest. I have been cleared to tell you—

"What is this all about?"

"Shh, watch."

—and that more arrests are imminent. I can't, however, give you the names of those Government officials until we have interviewed and charged them. Mr George Peterson, the former Minister for Defence, has been arrested and charged on two counts so far. Mr Peterson is cooperating fully with the police. Are there any—

'Doris' switched the TV off. The Commodore sagged back in his armchair. "Fuck me! The whole house of cards is falling down! Here I was thinking Peterson and Co. were untouchable! Do you know what the full story is?"

"Not a clue! One thing I do know for certain is that your options have taken a turn for the better. See, here's the thing, this job—me tidying up Peterson's fuck up—was on a kill-first-get-paid-later basis. Problem is, the paymaster is incarcerated. What to do? I've been tossing the quandary around in my head since I arrived here at 0200 hundred hours. Would you like to hear what I finally decided?"

"Do I have a choice?"

"Ah, hit the nail on the head in one!

"Yes, Commodore, you do. Here are your options; one—you can pay me what Peterson offered plus fifteen percent for incidentals and then hightail it out of Dodge or; two—you can tell me to fuck off in which case I'll report that someone fitting the description of Commodore Peter Fleming is living at this address to the Federal Police. There is a third option, of course, you commit suicide and save yourself a lot of embarrassment when the Feds finally track you down."

"How much?"

"I love a hopeful pragmatist! $57,250."

"$50,000—you know you're a cheap assassin!"

"Well, there were other incentives but who wants to live in fucking Argentina?"

"I'll need to go to the bank."

"Fine. In the meantime, what's for breakfast?"

Epilogue

A week after George Peterson's arrest, the Australian Federal Police team returned to Canberra and Barclay's Creek Police Station settled back into its normal small-town policing routine—apart from the fact that Senior Sergeant Rogers relinquished weekend command of the station to Senior Constable Ahearn. The lingering aroma of fried bacon slowly disappeared over time.

Bill and Moira Williams were annoyed when heavy machinery started moving onto the 'Ferris' property and began demolishing the abandoned farmhouse. Their annoyance turned to anger when large trucks came and went from the property day and night for two weeks. However, their anger turned to joy when the NSW Lands Department advised them that the sale of the land to the bogus Peter Ferris was invalid and that the title of the land reverted to them.

A week after being released from the cell in the Barclay's Creek Police Station, Bobby Massey voluntarily committed himself back into Cumberland Lunatic Asylum. While he was physically OK, if he and Linda were going to be in a lasting relationship, he wanted to be 100% sure that the mental side effects of the last few months wouldn't manifest themselves into another psychotic attack.

After ten days he was given a clean bill of health—much to the psychiatrist's disbelief. Doctor Wright in consultation with Doctor Garland had concluded that the over-stimulation his mind had experienced since being abducted and then being the abductor had, in fact, been cathartic and there was absolutely no reason for Bobby to receive any ongoing therapy or continue taking his medication!

Bobby and Linda both took some well-earned time off work to rest and recuperate. Linda stayed with Bobby and his parents—much to Mary Massey's delight. He introduced Linda to all his old mates who reminded him constantly that he was batting way, way above his average and that surely Linda had a vision impairment!

The couple surfed and sunbathed, drank, dined and danced—and did what lovers do the world over—drowned in waves of passion and an utter sense of oneness!

They both returned to Sydney after three weeks; Bobby was welcomed back to his old job in Lidcombe and Linda carried on her practice at Concord Repatriation Hospital—with the warning from Bobby not to 'flirt with those randy soldiers!' One thing did change though; Bobby's 1965 Mk1 metallic British Racing Green GT Cortina was no longer parked in Strathfield but joined the 1966 XY Ebony Black Ford Falcon 500 in Mortlake.

"Why buy new furniture when we can save money and use mine?" Linda said with her best Groucho Marx eyebrow wiggle. Funnily enough, Bobby agreed with her, "But we will need a bigger bed!"

On Saturday 23 May 1970, Bobby and Linda were married in St Paul's church in Shell Bay. Senior Sergeant Vic Rogers gladly accepted the honour of escorting Linda down the aisle.

All Bobby's mates were there 'just in case Linda came to her senses at the last minute'. The Best Man, resplendent in his Royal Australian Navy Commander's uniform, but alas confined to a wheelchair, beamed proudly with the knowledge that everyone in the bridal party had gone through hell and back as the beautiful couple exchanged vows and wedding rings.

As Bobby and Linda were leaving the wedding reception to drive to Surfers Paradise for their honeymoon, Linda bent down to kiss Jerry goodbye and slipped something into his coat pocket, "This may come in handy one day. I suggest leaving it in your pocket until you're somewhere private." She kissed his cheek, gave him a hug and a smile and then joined Bobby in the sparkling clean black Ford Falcon 500—Linda much preferred the front bench seat to the bucket seats of the Cortina.

Jerry waved them goodbye then wheeled himself to a quiet corner of the Shell Bay Hotel. Reaching into his pocket, he pulled out a small, empty Army Olive Drab box. Inside was George Fielding's Laboratory Report.

"Well, I'll be damned!"

****

In the weeks and months following George Peterson's arrest, the National and International press was awash with the story that had rocked the foundations of the Australian Government. In the final wash-up, one other serving politician joined the ex-Minister for Defence behind bars but the carnage didn't stop there. Two senior public servants, including the long-serving Secretary of the Department of Defence and the Deputy Secretary of Foreign Affairs, Mr John Forrester, were also charged with crimes against the Commonwealth.

Thanks to the information provided by the former Minister for Defence's Private Secretary, Henry Edwards, Raymond Brauer AKA 'Doris' was detained by NSW Police at Kingsford Smith International Airport while trying to board a flight to Thailand. He was once again handed over to the Military Police and escorted back to the 1st Military Correctional Establishment at Holsworthy. Hoping to reduce his lengthy sentence, he notified the Military Police where the missing Commodore Peter Fleming was currently residing.

Eighteen months later, the ABC's *Four Corners* program revealed the complete sorry saga on Australian National television. From the development of the biological weapon itself, the complicity of the British Ministry of Defence, the United States Defence Department and the Australian Department of Defence during the latter stages of World War Two, in their attempt to conceal the existence of the weapon and the subsequent and continuing cover-up of the fact that a secret cache of those weapons was—as far as the researchers for the program could ascertain—still being stored on Australian soil.

"The Government does not comment on matters of National Security," was the Prime Minister's only comment.

The producers of the program had gained an exclusive interview with the now-imprisoned architect of the deadly virus that was intended to bring about the demise of the Third Reich, Doctor Stefan Jensen. After the reporter had covered Doctor Jensen's life, including his abduction from Auschwitz, the interview moved on to the development of the biological weapon itself.

Doctor Jensen: "As you know, British MI5 interrogated and tortured me for over three months before I came to my senses and devised a plan to save my life."

Interviewer: "Doctor, you say you 'devised a plan'; hadn't you already created the virus?"

Doctor Jensen: "Yes, you are correct, but the derivative of the Spanish Flu virus itself wasn't the problem—placing it into hibernation was."

Interviewer: "So you were released on the proviso that you could bring that about."

Doctor Jensen: "Yes."

Interviewer: "And the 500,000 vials of deadly biological agent that were stored in an Australian abandoned quarry are proof of your success?"

Doctor Jensen: "No."

Interviewer: "No! Are you saying that the 5,000 crates didn't contain biological weapons?"

Doctor Jensen: "No."

Interviewer: "Forgive me, Doctor, but aren't you contradicting yourself?"

Doctor Jensen: "Young lady, one thing MI5 couldn't do was break my belief at the time, that the Nazi Party was the best thing that had happened for the Fatherland. As I said, the plan to stop the torture was simply to save my life, not some altruistic effort to bring peace to the world.

"The so-called 'deadly virus', or 'Spanish Flu II' if you like, was impossible to manipulate outside of highly controlled laboratory conditions, but MI5 and British scientists brought the dream of an early end to the war, lock, stock and barrel! While the 500,000 vials do actually contain bacteria in hibernation and a virulent growth stimulant, when mixed, it is no more 'deadly' than a jar of yoghurt!"